<u>Books by Ron Mueller</u>

Bram Nielson Series-Science Fiction
- The Fold
- The Message
- Fold Wormhole
- Negative Fold
- Ripples in Time

The Alex Evercrest Series-Detective
- The River Front
- The Girl on the Grill
- Missing
- Maggot
- Racist
- Votive Candles
- Windy City
- Country Road
- Pool of Blood
- Sins of the Daughter

The Taelo Series-Prehistory America
- Taelo: The Early Years
- Taelo: The Golden Feather
- Taelo: Journey of Discovery
- Taelo: Dangerous Passage
- Taelo: Condor Clan Slingers
- Taelo: Circumvention
- Taelo: The Journey of Sages

A Taelo Story
- The Name of the Child
- White Swan and Quiet Pheasant
- Broken Spear
- Floating Cloud
- Quiet Rabbit
- Busy Bee
- Little Otter& Talking Wren
- Burley Bear & Meadow Flower

A Feather-in-the-Wind Story
- The Eastern Elk Clan

The Door Series-Science Fiction
- The Door
- Delivery
- Journey Beyond

The Savitar Series-Science Fiction
- Journey's End
- Savitar
- Confluence

The Problem Solver Series-Secret Agent
- The Beginning
- Drug Lords
- Border Crosser

Current Past and Future-Science Fiction
Event Survivors-Science Fiction
The Door-Science Fiction
Viajante 7 -Science Fiction
Imagination by Courtney Huynh and Chloe Parker

The Message
By: *Ron Mueller*

Around the World Publishing LLC
4914 Cooper Road Suite 144
Cincinnati, Ohio 45242-9998

ISBN 13: 978-1-68223-311-5
ISBN 10: 1-68223-311-1

Distributed by Ingram
Cover Picture by: NASA
Cover Design by: Ron Mueller

Ron Mueller

Dedicated to those who seek other intelligences

in the Universe

The Message

Table of Content

Ron Mueller

Chapter 1: Success Celebration

This was Bram's first Fold. He, Zuri, Orlando, Eric, and Zoe were the newbies in the bubble.

Bram sat next to Nuri looking out at the surface of the far side of the moon. He was explaining to everyone that what was most often referred to as the dark side of the moon was no darker than any other part of the moon. In the course of a month, Sun light fell equally on all sides of the Moon and that the lunar day lasted about two Earth weeks.

He then shared the fact that they were being shielded from the noise of Earth and were in what was called the "radio dark." It was a location that was shielded from the noise of the Earth and the weak signals from the universe could be measured more easily at this location.

In fact, the systems on Wheel One were scanning out into the universe and when they returned to Earth the data would be closely scoured to see what they could learn.

He went on to have everyone look at the difference between the more heavily cratered backside surface and the fact that it lacked the maria or seas that made up the familiar man in the moon face.

He shared the fact that it was thought that the differences were caused by a wayward dwarf planet colliding with the moon in the early history of the solar system.

Orlando thanked Professor Bram for the great story that he had just shared.

Nuro squeezed Bram's hand and thanked him for giving them all a quick education about the moon. She said that it was all new to her and that she would have to do a little more study and research before the next Fold out to the edge of the solar system.

The Fold they were on was a top-secret Fold to test the ability to Fold over a long distance through space. In reality the distance to the back of the Moon was a miniscule distance as compared to the subsequent distances that were in upcoming Fold plans. The Fold implementation order was to go first to the edge of the Solar System, then to the nearest next solar system and finally to a different galaxy.

Since a Fold took relatively no time, it was possible to do the three planned Folds in the coming year. It could be done as quickly as doing them on three subsequent days but there was data analysis time put between each Fold. It would be important to analyze the data and apply any improvements that the data might provide insights about.

The Message

The successful Fold to the back of the moon pleased Bram. It was to have been the first Fold of the two Wheels but in reality, it was the third. The first two folds occurred in getting each wheel out of the Seattle area when a throng of rioters threatened to expose the technology that was a top US government secret. So, the official Fold that would be recorded for the history books was really the third one.

It was his first, but it was the second for each of the Wheel Crews.

He had let them all know that the people taking part on this Fold would have their names and biographies recorded in the history books.

He had been as inclusive as possible, but it was not possible to take everyone on the project. He took all the top players. He eventually would offer the Fold experience to all those who desired.

The Fold was a moment of relief for him but the lead up to it had been extremely stressful.

He had not intended the days leading up to the Fold to have been so hectic and stressful. He had envisioned a rather controlled, full schedule but one that focused on making the Fold to the back of the Moon safe as well as successful.

One concern was the safety of the crew members. Since relocating the Fold project to Dallas, Oregon he and his team had been attacked several times.

He and his close team had been attacked when they went on a fishing trip to the Mt. Jefferson resort along the Rushing River. He, his team, the Marines guarding him, and the resort owners fought and defeated a group of mercenaries that had arrived in a helicopter gunship and had a tripod large caliber machine gun on the ground. The battle had been fierce but ended in a few minutes as Bram and his two Marine guards took out the attackers.

The next attack had been at the Fold neighborhood swim party. Three shooters opened fire from the parking lot. Bram, unarmed, took immediate action, and killed one of the attackers and his FBI bodyguards took out the other two.

He had gone into action when he realized that Pat was the next target after the first two people had been shot.

A third attack, by a gunman shooting at him from a boat, had occurred out on Celio Lake during a fishing party. Orlando and Castor turned the attacking boat and its occupants into Swiss cheese.

The final attack had been thwarted when he reported seeing a flicker from the top of a semi parked in the orchard that bordered the Fold community housing. A Marine marksman killed the attacker from a patrol helicopter before he could act.

Bram figured that some rich and powerful people were trying hard to stop the Fold development from making any progress and he was the bullseye of the project.

These attacks had made him very cautious about everything associated with the project.

The attacks were disturbing and of concern to him but not as disturbing as being accused of being a child molester by the wife of his genius Astronomer and Fold coordinate planner, Marcus Smith.

He had worked hard at making the Fold community into a caring, sharing, and fun group.

The accusation if it was shared would have a very negative impact and he acted to immediately address and resolve it.

It turned out that Myla, Marcus's wife, had been molested as a child and had a hysterical reaction when she saw him hugging Zuri, a young autistic savant constrained to a wheelchair. He told Marcus to get help for Myla or both of them would be transferred to another project or job. It was a huge relief when Mallica got Myla to accept counseling to deal with the child abuse she had suffered. He was hopeful that with the counseling, she would resolve her mental issues.

After that he turned his attention to the planning of a celebratory fishing trip.

Lacy his secretarial support had worked out the schedule with her father for another fishing trip.

Bram had her invite several dignitaries all the way up to and including the President. He did not expect most of them to accept but he asked Lacy to make sure that she arranged enough fishing boats to handle everyone that accepted the invitation.

She let him know that her father, and brothers were all committed, and a picnic lunch would be arranged as well. They had all sent their greetings and had said that they hoped for another successful fishing outing without the associated fireworks of the last one.

On the Fold's return from the back of the Moon, Zuri commented that though she had learned a lot about the moon, she was a little let down that the Fold experience was no different than taking a ride in a car.

Bram gave a little laugh and said that he agreed with her and that the only thing that had made it the least bit interesting for him was Orlando constantly joking with her.

He said that getting the math and the means to make a Fold occur had been the part that had engaged him. Taking the ride out to the back of the moon had been very anticlimactic.

He asked if a fishing trip might excite her more.

That brought out an immediate and loud yes and she commented that the last time, her first-time fishing, had been a blast. She said that Orlando had really caught all her fish because she was too weak to pull them in. He would have her hold the pole, but he would reel in the fish.

She said that Captain Ted had done a great job in making the boat wheelchair friendly and he had made sure that she was safely strapped in. Then he had zoomed at top speed and made sweeping turns to give her a thrill sitting in her wheelchair. A ride in his boat was more fun than a ride in Wheel One to the back of the moon.

Bram said he agreed with her.

He then asked her if she wondered why the trip to the moon had been so short.

Zuri replied that she had no idea.

He then shared the fact that the current Fold was frozen to one coordinate location and could not move. He wanted to add the capability of motion to the Fold process.

Zuri looked at him and said that if he solved that problem, he would create a Fold wormhole that would turn Wheel One into a Fold spaceship. It would be a spaceship that could move through time and space free of the conventional limitations of the speed of light.

She asked what he was waiting for.

He looked at her and asked her for her IQ then reminded her that hers was much higher than his and that she was the smart one in the room that needed to solve the problem.

She gave a little laugh and joked that he was the smart one she was just the clueless one that asked the right questions.

Pat, Amy, and Elizabeth walked into the office and commented that the journey of Wheel One and Two had been anticlimactic and that it seemed surreal as if it had just been a dream. They commented that getting the two Wheels out of the hanger in Seattle into the Dallas hanger had been more exciting.

Bram said that Fold had been more exciting for him too since he had almost left them somewhere in-between. He made the point that he had no idea if an in-between existed or if the wheels would have just disappeared and never been found again.

Elizabeth looked over to Zuri and told her to watch out for Bram because he might have a great mind, but he often moved faster that the technology around him. She shared that she had gone and looked at the charred power transformers that Bram had fried when the first Fold was done. She said she had gone out and bought a dozen lotto tickets hoping to cash in on her good luck at being alive, but the lotto had won, and she was still poor.

Zuri smiled and said she would pay close attention to what Bram was concocting since even his fishing trips were more exciting than she had expected.

Lacy called and asked if Bram was able to meet with Myla.

He was surprised but he said that he would be free in about five minutes.

Pat said that she would take Zuri and look to see if anything had been done with her future office area and that afterwards she would have Orlando take Zuri home.

The Message

Elizabeth said she was going to see about the new Bramlets that were being assembled. She commented that the next set of Bramlet scouts for the Neptune Fold were almost all ready for testing.

Bram asked Lacy to send Myla in.

When she came in, he saw that her hands were shaking, and he knew immediately that she was very nervous.

He asked if they should shake hands or just go for a hug and put the past behind them and look forward to a long friendship.

Myla began crying but stepped forward and they hugged.

She began to apologize.

Bram stopped her and said that she should relax. He had no grudge and was not looking for an apology. He was looking forward to the long and good relationship the two of them would enjoy.

Myla thanked him and asked if there was anything she could do that would be appropriate.

Bram said that she should talk to Lacy on the way out and get the information about the upcoming fishing party and that he would expect the Smith family to catch the biggest fish.

Myla thanked him and said that she loved fishing, but she seldom caught one. She said that it was the sitting and enjoying the motion of the boat that pleased her.

Bram agreed with her and said that what he enjoyed most was to watch folks fishing, talking, and teasing each other about the one that got away.

He escorted Myla from his office and told her to stop by Marcus's office and let him know that his rather eccentric scientist was waiting to find out what the future travel plans would be.

He already knew the plan, but he wanted to have Myla stop and talk with Marcus before going home. He had told Marcus to finish what he was doing and then go home to Myla. He figured Marcus would figure out that he did not have a meeting with him.

Pat came back and said that Orlando and Zuri had left. She commented that Orlando and Zuri seemed to have bonded and become fast friends.

Bram said that in fact he had replaced Orlando with a new Marine guard, Donna because Orlando had suggested that Zuri rated at least one person guarding her at all times and he was stepping up and volunteering to do so. Orlando had been the one to recruit Donna, who seemed to have her eyes on him.

Pat gave a small laugh and suggested that they both stay out of the love triangle.

He nodded and said he had all he could handle with his own love affair.

He suggested that since it was a nice day they walk home.

The Message

Walking home was not a simple affair, Castor, and Donna the two Marine guards, in full battle gear, were in front, and on this day, Eric and Zoe his two FBI bodyguards were walking in back and Bob and Thomas the other two FBI guards were driving the van that was most often the mode of transportation in the afternoon.

The morning always consisted in a slow jog to work.

The attacks aimed at killing him had resulted in the current mode of increased protection. This had been the routine for several months.

The level of security around Bram had always been high and though he sometimes felt constrained by it, the attacks that he had experienced made it clear that he was at the center of the bullseye to his adversaries and his adversaries seemed to have some deep political connections that surprised him. He wondered how he might find out who they were and see if there was a way to stop them.

The walk gave him time to think and to allow his mind to sort through what he needed to do to make the Fold program successful. He had stepped back from being the only one making it all happen and had split the responsibilities with various other members.

The Fold program's overall management on site was now being handled by Erica and back on the East coast by Jeffrey.

He had embraced the role of being the scientist that managed the data analysis and its interpretation, and he was the lead in making improvements to the Fold program.

Now all he needed was for his mind to open up and participate in solving the problem of developing a means to propel a Fold enclosure.

<u>Chapter 2: Fishing</u>

Almost everyone of the team members signed on with Linda to go fishing. There was high enthusiasm among all the participants and a common groan when they found out the time that the fishing boats would leave the dock.

Lake Celio was really the Columbia River up stream of the Dallas hydro-electric dam. The river was somewhere around a mile across, and the current was slow and easy.

It was still dark when the boats left the Celio park docks. The moon light etched the far bank a dark black. Home lights twinkled as if the bank had its own stars competing with the millions of the ones overhead.

The rising sun was battling the night and slowly bringing in the day.

As it rose ahead, the seven boats went single file toward it.

Then the far horizon looked as if it had burst into flame and the sun rose red behind a thin layer of clouds.

The saying, "Red sun in the morning, sailors warning" went through his mind.

The rising white steam going up from the lake seemed to be trying to warm the cool and somewhat nippy air.

Ted gave a hand signal and the six boats behind him moved into a V formation. He began weaving back and forth and the other boats all followed and did the same. He was making it as exciting as he dared.

Zuri had thanked him for an exciting ride the last time he had taken her fishing. He planned to get her to thank him again. He was personally pleased that he had made a positive connection.

It was hard for him to treat her like he would anyone else. He needed to get rid of his lifetime feeling of alienation when he saw someone who was crippled. He needed to realize that the people in their wheelchairs had their own talents, ambitions, and dreams.

He loved fishing and so did Zuri. He figured that would give them a common bond. A good start. He shook his head; he was just an old foggy that needed to be around people like Bram and Zuri.

Bram was sitting next to Pat and holding her hand as they let themselves be absorbed by the moment. He alternated between watching the occupants of the other boats, enjoying the motion of Captain Ted's boat, and the feel the wind blowing his hair gave him.

The Message

The majestic scenery of the snowcapped mountains and the skirt of green forest that swept gracefully down to the edge of the water was spell binding. The experience seemed to tease his mind to let go of other thoughts.

The zigzagging brought him out of his daydreaming, and he paid attention to what was going on. He laughed when he realized that all the boats were copying what Captain Ted was doing.

He shouted out to Ted and asked if help was needed in guiding the boat.

Ted smiled and said he had no choice because he was following Zuri's order to make fishing fun.

Zuri shouted out that she had not given any such order, but he should continue doing what he was doing.

Bram noted that the seven fishing boats formed a V as they made their way eastward along the lake. He wondered what the formation looked like from an arial view. He looked up to see a small drone following above them. He pointed it out to Ted who nodded and pointed to himself and to the drone to indicate it was one of his.

Bram later found out that Lacy was the one flying the drone. It had been her idea to film the entire fishing trip.

Lacy had informed him that Jeffery and Major General Lester Tilson would be joining in on the fishing trip. She also let him know that every one of the big shots up to and including the President had sent him and the fishing party good luck and that they regretted not being able to join in personally.

Jeffery had called when he had landed and let him know that he and the General had been parked out on the tarmac for almost an hour waiting for some gate keepers to get to work and work the bridge that connected the plane with the terminal. The Pilot finally let everyone off via the planes own steps.

The fishing had just started when Jeffery and Major General Lester Tilson arrived in the eighth boat. They pulled alongside and apologized for having been late.

Bram let them know that no apologies were necessary but that they needed to get their lines in the water so they could try for one of three prizes, the largest fish, the most fish and the smallest keeper fish.

They both gave him a salute and their boat went out to the edge of the group and threw in their lines.

By noon everyone had caught a fish and Ted called a halt to the fishing and said it was time for the picnic to begin. He pointed to the darkening sky and said that it looked like a rain squall was coming in over the lake.

He called ahead and asked that the tent to cover the picnic area get set up in case they got rain.

The Message

The ride back was fast and straight. They all had their eyes on the black clouds slowly gathering down by the hydro-electric dam.

They had all just gotten out and helped finish putting up the very large tent when the rain started and soon it was pouring. The far side of the lake disappeared. It was hard to see to the end of the dock. The boats had their rain covers on, and all fishing poles had been put away.

Ted said that the amount of rain they had been getting was unusual.

The three grills were just outside of the tent and the three doing the grilling got wet every time they got a serving of what was on the grill.

Zuri was sitting by the edge of the tent looking out to the lake with her parents helping her eat. They were all listening to Orlando tell a story about the time he was on patrol and the rain had started. He made the point that the patrol was in the middle of the desert and had not come prepared for the rain that fell as heavy as the one that they were now sitting and watching. He went on to share that after the rain the desert was covered in flowers. It was as if a miracle had happened.

Bram enjoyed the story and noticed that Orlando had captured everyone's attention.

He took the opportunity to let everyone know that they would wait until after lunch and after the rain they would see who had qualified for the prizes that were being offered.

The tent and the food seemed to bring everyone closer. Pat commented that the rain only added charm to the event.

The thunder and lightning seemed to have the effect of making everyone speak softly. Rita, Ted's wife, asked if it was all right for her to play some music.

Lacy gave a small groan and then said that it would be country western, or old crooners singing songs of the sixties or before.

Major General Tilson said that it would be great to hear some music that he could understand.

The intensity of the rain lessened. The music was just what everyone needed, and the conversations seemed to well up like a dry sponge getting water put on it as everyone listened to Rita.

Bram then heard a loud explosion and as he looked back along the shoreline, he watched what looked like a small atom bomb's plume rising brightly up into the grey of the clouds.

Everyone under the tent quit talking.

He knew immediately that the location was back at the Fold property.

The silence was louder than the thunder and lightning that seemed to have risen.

Everyone turned and looked at Castor as his phone rang. He put it on speaker mode and answered the call. It was the Marine site leader calling to inform him that an attack on the compound had taken place but had been thwarted.

The explosion had been one of the attack vehicles exploding in the back of the compound area and other than being spectacular, the explosion had killed all the attackers that had retreated to it, but it had done no damage. He said that each attacking van had four gunmen and all but one of the attackers were dead.

He reported that USS Hood, Wheel One had been tipped on its side, but it did not seem to be damaged.

When Jeffery asked if they should return to the compound, Bram was about to say no, when Pat spoke up and said that they should finish their fishing picnic. She went on to say that if the wheel was not damaged, she would later do a Fold and then land to bring the Wheel back up right.

Major General Tilson asked the Site commander to have a twelve-person patrol sent to the picnic area and set up a defensive perimeter. He looked around at the group and said that it was just precautionary.

Bram looked out at the rain and the lake and said that if there was to be an attack they should be expecting the action to come from the lake.

Orlando suggested that they prepare for that possibility, and he asked if the Marine bodyguards had their weapons. He knew the answer but asked so that he could ask that of all the others would know that they had come prepared.

He then looked to the FBI bodyguards and asked them the same thing.

They all responded in the affirmative.

He then asked the boat captains if they would allow their boats to be used and got a unanimous response that they could but only if they were doing the driving and they got to shoot as well.

Bram watched in amazement as the boats loaded up and went out in the rain. He had been turned down when he had volunteered to go with Ted.

The General simply said that he could not justify risking either Bram or any of the other brains running the program.

Jeffery agreed and when he volunteered to go out, he was also turned down.

Rita said that she wanted those that were staying under the tent to round up all the extra tables that were in the park and bring them to the edge of the tent on the lake side and tip them so that they made a protective barrier.

She then went to the van and the trailer and returned with several shot guns and boxes of shells.

The Message

She handed one to Bram and said that she had heard that he was rather deadly in a gun battle and that her Ted had said that he was almost certain that once the rain let up there would be an attack.

Bram had a second set of tables tilted in the center of the tent and had Zuri and everyone else get behind the second barrier.

He asked that Lisa help Zuri to rest on the ground and instructed everyone to lay down flat if the fighting came their way.

The storm must have been listening because almost immediately after his announcement the rain stopped and as if it were providing better fighting conditions, the sun seemed to be pushing the clouds west along the lake.

Bram then saw what looked like a dark grey blanket being lifted from a fleet of boats coming in at full speed from the west.

Pat was looking through a set of binoculars and commented that there seemed to be more than a dozen and that two had what seemed to be heavy duty machine guns and two had mortars mounted on the bow.

Lacy excused herself and asked Linda to look after Zuri. She took the opportunity to launch her camera drone. She said she would take a closer look and she could help guide the gun fire from their boats.

Elizabeth said she would talk with Orlando and Pat said she would talk with Castor.

Bram had several tables moved to the two launch ramps and had two shooters positioned behind each.

Rita and Marial were also out at the two tables to help support them in case of a gun battle.

Amy, the helicopter pilot turned wheel two captain became the play-by-play announcer and shared what she was seeing on the computer screen.

Bram quickly realized that their boats were outnumbered and out gunned. The only advantage seemed to be that Stacey was an expert in flying the drone and in providing critical information.

The two boats carrying mortars were sunk in the first round of fighting. Then those out in their boats were able to take out one of the boats with a fifty caliber machine gun.

The remaining boat with the fifty turned toward the docks.

All the attacking boats that remained had shooters with either AR 15's or high-powered rifles.

Bram realized that the one boat that had a fifty-caliber gun was fast approaching the ramp area.

Lacy saw the same thing and her drone made a sweeping turn and returned to the tent area.

When the first round of the fifty caliber was fired, the splinters from the first set of tables flew past Bram as if they were sent to make him into a porcupine.

Lacy flew the camera drone directly at the gunman and turned so close to his face that he turned to avoid getting hit. She then took the drone on a sharp turn and flew the drone toward the boat driver and crashed it into his face.

The boat swerved and hit the end of the dock. The fifty-caliber gunman hit the grips of the gun chest first and was most likely critically injured but Bram's shotgun blast sent him flying back over the boats low wind shield where the shooter behind him accidently shot him in the back.

Bram rushed toward the boat in a continuous pump and shoot fashion and then the click of the trigger made him realize his gun was empty and he was now a sitting duck. He was about to jump into the water when Pat handed him another shotgun as she took the empty.

Rita had done the same back up with a second shotgun for the grill master that had done the same thing as Bram, but on the adjacent dock.

Bram continued on toward the boat as he pumped and fired. There was no response, but he made sure everyone was dead.

Lacy ran down the pier, jumped into the boat, retrieved her drone, did a quick check, and used some duct tape and then launched it and sent it out to the boats where the battle was still going at an intensive battle.

Bram stood and watched as she flew her drone as if it was a combat plane.

Stacy's harassing drone seemed to turn the tide and the battle slowly came to an end as the only surviving attacking boat surrendered.

Stacy did a slow sweep of the boats and noted that all of their boats were full of holes, but the design of the boats kept them afloat. They might fill with water, but they would not sink.

Only Ted's boat had an engine that came to life and allowed him to slowly tow the other boats into the dock area. All the boats were tied bow to tail as Ted slowly pulled them back.

Bram had the ramp area cleared of the tables. He was about to get Zuri sent home when the Marines from the Fold compound arrived.

They took over. They had an EMT group with them and as the boats came in, they began checking on the wounded.

Almost everyone out on the boats had some sort of wound. They were treated and then those needing to get transported to the hospital were taken by the first unit. It was designed for battle conditions and could transport six and they were full as they departed.

Another EMT unit was on its way.

Bram was listening as Orlando was telling his version of the battle to Zuri. Castor kept throwing in color comments and Donna kept saying that they shouldn't try to pull the wool over a person's eyes who was ten times smarter than they were.

He saw that Zuri was really enjoying the banter.

Niro and Jina were standing next to him, and they commented that Zuri was really blossoming into a very social person and even with what had just happened they thought that she was where she should be.

Jina looked at him and said that she had not expected to see the dark side of such a bright mind, but she was relieved that he was a person of action.

Pat came over and pointed to Bram's leg and asked him if he knew he had a splinter the size of a chop stick that gone through his leg.

Bram looked down and realized that the shower of splinters created by the fifty caliper bullets had not all missed him. He was surprised by the size of the splinter and the fact that it was not bleeding.

Jina gasped when she saw the splinter.

They had all been so intend on listening to Orlando that Bram's injury was missed.

Pat had motioned to one of the EMT's and pointed to Bram.

He came over and asked Bram to come over to the Emergency Vehicle and get the splinter removed.

He wanted Bram to go to the hospital, but Bram refused. He asked them to remove the splinter and later he would go to the hospital.

The EMT went over to the General and after a brief discussion he returned and told Bram that removing the splinter was going to cause some pain.

By this time everyone was standing around watching.

Orlando was reassuring Zuri that Bram was going to be alright and that he was going to demonstrate the bravery of a Marine.

Bram reached into his shirt pocket and took out a large piece of hard jerky and put it between his teeth.

The EMT use some Novocain to numb the area around both ends of the splinter. After a few minutes he said that he was going to pull it out in one fast pull and that his assistant would put some gel and gauze to prevent the wound from bleeding.

Orlando began a chant.
> *Fifty caliper no big deal.*
> *Bram is shooting,*
> *Bram is real.*
> *Fifty Caliper missed the mark.*
> *Splintered the table,*
> *Angry table, Angry table,*
> *Tried for Bram but missed the mark.*
> *Little splinter, Little splinter*
> *Does not bother.*
> *Bram is real.*
> *Bram, Bram is a true Fold hero.*

Everyone at the outing took up the chant.

The EMT waited until "hero" and then swiftly pulled he splinter out.

The pain caught Bram by surprise. He bit down on the hard beef jerky and thought about a Fold to the Alien world.

Pat put her hand on his shoulder and asked if the contest was still on. She knew that Bram had used his powerful mind to ignore most of the pain and she wanted to distract him as the EMT's finished binding the wound.

Bram looked at her and smiled. He thanked her for being such a brave backup. It had saved his life.

Pat had not expected the reply, but she smiled and said that she always had his back.

He then replied that everyone had won and that they would all share first prize.

Chapter 3: Aftermath

It felt to Bram like the drive back to the compound took twice as long as the trip out to go fishing. An armored Marine vehicle was in front, and one was in back. There were three vans transporting the fishing party back to the Fold living area in the middle.

He was still recovering from the removal of the large splinter, and he was also feeling the emotional aftereffects of having shot and killed several of the attackers. He was feeling fine, but he was already thinking about the discussion he would have with Dr. Windal the Fold phycologist. He had no remorse about his actions so much as it nagged him that he was constantly under attack by an unknown but seemingly powerful group of people and that his side was constantly in a defensive posture.

He was also thinking about the action that Lacy had taken with her camera drone. She had played a huge part in thwarting the attack.

He wondered if she were up for a new role on the team. He would ask her and see if she would lead a team assigned to identify potential enemies of the Fold program.

He had voiced his concern before about always being on defense instead of being on offense. He figured that Lacy was the one that could lead a team to develop a Fold offense.

When the caravan arrived at the Fold work area, Bram asked it to stop by the gate area where two of the vans had been stopped. He took in the crumpled entrance gate.

He figured that the van had run through the gate at a high speed. He decided that the entrance would need to be redesigned to make it impossible to just run through at high speed.

The bodies of several of the attackers were still on the ground or in the bullet riddled vans. Bram looked at all the bullet holes in the vans, he looked around and saw all the bullet hits on the entry booth and he was sure that if he walked around the entry area he would find a ton of bullet casings from the guns that the Marines had fired.

He asked the Marine guards if any Marine had been wounded or killed. He was relieved to learn that there were no injuries on their side.

He was thinking of walking the rest of the way in but realized that the wound in his leg was flaring up. His protection group jumped out and helped him back into the van.

The Message

The driver drove toward the rear of the compound to where the remains of the third mangled and blackened attack van rested looking like a high diver that had missed the water and had instead hit the pool side headfirst. It looked like the van had a black accordion body design. Bram saw the blackened arm of the person who must have been inside at the time and several blacked bodies were still on the ground where the explosion had hurled their bodies.

The van then drove into the hanger where the two Wheels were housed.

He was processing the events of the day. He was sure that he had someone on the inside of the Fold organization that was giving information to his adversaries. He was sure he had a spy in the Fold organization. He thought through how he would expose this spy. He mentally put together a list people that would potentially have a reason to be the spy.

When he stepped out of the van, the sight of Wheel One laying on its side put the list out of his mind. He limped to the Wheels entrance ramp and pressed the open button. The ramp went to its down position. He was about to climb in to see if there was any internal damage, but Pat stopped him and said that she would see what the damage was.

Bram heard her laugh as she called out that the only damage was the broken Boston Starbucks coffee mug that Bram had given to her. She came out, shook her head, and commented that the attackers had lost their lives and the most they had accomplished was to shatter her favorite coffee mug.

She thought through how to get the wheel back to its upright condition as she exited and pushed the ramp's close button. She remembered the lab demonstration that Bram had done for Remi and the lab group to show them how the Fold process could be used to move a bubble. She realized that she could create a Fold inside the hanger and be able to get Wheel One back to its upright position.

Bram felt a hand on his shoulder and realized that Pat was talking to him.

She was telling him that she would do a Fold inside the hangar to upright Wheel One.

He let her know he would go online and order a replacement Boston Mug.

Pat started to laugh. She pointed to the Wheel and asked whether they were going to put it back upright.

Bram replied that of course they were and that her idea of doing a little Fold was right on. He said that the first Fold would be to an upright position one foot off floor and the second Fold would be to a position on the floor. He looked around and signaled to Marcus and asked him to determine the coordinates for the two Folds.

It was Marcus's turn to laugh. He shook his head and said that he had discussed getting Wheel One upright with Pat and he had the co-ordinates already programmed. He shared that the Fold would take almost no power.

Bram agreed and walked over to where Lacy was standing and asked her to set up a meeting with the Fold leadership to start immediately after Wheel One was back upright. He asked that she plan to attend as well.

Pat entered Wheel One and strapped herself into the pilots control chair. She called the control center and asked if everything was a go.

Marcus gave her the green light and she pressed the Fold button.

As the Wheel seemed to magically move into an upright position and levitated one foot off the floor, a cheer went up, from everyone that had gone fishing and were standing in the observation area. A second cheer went up when the Wheel moved onto the floor and was back to its upright position and Wheel One was secured with its holding cables.

Lacy let him know that she had arranged for the leaders to be in the meeting room and that everyone else was going home.

Bram took a moment and asked Lacy if she was willing to take on a new role. It would be a promotion and it would put her in charge of a team that would focus on taking an offensive posture against the people trying to subvert the work of the Fold project.

Lacy replied that she was excited about being more active in the Fold project and that she would do her best to fulfill his expectations.

He deflected her question about the details of the role and said that they should go to the meeting, and she would learn what he had in mind.

The meeting room was uncharacteristically silent. Everyone seemed to be concentrating on their drink or silently looking around.

Bram walked in, sat down, and used the old line, "I guess you're all wondering why I called this meeting."

Erica smiled and quietly said that she hoped that this time it wasn't about her.

Bram gave a little chuckle and replied that "No," this time it was about the fact that the Fold team lacked an Offense and an Offense coordinator, and he was determined to change that situation.

He pointed to Lacy and said, "let me introduce, Lacy Stetson, the superior and excellent drone fighter that was a key participant in defeating the attackers. I am promoting her into the new position of Offense coordinator."

Today in the battle by the lake, Lacy single handedly put offense in the air with nothing more than a camera drone. She disrupted the attack and gave our side the upper hand. It was an arial performance that you will all need to watch.

Her actions saved the day.

I want the upper hand against those who have repeatedly acted against the Fold project.

I would like Lacy to lead a team of five, have an appropriate number of Fold bubbles and anything else that she and her team determine will make them a potent offensive force.

I now request that the rest of you work with Lacy and put the Fold offense team on the field. She will lead and manage but she should be coaching a professional and superior team.

Jeffery asked if a person in the meeting could be on the team.

Bram once again pointed to Lacy and said that it was up to her. She would review the qualifications of those wishing to be on the team and insure that the participant brought the resources that contributed to winning.

Bram stood up and said that he was now leaving the meeting, and Lacy would manage getting the Fold offense team established and organized.

He looked at Lacy and asked if his way of explaining her new role made it clear to her what he was asking her to do.

Lacy looked at Erica and asked if this is what she had meant when she commented that she hoped it was not about her.

Erica replied, "Yes and now you know how Bram can knock you off your pace."

Bram looked at Erica as he got up to leave, "It's her first moment in this new role, give her a hand and then get out of the way."

The conversation in the meeting room rose to a robust level as everyone began talking about the way to get to their adversaries.

Bram left the meeting room and was greeted by his Marine and FBI bodyguards. He uncharacteristically gave each of them a high five slap and said that it was time to go home and have a cold one and then prepare dinner. He looked at Donna and suggested that she check with Orlando to see if he wanted to join in.

The ride to the house was short but his Marine and FBI bodyguards carried on a constant discussion as each described their experience in the gun battle on the lake.

Bram knew that, like himself, all of them were still on an adrenaline high.

Castor pointed to two large red coolers, three cases of beer and a large watermelon and said that the picnic should continue when they got to the house.

He then lifted the cooler lid and said that the warm food was still warm, and they could all just sit back and continue the party.

Bram stopped him and said that the picnic should continue at the house, but he wanted all weapons turned in so that he wouldn't worry about having anyone animating the action of the gun fight that they had all survived.

That got a laugh out of everyone.

The Message

Bram led the way up the stairs from their basement parking area. He knew he was supposed to get his leg checked out, but he did not want to sit and find out from the Doctor that time would heal his wound and he could have pain pills if the pain was too great.

He was more interested in getting his protectors back into the partying mode. He thought that some watermelon and some of the grilled broccoli and baked beans would make a great snack.

He would then sit down in his study and think through his bubble problem.

The team insisted he have a beer with them as they all put their weapons on the dining room table.

Bram had to laugh when Orlando came in and said that he was still armed and would protect him if his regular guards were too drunk to do so.

After he had his "snack," he picked up his half-finished beer and said that he was going into the study to work through his current problem with how the Fold vehicles were frozen at the coordinates that they Folded to.

He had to laugh when the whole group in unison said that perhaps another beer would help to solve the problem.

Bram went into the study and turned on the pot to make some tea. Eric and Zoe had followed him in, and Eric came and took over getting the teacups ready for the hot water. He said that he was making a cup for himself, and Zoe and he would include Bram as well.

He said it was their day on guard duty and they had only taken a sip of their beers.

Bram thanked him and sat down at his desk. He turned on his computer and began going through the equations on the spreadsheet that he had created.

He could just as easily have settled into his easy chair and gone through the equation in his mind and if Pat had been present, he would most likely have chosen to do so. But since she was back working with the rest of the leadership team on how to set up the offense for the Fold project he chose to sit at his desk.

He had been reviewing his equation and the assumptions he had made to connect space position with time for more than an hour when Pat knocked on the door.

As she entered he heard the group in the dining room say, "Tell us that half a beer didn't knock him out."

Bram knew that his guards were enjoying the remainder of the day. He got up and gave Pat a hug and asked how things in the meeting had gone.

Pat commented that Lacy had taken charge and had done a great job on insisting that the focus stay on identifying the members of the Fold Offense Team. She had limited the number of members to one from each organization and insisted that each provide some expertise or connection needed to provide the team with the ability to take action. She had made the point that she was not inclined to work with a team that talked more than they acted.

Pat went on to praise Erica for supporting Lacy in how the members should be selected.

Bram asked if the group had provided the names of members to Lacy.

Pat shared that Major General Lester Tyson, John Morgan, Elizabeth, and Lacy's father Ted were currently on the list.

Brian thought for a minute and asked how Ted had gotten on the list.

Pat said that Lacy had made a call during the meeting and asked if her father had recognized any of the attackers. She then hung up and put his name on the list.

Bram asked whether she was going to stay in the office or go and party out in the dining room.

Pat pointed to her side of the recliner and said that she had all the partying that she could take and that a cup of tea and some quiet time was what she was looking forward to.

Bram turned off his computer and made her a cup of tea. He was now looking forward to having her lean against him and feel her warmth.

<u>Chapter 4: The Bubble Problem</u>

The next morning when Bram arrived at his office, Lacy was sitting at her desk. After greeting her, he asked her to come into his office.

He let her know that he had heard from Pat and early this morning from Erica what a great job she had done in guiding the leadership meeting and with organizing the Fold Offense Team. He then asked if she had any recommendations for someone to replace her and he said that he wanted her to remodel the room next to Marcus's and appoint it in the manner that pleased her, but she had to make it a better office than Marcus's.

Lacy admitted that the change was happening in a very fast but exciting way. She was a little overwhelmed at the role that he had carved out for her. She admitted that she had to overcome the fact that many of her team had positions that were at the top of the organization.

He nodded and said that he had thought about the change all the way from the picnic area until they got to the gate. Seeing the attack vans and the bodies and then seeing the wheel on its side had coalesced the idea of an Fold team offense. He wanted an attack team and as soon as that thought came to him, her attack with her camera drone and the expertise she demonstrated using it had made her his choice of who would lead that attack team. He made the point that his one desire was that she develop the expertise of the Fold Offense Team with as much skill as she had demonstrated flying the camera drone in an attack mode.

He told her that on her team, her members answered to her no matter where they sat in the organization hierarchy.

He suggested that she identify what she needed to learn. He let her know that he was not going to get involved in all the details that she would be working through, and she should look to Elizabeth for support guidance. He would be available as well but expected to only get called on if a barrier seemed insurmountable.

The vacant support position was one that he identified needed to be addressed before she would be able to assume her new role. He asked if she had anyone who might be able to fill the role. He made the point that it would be good if that person was already in the Fold organization.

Lacy was silent for a moment and then said that she knew of several persons capable of filling her positions. After a moment she asked if it could be someone in her family.

Bram smiled and said the Stetson family was in good standing with him and who did she have in mind.

Lacy, said that it was her older sister, who had asked if she could interview for the position, when she heard about the promotion.

Bram pointed out that Linda was a social worker.

Lacy nodded and said that Linda had done a little secretarial support before becoming a nurse and going into the social work force. She was the smart one in the family and had always gotten better grades than her. They both had been on their high school lacrosse team, and Linda was seen as the leader of the team. Lacy gave a short laugh and said that Linda had expressed the fact that her younger sister had been the lucky one to land a job with the Fold Organization and that luck paid better than skill.

Bram said he was a believer in luck and that it was good to be lucky but usually luck was the result of good preparation and hard work.

He asked when Linda would be available for a personal discussion with him.

Lacy smiled as she said that she could be in his office in as little as fifteen minutes from now.

Bram replied that he was not going to cause someone to get a traffic ticket and that he would like to talk with Linda at one hour before the end of the normal workday.

He then tilted his head and asked what Lacy's new salary would need to be for him to keep her from jumping ship to one of the outside support organizations that he was sure would make her salary offers that might make her head spin.

Lacy replied that she was already getting one of the best salaries that she could imagine for someone with her skills.

Bram smiled and said that her sister was most likely going to get something close to what she was currently earning, but he expected to give her a salary closer to what Marcus was earning. He knew that Lacy had seen the pay level of several of his staff.

Her face went red. She pointed out that would mean that her pay would almost double. She said that she would love it, but she would settle for much less.

Bram nodded and said that when she got into her new role and experienced the intensity of the work, she would have a different opinion.

He said that it was time for her to call her sister, organize her transition to her new role and for him to meet with Zuri, Mallica, Marcus, and Jina and organize the review of the Fold equations.

He stood up and walked to the door, opened it, and waved her out.

Lacy walked out and immediately called Linda.

Bram could hear Lacy saying that yes, yes, she had the interview.

He was looking forward to having Linda as his new support. He had been impressed with her ability to recognize that Zuri was a mental genius and how she had persisted in telling everyone so. He had also noted that Zuri had a close relationship with Linda. He figured all Linda had to do was show up for the interview and she would have the support role that Lacy currently held.

It came to him that the Stetsons were slowly penetrating the Fold organization. By the end of the day, three of them would have active positions in support roles.

Orlando was joking with Zuri as he wheeled her into the office. He pointed at Bram and commented that he was the one that had twisted his arm and made him drink too much.

Zuri gave her soft laugh and said that Bram was too weak to twist Orlando's little finger let alone his arm.

Bram joined in and said that Orlando and his cohorts had consumed so much alcohol that he was amazed that Orlando was even capable of pushing her in and he would understand if Orlando were to pass out to the floor.

He then suggested that Orlando sit down and enjoy a cup of coffee or tea while the rest of the Equation Analysis Team (EAT) reviewed the Fold equations.

Orlando said that the review of the equations was sure to put him to sleep and most likely he would have nightmares. He walked to the door and said he was going to go to the cafeteria and make up a ditty about the EAT team that were trying to eat their way through the Fold equations.

Everyone laughed and Bram insinuated that he was probably going to engage in a pleasant endeavor while the rest of them drank tea or coffee and tried to stay awake.

Elizabeth called the EAT members to order and suggested they all get comfortable, and that Zuri would be expected to ask the why questions and as often as possible suggest a reason. Everyone else should ask questions for understanding or clearly state that they were lost and needed to be told what a specific part of the overall equation meant.

She then pointed at Bram and said that he would have to answer Zuri and the rest of them and needed to make everyone have at least a general understanding of the concept that each part of the equation represented.

It soon became clear that those in attendance were struggling like maple syrup sap trying to flow out of the tree on a cold winter day. Their sap, drip pan minds were mostly empty. The sap was just too thick.

Zuri was the only one that seemed to grasp the concepts and her why's caused Bram to stop and think about the reasons why he had linked certain parts of the equation together and what assumption had led him to do so.

Bram came to realize that he had been very lucky to have made the breakthrough. He thought back to his conversations with Einstein at the desert location when they sat together on the boulder where he had finally achieved the breakthrough.

Einstein his pet mouse was still with him. He had the urge to share this fact but decided that would wait until he and Zuri were working through the answers to her questions and share it only with her.

After an hour, Elizabeth called an end to the meeting and suggested that they reconvene in two days or when Zuri had answers to all her questions.

Bram thanked Elizabeth for having led them through the hour. He thanked, Jina for having recorded all the questions. Then he thanked everyone else for having added their questions.

Mallica commented that she felt that getting the answers to Zuri's questions would make a huge difference in her understanding the basics of the equation. She admitted that it was hard for her to understand how many of the assumption allowed the connection between the concepts.

Bram nodded and said that luck had a lot to do with his success.

Zuri shook her head and added luck and a brain that worked in a nonlinear fashion. She then emphasized, "in a fashion distinctly different, and more like that of a savant on drugs."

He asked Zuri to stay for a few moments and then asked Elizabeth to let Orlando know that they were done but that he should wait about fifteen minutes before coming to get her.

Zuri was in the process of asking what he wanted to talk about when Bram raised his hand to stop her.

He walked over to his bookcase and opened a small door and a small grey mouse walked out and got on his hand.

He carried it over to Zuri and introduced Einstein the coinventor of the Fold technology. He then described sitting on a large boulder in the middle of the desert in the dark, early in the morning waiting for the sun to rise. A few minutes after the sun hit the boulder, Einstein would come and sit with him and nibble on a piece of cookie.

He would always share the problem that he had with Einstein and ask for his advice.

Einstein never failed him and in time guided him to the Fold equation.

He explained that when he claimed not to know an answer it was because Einstein had never told him why an assumption would work.

Zuri had been gently petting Einstein, who had settled in her lap. She asked if she could give him a piece of cookie and ask him a question.

Bram gave her a cookie from the refreshment area.

Zuri gave a small section to Einstein and then asked why he had never explained the assumptions to the brilliant but definitely loony person named Bram.

"Oh, you say because you didn't think he was smart enough to understand. I get it from now on you want us to come to you with the questions needing answers and you will help us get to the answer. OK, you have a deal," Zuri said in a soft voice to Einstein.

Bram had a huge smile on his face when she lifted Einstein and place him in his hand.

There was a knock on the door as Bram put Einstein back into his palace and closed the little door.

He walked over and let Orlando in.

Lacy was standing right behind Orlando and when he wheeled Zuri out, she let him know that Linda had arrived and was ready.

Bram asked for five minutes and then to bring her in. He called up her resume and reviewed her work history. A picture of a very smart and hard-working person formed in his mind. He also was impressed with her focus and dedication to helping the most disadvantaged younger persons. He gave her a lot of credit for having insisted that Zuri was brilliant in spite of everyone doubting her.

He figured she had the job, but he wanted her to make her case and feel that she had sold herself.

The knock on the door caused him to rise and walk around the desk to greet Linda.

He went directly to the key question. He asked why she wanted the support role.

Linda responded that from all the stories that Lacy had shared working on the Fold project was the most challenging and provided the biggest opportunity to grow. She pointed out that Lacy was now moving on to a role that had not existed and that neither had ever dreamt of such a role.

Bram commented that such an opportunity might not happen again for a long time.

Linda smiled and said that she had only experienced a slice of the action that went on and it was a slice bigger than she had experienced in her whole working career.

Bram asked when she could start.

Linda said that she would ask Lacy to vacate her desk as soon as the interview was over.

Bram asked if she had any other questions.

Linda asked if she could move in with Lacy in her apartment.

Bram said that she could have her own apartment.

Linda replied that she and Lacy preferred to share since it would give them a chance to interact with each other every evening. Later if either of their situations changed one of them might want an apartment.

She gave a little laugh and said that neither of them had any love life and figured that it was because of their reluctance to be the weak member of a romance.

She then asked if he might want to change any support items.

Bram said that there was one small change that was due to the current effort of reviewing and improving the Fold equations. He normally ran an open-door office but for the duration of the review, he would like to have a scheduled ten minute warning for the next item on his calendar. She would schedule, let him know and then give him the ten-minute warning when appropriate.

Linda thanked him for the opportunity and stood up and walked toward the door.

Bram asked her to send Lacy in.

Lacy was all smiles when she entered. She thanked Bram and let him know that she and Linda were going to have a celebration dinner at their apartment that evening.

Bram smiled and said it was an easy hire. He knew that Zuri would be ecstatic about his new support since she would also be her support.

Lacy agreed and asked what he wanted to talk about.

Bram nodded and said that he wanted to apologize for having underpaid her in the past for her talents.

Lacy spoke up and asked if he were kidding. She was the highest paid support on the Fold team and made at least twice as much as she could get on the outside.

Bram said, "Oh" as if he were surprised. He then asked if her salary would satisfy Linda.

Lacy let him know that she made twice the salary that Linda currently got.

"Oh," so you think your current salary would be too much for Linda, he asked?

Lacy gave a small laugh and told him to pay Linda whatever he thought was fair.

Bram smiled; he had enjoyed baiting Lacy. He let her know that Linda would start at her current salary.

He then asked what he should pay her for her new role.

Lacy nodded and answered, "Whatever you think is fair."

Bram threw out the figure that he had determined fit with the role into which she was moving. It was just below Erica's, Elizabeth's, and Marcus's salaries but almost twice as much as she was currently making.

"Wow," I am shocked, "Wow" let me catch my breath before I faint," Lacy said as she closed her eyes.

Bram felt good about everything that had gone on during the day and the ending was especially rewarding. He suggested that Lacy go and celebrate and let him get home and get some rest so he could work on the most important issue at hand.

Chapter 5: Change

It was clear to Bram that the change in his role was opening up more time for him. He wondered how the change was affecting some of his key people. He invited those closest to him to give him their opinion on the change.

He asked Pat and Amy to meet with him. Amy wondered what the meeting was about, and he said that he wanted to get the impression from the two of them about the organizational change impact.

Amy said that overall, it seemed that Erica had become a new person. She was still hard driving, but her current approach was much more into making sure that everyone was getting coached, developed, and was enjoying their work.

He knew Pat's assessment already but asked her for her impression. Pat smiled and agreed with Amy. She did not have the desert experience where Amy had described Erica as the wicket witch from the east but what she saw now was a caring person and one that was trying to embrace the social environment that he had created.

Amy then said that she had heard from Elizabeth that during the Fold equation review, whenever you didn't have an answer to a question about why or how you had decided to combine concepts, you always replied that only Einstein would know and that Zuri would often repeat, "yes only Einstein would know."

The only Einstein that I ever met was a little mouse that came and sat with us on the morning that you revealed that you had solved the problem of creating a Fold. We two ate our treat and Einstein ate his cookie crumb.

I went on to become an Fold pilot. I forgot all about Einstein until Elizabeth shared what was happening in the Fold review.

Is Einstein still alive?

Bram looked at Pat and said that he had shared the story about talking to Einstein with her, but he had not shared the fact that Einstein was the most experienced Fold traveler among them.

One of the side effects to going through the Fold seemed to affect aging. He said that Einstein had volunteered to be a Fold traveler, so Bram had used him to make sure the Fold process did not prove fatal to a living organism. He had Folded him more than a dozen times and other than his friend turning grey as he aged, he physically was not deteriorating.

Pat smiled and asked if he had Einstein in the office.

Bram got up and went to the bookcase, moved a few books, and opened the little door. Einstein sniffed his way out and hopped into Bram's open hand.

He carried him over and handed him to Amy. Einstein sniffed her hand and then curled up in her palm.

Bram pointed out that it was Einstein's way of greeting an old friend.

Amy had tears in her eyes as she handed Einstein to Pat. She said that her trip to the rock in the desert that Bram went to every morning had been the turning point of her life and she was still on the launch trajectory he had urged her to take and hoped that it would take all her life to reach orbit. Einstein is the jewel that I think about often and it doesn't surprise me that he is smarter than the mad scientist he coaches.

Bram gave a light laugh and agreed about Einstein being the genius. He was now in the process of coaching Zuri and he, as they examined the assumptions that had been made during the Fold equation development.

Bram went on to share that the reason that he and Zuri were examining the equation so closely was that their goal was to create the ability that an object in a Fold would be able to move the Fold coordinates from their Fold location but not have to use additional energy to do so.

Pat put up her hand and asked whether that would allow her to move positions at will.

Bram answered that Zuri described it as creating a portal that allowed the Fold vessel to travel through a time and space portal.

Amy shook her head and said that she was lost in how it would work but she was eager to see him succeed and if Einstein was the critical thinker, then she would bring him a cookie crumb every day if that would help.

Bram replied that Einstein had agreed to a strict diet and did not want to eat too many cookies and gain weight. He said that he had also volunteered to be the first to travel through the time-space wormhole as soon as what allowed that to happen was discovered.

Pat came over and gave him a kiss and said that she thought that he had told her everything but now she had learned that he had kept a secret.

Bram said yes he had but he lifted Einstein and pointed out that it was a little secret.

After they left Bram asked Linda to come meet with him.

It had been a week since she had become his and Zuri's support. He asked her how she felt about the week and whether the pay was adequate.

Linda had learned what her pay was going to be from Lacy when they both celebrated their new jobs. She was very happy to be getting her sister's old job. She was surprised at how much she was to get paid. Was the pay adequate? She then shared that it was a fifty percent increase over the pay she had received as a nurse.

It was more than adequate.

She finally verbalized that yes, the pay was more than adequate and that if Zuri and he did not generate more work she would need to bring in large books to read.

The Message

Bram nodded and said that she should embrace the moment and that it most likely was the quiet before the storm.

He then asked if he and Erica were still scheduled to meet.

He walked to Erica's office to meet with her. This was the first time for them to meet with just each other and it was the first time he would get to see her office.

He knocked on the door and entered when her heard Erica say come in. He took in a simple and efficient looking office. It seemed somewhat Spartan. He sat down and asked how the first week had gone.

Erica commented that she had no idea how he had kept things going on his own. The bubble assembly work alone could take all of her time if she let it. But she was also in the process of contacting the companies that they might choose to produce the future bubbles.

She asked whether any additional wheels would be needed.

Bram replied to the last question and said that if he and Zuri were able to make a breakthrough in the Fold equation that the wheel might be of interest but at the moment two wheels seemed to be two too many.

He said he felt bad about having started with them, but they had been successful and would be useful if staying out in a Fold for some length of time were the objective.

Erica then asked him what he was hearing about her leadership.

Bram replied that she was seen as a hard driver but one who seemed fair and developmental. He made the point that his informants were tough critics and their positive assessment meant that she was doing a good job in her role.

He thanked her for having chosen to come to the Dallas Fold complex.

He asked her how she liked her living accommodations.

Erica was overjoyed at the comfort of and the view from her top-level apartment. She let him know that the tension overload that she had accumulated working in Washington was leaving her body on a daily basis. She laughed and said that she was waiting for a breakfast pancake, eggs and sausage invite.

Bram felt relieved that Erica was making the transition into being the kind of leader he had always envisioned she could be. He was pleased to hear that she was finding the Fold environment to her liking.

He then invited her for a Sunday brunch. He said he was not sure who would be present, but he would make sure there would be plenty for everyone.

Erica thanked him and said she would put it on her really busy Sunday schedule.

Bram said his would be busy as well. He had breakfast, lunch, and dinner to deal with and maybe a dip in the pool.

He then stood and said that he was going to go to the bubble assembly area to get a look at the bubbles. He said the bubbles helped him to think physically about the mathematical concepts with which he was struggling.

Erica asked if she could join in on his visit.

Bram was greeted in the lab with a Marine "Hurrah" that had become a common way for the folks there. He gave the Hawaiian finger waggle and walked over to where Bramlet One was still in its chamber with the large black object merged in its bubble.

He asked Erica what was planned for Bramlet One.

She said that the following week Bramlet One would be taken to a sterile lab and disassembled. She said that there was a great deal of interest to learn if the plastic was merged with the asteroid material or if it had been melted and formed around the asteroid.

Bram said that he would bet on the two materials having merged all the way through and the shape of the bubble would be found in the asteroid.

Erica said she would let him know as soon as she found out.

Bram then went around the lab and asked if what he saw was the total production to date.

Remi said that they had started to put the bubbles out by the Wheel area. He wondered how many more his group should plan on.

Bram said that Erica and Marcus would be the ones that would determine how many more would be needed.

Erica replied that the current production was based on Marcus's projection of where he wanted to send the bramlet scouts. She was working the longer term and was working with external folks to set up production. That longer term need would be based on what the Fold expansion would look like.

Bram nodded and said that if he had anything to do with it, they would need a lifetime of bubbles, but he was not sure what the specifications would be.

Chapter 6: The Message

The team analyzing the Fold equation decided that viewing the equation on paper might be easier than viewing it on the large screen. Bram agreed that an analog way of seeing the whole equation allowed the assumption points connecting various concepts to be seen all at once. He suggested they move their review to Zuri's office.

Linda let them know that only the area around Zuri's desk area was complete. The window area across from her desk was due to get painted and a long flower tray would be built in front of it.

Bram asked Linda to have the contractor put some plywood across the windows and to leave the end walls open. He then asked her to find a large roll of thick white paper to put on the wall and across the windows to create a giant white board that he could write his equation on. He asked for several large black felt pens and some white out in case he messed up a part of the equation and wanted to correct it.

Linda commented that she had never seen white out and was surprised he even knew about it.

Bram laughed and let her know that he had gone to a sandstone walled, one room school for his first eight years. There he had used chalk on a black board. He had used his teacher's manual typewriter and often used whiteout because he was terrible at typing.

He asked that the work on the white board take priority and get done that day.

He then asked Linda to have a messaging tube like those used at the mobile banking stands installed between his office and Zuri's office and to locate the tube exit behind Zuri's desk. He said this would allow the two of them to send material back and forth and save them time. He added that he wanted the tube to be in the wall and basically invisible.

He and Zuri had come up with this as an excuse and were really planning to use it as Einstein's private subway system.

The next day he spent the day carefully writing the Fold equation on the white paper. Mallica, Jina and Zuri stayed and watched but Marcus excused himself so he could go focus on where he was planning to send the Bramlet scouts.

Bram started writing on the upper left corner at head height. He thought that the equation was complicated and long enough that he would be having to be on his knees writing to get the equation on the space that the paper provided.

When he got to the first connecting assumption, Zuri suggested leaving a wide-open space so they could add a linking equation that might be needed to create the Fold location motion.

Bram let her know he liked that suggestion and wondered how much space he should leave.

Mallica suggested leaving at least three feet of space.

Bram worked hard at keeping the equation going straight across the room.

Jina joked that it reminded her about her writing lessons where the paper had guidelines to guide the writer.

Bram stopped and asked if Jina would put the guidelines up so that he could concentrate on the equation versus on trying to keep it level.

At ten, Linda brought in break refreshments and asked if she should order lunch in.

Bram shook his head and said that he was looking forward to going to the cafeteria for lunch and that Linda should take the lunch order and make sure they had a table reserved.

By lunch Bram was only a third of the way through the equation.

Mallica commented that Einstein had written his E=MC^2 that had stood for most of a century and wondered why Bram's was so long.

Bram replied that the next layer of equations that Einstein had written as the proof for that equation was about as long as what he had written on the wall.

He made the point that his equation took everything that Einstein had done and merged it with the works of several other scientists and that he had to modify some parts of each of those equations. This meant that his equation was roughly three times longer than Einstein's proof equations.

By noon Bram had made it about halfway and the going was slowing down. Zuri commented that they needed Einstein's guidance, and everyone agreed.

Bram smiled because what everyone else had heard was not what he had heard. He knew that Zuri was telling him that she wanted to hold Einstein, the mouse.

He suggested that after lunch, he would continue on his own, and they would all reconvene in the morning.

Mallica thought that was a good suggestion and said she was going to check on the progress of the next set of Bramlet scouts and see how Marcus was doing with getting the coordinates ready.

Jina asked Mallica if she could tag along.

Zuri said since she was in her office she would sit, and watch Bram put up the equation until it was time to go home.

Bram led the way to the cafeteria and spotted Linda sitting at a table that she had reserved.

He had a leisurely lunch and then he pushed Zuri back to her office.

He then went to his office and carried Einstein back in his pocket and hand him to Zuri who held him in her lap and lightly stroked him.

He spent the rest of the day writing his equation along the lines that Jina had drawn for him.

Zuri would periodically pose a question to Einstein about the equation and Bram would answer if he knew the answer or he would write her question down on a separate easel that they had set up for that purpose.

He stopped writing when he came to the last equation link assumption. He figured that he had at least a half day left of writing and that the link was a good stopping point.

The next morning everyone was back in Zuri's office and Bram concentrated on writing the last series of equations. He was down to the last few mathematical statements when there was a knock on the door and Linda announced that Erica had called and let her know that she had received a call from the analysis team saying they needed help and that she needed to meet with him.

Bram held up his hand and said that he would speak with Erica after lunch because he was at the end of writing his equations and it would take that long to finish.

Linda replied that she would let Erica know.

Bram wondered what the analysis team could possibly have found that would cause Erica to want to immediately talk with him.

He sped up his writing and by lunch he emphatically drew a large black circle and put the words "The End" at the end of the last mathematical symbol.

He looked around at Mallica, Jina and Zuri and declared that he was done writing and that now all they had to do was to step through each part of the equation and answer all the questions that they had captured on the chart pad, and they had to determine if the transition points were where they would be able to put transition equations that would alter the Fold from being stationary to one that would allow movement in the desired direction that could be programed in.

He declared that after lunch they would get into the thick of things and see if they could make the desired breakthrough.

They were all just finishing their meals when Erica entered the cafeteria and came over to their table.

She was about to engage them when Bram put up his hand and asked that they all go meet in Zuri's office.

He pushed Zuri back to her office and once there he took a seat and asked about the urgent request from the analysts.

Erica said that the analysis team that was examining the tremendous amount of data from the first set of Folds that Bram had conducted with the Bramlets. The team had called her and said that they needed help in deciphering what they were sure was a message from an alien race.

The Message

They had sent her the recorded section that held the message, and they were asking for help in deciphering it. They admitted that they had hit a wall, and no one knew what to do next.

The meeting had gone silent. They were all looking at Bram.

Bram looked around the room and asked which branch in the road should the team take. Should they continue to work on the Fold equation, or should they see if it was a message from an Alien race and decipher it.

Zuri spoke up and said that they should address the message, but they needed first to determine if the message was fresh, and she clarified that fresh meant that it was within her lifetime and was not a message that was sent millions of years or longer ago. If it was fresh, they should decipher it otherwise they should focus on finishing the work on the Fold equation. She commented that a million year old message was like finding a message floating in a bottle that had been thrown off a sailing vessel three hundred year in the past.

Bram nodded and said he agreed and then asked how they would determine if it was a fresh or ancient.

The room was quiet.

Zuri asked how many times the message repeated.

Erica said she had no idea. She had received only one copy of what the analysis team said was a message.

Bram suggested that they set up a meeting with the analysis team so they could learn what they had done and could answer any questions that the Fold team might have.

He asked Erica to work with Linda to set up a meeting for the following morning.

He let her know that the Review Team would generate a list of questions for the Analysis team, and they would finish the day reviewing the Fold equations and determining what the next steps would be.

He then asked Mallica to lead the preparation for the meeting with the Analysis Team.

Mallica excused herself saying she would work with Elizabeth and Jina on the meeting with the analysis team.

Bram realized that only Zuri was still in the office. He said that he was going to get Einstein and they would set up the equation review so that they could return to it and determine how to dynamically connect the transition points in the equation. Then they would focus on setting up a test plan to determine if any transition point was the key to allowing them to create what Zuri had labeled a moving Fold.

Pat knocked at the office door and then entered. She pointed at the clock and asked if the two of them were going to call it a day.

She said that she had joined Mallica and had worked on getting ready to work with the Analysis team. She had listened to the one cycle of the message and wondered how that team had decided that it was a message.

Bram and Zuri both started to answer. Bram waved to Zuri to indicate she should answer.

The Message

Zuri said there was no way to know if it was a message until they listened to the entire transmission that was received and that even then it would be hard to determine if it was a message or if it was a random signal being generated by some rotating object that was emitting a radio signal.

Bram agreed and said that he planned to get the entire transmission and that he had the original saved in Dallas and they would make sure that no corruption of the signal had occurred.

He agreed that it was time to quit. He took Einstein from Zuri and handed him to Pat for a moment.

Pat asked if Einstein had helped to solve any of the questions generated by the Fold equation review.

Bram pointed to Zuri and said that Einstein had calmed her down enough that she had stopped shouting insults about how poorly he actually understood his own equation and assumptions.

Zuri gave a small laugh and said that talking to Einstein was the only way for her to come close to understanding what Bram had developed since he was somewhat smarter than either of them.

Bram took Einstein and put him in his pocket and said he was returning Einstein to his castle for the night and then he was ready to head home.

He asked Pat to get the van pulled to the door and notify Orlando that it was time to get Zuri home.

The next morning as they jogged into work, Bram asked that they think up a ditty about a message from space. Caster started with,

There are aliens out in space.
They've no idea about the human race.
There are aliens in out space.
They may be smart or maybe not,
There are aliens in outer space,
They have no idea of what they now may face.
The human race, the human race, will make fodder of the alien race."

Bram was surprised at how fast the ditty came out and except for the last line he liked it.

Linda was waiting when he arrived and let him know that she had arranged a large table on the stage of the auditorium. She had determined that every member that had made the Fold to the back of the moon had requested a seat.

Bram asked her to establish the protocol that only he, Erica and Zuri would ask questions of the Analysis team members until they were at the end and then there would be an open question and answer period.

When they got to the table, Linda made the announcement.

Bram asked Erica to manage the meeting.

He handed Zuri an I-pad and said that the two of them could talk back and forth on it. He said that they were the code breakers and just like the ones made so famous in World War Two, the two of them needed to become as good as they were and needed to do it much faster.

The Message

Erica opened the meeting by having the Analysis Team introduce themselves.

She asked that they begin by listening to the entire message cycle.

The team leader replied that the entire message would take several hours and did they really want to start there.

Bram nodded in the affirmative.

Erica replied that they begin at the beginning of the message cycle.

The message indeed seemed to repeat but Zuri picket up that one passage only repeated every tenth time and each of the repeats in between seemed to have a slightly different tone at the beginning. She noted that the other nine distinct sections remained unchanged when they repeated.

She said that she believed the unchanged part was the message being repeated and the one changing was the key for them to unravel the message.

She was typing away as fast as her fingers would allow her to. She pointed out that the one repeating every tenth time was most likely the Rosetta stone that would allow them to decipher the message.

Erica picked up on the fact that Bram and Zuri were communicating with each other, and she was watching for signs of some sort of breakthrough. It was clear to her that they had discovered something, and she was dying to know what that might be, but she knew to keep out of their way.

It was hard for her to listen to what seemed to her to be a monotonous signal repetition.

Brian noted that most of the participants were having difficulty listening to the seemingly monotonous, repetitive signal. He wanted to share that there were slight nuances that would most likely lead to the ability to decipher the message.

He now began to wonder how he and Zuri would be able to determine when the message was sent. He did not want to spend time on a message that might be millions to billions of years old. If, as Zuri had suggested, that if it was fresh then they should focus on it and determine what was being sent.

She had jokingly suggested if it was a fresh message, she wanted to be certain that it was not a bogeyman race letting Earth know that they were on the way to ravish the planet.

Linda escorted her father, brother, and mother in as they set up some tables and put a variety of snacks and drinks out for everyone. They then returned with a variety of pizza's and a large bowl of mixed greens.

Bram thanked her for going the extra mile.

He was still trying to figure out how to time stamp the origin time of the message.

Linda pointed to one end of the table and mouthed the words, start here.

Bram suddenly had a flash of how to identify what was on the "Alien Rosetta Stone." He stood up and suggested they take a break.

The Message

Erica knew the look on Bram's face as she called for a break. As the team headed for the refreshment and pizza table, she approached Bram who was talking to Zuri.

She asked him what had just happened.

Bram pointed to Linda and said that she had solved the conundrum of how to decode the message.

Erica looked at him and said that she was confused since Linda had never said a word.

Bram laughed and agreed but he said that she had pointed at the end of the table and mouthed, "start here."

Erica asked how that had triggered Bram to ask for a stop.

Bram said that they had to go back to the beginning of the message and take a few steps back so they could start at the beginning. He said that he believed they may have started after the tutorial on how to decipher the Rosetta. They had to go back and get the very first part of the message and take a step back to get the start here section. Then they would be able to decipher the message.

He commented that the question of when the message was sent still needed to be resolved.

He suggested a fresh start on the following morning. He said that he and Zuri would spend the afternoon organizing their thoughts and on stepping back to the very first point of the message.

He also planned to have Marcus send a bubble out to that original location and see if they could look back farther and get the very beginning of the message.

Erica replied that she would manage the change and he could get Marcus going on Folding a bubble to the desired location.

Bram thanked her and after asking Linda to have Marcus come to Zuri's office and to also bring some pizza to her office, he wheeled Zuri out of the auditorium.

Chapter 7: Time Marker

Bram had just handed Einstein to Zuri when Marcus knocked on the door. Bram walked over and opened the door and let Marcus enter.

Once Marcus had entered, Bram asked him to send out a bubble to the coordinates of the bubble that had picked up the message. He asked Marcus to pinpoint the direction from where the message originated. Once Marcus had those coordinates, Marcus should then Fold the next bubble at least half the distance to the origin of the message. While the bubble was in that location, he wanted a high-resolution picture of the stars and constellations in that area of space.

Marcus confirmed the request and said that he had several bubbles ready, and he would send at least two out simultaneously and try to get another one out to the halfway point.

He excused himself and said that he would be able to fulfill the request by late afternoon. He asked if he should share the results with the two of them then or wait until the following morning.

Bram said that he wanted the information that day.

Marcus let them know that he would get it to them immediately on return of the bubbles.

Once Marcus had departed, Bram took a wedge of pizza and pinched off a small piece, gave it to Einstein, and asked him if they were going to find out if the message was fresh.

Zuri responded that she wanted Bram to share what he had in mind with the information Marcus was gathering.

Bram replied that he was going to correlate the message origin with the star map of that area that was on record. He would then compare the message star pattern to the star pattern for that area captured by the bubble. If they were the same, they would have a fresh message and they would know how much energy they needed to assign to deciphering the message. He was also hoping that they had missed the very beginning of the message which he was sure would be a tutorial on how to read the message. He figured the tutorial would guide them on how to translate the Alien Rosetta Stone message.

Zuri asked how Linda's pointing to the end of the table and mouthing "start here" had triggered the action that he was now taking.

Bram replied that a few moments ago Einstein had replied, yes, to his question about whether the message was fresh. It had triggered the thought about the tutorial being at the beginning of the message, he had no clue why he had thought of it, but it just happened.

The Message

Zuri nodded and said that he had a weird mind that had allowed him to tie a variety of seemingly independent concepts together by talking to a mouse and now he had added lip reading to the mix. She said that she had no way to keep up with such a non-linear mind.

Bram made the point that the two were a good match since she would force him to take the kinks out of his thought process. He said they were like the couple where the man could eat no lean and the wife could eat no fat, so between the two they licked their platter clean.

Zuri gave a laughed and said that he had just proved her point about a nonlinear mind.

Bram poured each of them a cup of tea and then sat down. He suggested they listen to the message again and try to use its cadence to organize it into a structure that seemed to make sense.

It was late afternoon when Zuri suggested that they put Einstein back in his palace and get ready to go home.

Bram was returning to Zuri's office when he saw Marcus coming down the hallway in a slow jog. He asked him if the jog was meant to get him in shape

Marcus replied that he wanted to get the information to Zuri and him before the end of the workday and handed Bram four memory sticks each having the numbers one and two written on them.

He said that the one labeled one was the message and the one labeled two had the star constellation picture taken from the bubble and it also had the star constellation as seen from the Hubble telescope. He went on to say that he had run a statistical analysis that compared the two pictures that showed them to have a ninety-nine percent correlation. This seemed to suggest that the message was a recent one, but he did not know how to define recent.

Bram then said that perhaps they had started out wrong in listening to the message and thinking it was a written message needing an Alien Rosetta Stone to break the code. He then share the fact that some forty years in the past when the Arecibo telescope had been rebuilt they had sent out a very simple message on the celebration event day meant to be assembled as a graphic and then interpreted. It had been aimed at a very specific star cluster and was still on its way and would be traveling there for another twenty-five thousand years. There had also been the records sent out on the voyager spacecrafts. The records were more elaborate and had music, laughter, and messages in text and in voice.

Zuri commented that she had not known about either. She then asked how they should approach the message.

The Message

First let's think about who they are trying to reach. We have a signal that seems to be coming at us but in fact we need to look to see if there is a specific galaxy behind us. We might also need to develop a three-dimensional map of where else they are beaming the signal. If they are beaming in all dimensional planes, then they seem to be trying very hard to get a response. It makes me think about a ship beaming a Mayday signal in all directions.

He asked Marcus to send out his Bramlets to determine the signal distribution pattern. Meanwhile we can start at the very beginning of the message to see if we can begin to decipher the signal.

Zuri said she needed to absorb the morning's lesson about historic space messages before trying to learn an alien language.

Bram said that he understood and that he was as hesitant as she about learning a space language or perhaps figuring out a space drawing or a multi-piece puzzle. That is when it came to him that the messages could create a flat puzzle and the breaks in the message string might be there to guide the layout of the puzzle pieces.

He shared that with Zuri who put up her hand and suggested he get the rest of the people who had volunteered to help decipher the message.

Bram gave her a thumbs up.

By ten everyone had gathered in Zuri's office. Linda had brought in another large white board that Bram had requested.

He went to the board and drew a large rectangle and then divided it into nine parts. He then had Linda print out each section of the message that seemed to be preceded by a number and place it on the board. The first three went across the top from left to right, the second three went across the middle and the last three went across the bottom.

He then asked the team to examine the signal to see if the pattern remained the same or if there was a difference. He asked that they slow the signal speed down so they could listen for differences.

Jina immediately commented that there were differences in each section. Elizabeth confirmed that she too could discern differences. Mallica and Erica shook their heads and said they were not able to hear the differences.

Bram nodded and said that he could not hear differences either, but he was going to count on Jina and Elizabeth to create the picture that he now was sure was in the puzzle and he was certain the puzzle would be the message.

Linda suggested that they break for lunch since Chef D'Carluca

had sent her a message that he had made French Veal Cordon Bleu with mushrooms and scallions in a white wine sauce for the team and that it was on the verge of being ready.

Bram said he was ready as Elizabeth grabbed him by the arm and led the way out the door.

The Message

They were met by Eric and Zoe who immediately took the lead.

He looked back and saw Mallica pushing Zuri, so he relaxed and sauntered up the Hallway to the cafeteria.

Pat and Amy came over to the table and said that they had been invited to lunch and wondered if they could join the team in trying to translate the alien message.

Bram listened as Elizabeth said that she was eager to get the two to listen to the message to see if they could hear a difference between each segment.

Bram knew that Pat had a great ear for music and expected her to discern a difference. He hoped so. Having three persons able to hear a difference would be reassuring.

Chef D'Carluca came out with his team and served the Cordon Bleu.

Bram asked if there was something special about the day and found out that it was exactly two years since the pool attack.

The Chef pointed to Zoe, Eric and to him and said that he was recognizing the heroes that had saved the day.

Zuri gave a hand clap and the whole cafeteria responded in kind.

Bram acted as if he had forgotten the date but in reality, it was hard for him to forget anything that he considered significant. He had remembered but he had not expected anyone else to remember.

Pat came over to him and gave him a hug and whispered that he was a good actor, and she knew that he had not forgotten that it was the day that he had saved her life.

Bram smiled and thanked her for the hug.

He raised his glass of sparkling water and toasted Zoe and Eric for having both jumped the pool fence in their swimsuits and charged at two shooters who had long rifles and were shooting at them. He added that he had fallen down and accidently knocked into one of the gunmen and was lucky to have survived.

He had just finished the toast when Marcus entered the cafeteria and announced that he had sent out his Bramlets and had surrounded the source of the signal and all had returned with the same signal.

Marcus sat down and asked if there was enough of whatever they were having. Mallica said that she had plenty to share but Linda stopped her and signaled one of the cafeteria cooks and asked for an additional order.

Mallica commented that the two of them had spent a year isolated out in the desert and had learned to share everything.

Marcus asked if he should plan any more Bramlet missions. He said that if not he would really like to join the team trying to break the message.

Mallica said with his great musical ability he should definitely be part of the group.

Elizabeth answered and asked if he was good discerning slight differences in the flow of sounds.

Marcus replied that he thought so, but he was not sure why she was asking.

Bram explained that he thought each of the signal blocks held a different content and that the content would be graphical, but they would need to figure out how to interpret the sound.

Once back in Zuri's office, Bram asked that the message be played again and this time he wanted to go slow enough so that they could diagram each block with a different symbol for each sound. By going slow enough they were able to recognize the blank space between each sound. Elizabeth, Marcus, Pat, and Jina worked together to decide the symbol for each distinctively different sound. It soon became visibly apparent that some sort of alphabet was being used.

After the fourth block had been listened to it became clear that the alien alphabet was going to be longer than that of Earth's English alphabet.

Bram pointed to the number of symbols and commented that they had designated eighty-four different symbols. He said that the longest alphabet on Earth was only seventy-four letters long and that one of those languages was Vietnamese. He then pointed out that they were trying to put together a puzzle and puzzles were normally pictures. There were currently two active languages that used ideographic and pictographic forms of writing.

He said that Mandarin was an ideographic alphabet. It was a language that used graphic symbols that represented an idea or concept. He made the point that it was actually independent of any particular language, and specific words or phrases.

The other was Cantonese that was a pictographic alphabet. He made the point that it used pictorial drawings to represent concepts and ideas.

The Fold team had individuals that fit into each of the unique alphabetic groups. Bram decided these folks needed to be on the team.

Elizabeth pointed to the wall clock and said that it was time to close the meeting. She congratulated the listeners for having created a set of symbols for each sound.

Bram said he was going to recruit members that were on the Fold staff that were familiar with each and have them come and listen to the message.

He declared the following day to be free for everyone including Zuri if she decided to take it off.

Zuri responded that she was not going to miss out on her moment to become smarter. Everyone but Marcus agreed that they wanted to attend.

He said that he would spend the day reviewing where to send the Bramlets.

Bram asked Linda to set them up in the auditorium. He said that there would be ten additional people that he was inviting for the next day.

The Message

He let the rest of the team know that he wanted the early part of the morning until ten to interview the folks he was going to recruit. He wanted to make sure they could hear the nuances in the message. Then they would listen to the entire message again.

He listed the people that he was planning to invite and asked Linda to contact them before the end of the day and invite them to the auditorium. He let her know that she should let them know that it took priority over everything else they might be doing.

Chapter 8: Visual Language

Bram decided to walk back to his house and once again he was following Castor and Donna in their battle gear. He had asked them if it was really necessary, and Castor had responded that Bram should stop asking that question or show them his superman costume.

Bob piped up that Bram didn't have a superman costume but instead wore a bull's eye target on his back and that was why the FBI ran in back. Zoe and Eric were in the armored truck behind all of them and had heard the exchange and blinked the headlights.

Pat gave a pull-on Bram's arm and quietly told him he had asked for it.

Bram nodded but said he really worried about the weight that the two carried and that the heat was very oppressive.

He then went silent and concentrated on the Alien signal. He was feeling more and more positive that in the next several days they were going to break the message.

He had the resources; he had the right people now and they all had to listen to the tutorial and learn how to decode the message.

He wondered if they should have started with the tutorial but felt that they would have had to do the same thing and now that they were more familiar with the message, the tutorial should be easier to decipher. He also felt that having the additional new folks would make a huge difference.

Pat knew that Bram was off in a different world and walking in automatic.

It was his day to cook but she wondered if he were up to it. She thought it would be better for him to spend the time in his office and sit on the couch and think.

She sent a text to the team and asked who was up to take Bram's cooking duty. Everyone responded in the affirmative.

When they got to the house, they all entered through the basement garage. As they got to the kitchen, she pushed Bram past it into the office and said she wanted a cup of tea to go with her biscuit.

It was clear to her that he was still in his other state.

She took the cup when he handed it to her and had him take his seat. She leaned against him and asked what he was thinking about.

Bram was silent for quite some time and Pat wondered if he had heard her. She was sure he had but had put her question at a lower priority than what he was working on.

The Message

He finally said that he thought he knew what the message was about, but he had to think through it some more and he would wait until the following day and the next pass through that message.

Zoe had been standing quietly on one side of the office and Eric was on the other. She commented that she knew when Bram was in this mode that he was in she could do almost anything and he would not bother to react to her.

Bram opened his eyes and replied that he remembered every action that she had taken when he was thinking and someday, he would get even.

The call to dinner stopped the exchange and they all went into the dining area.

Bram reminded everyone that the following day was going to be grueling and that he planned to retire early, and they should make sure he did not oversleep.

The next morning, he asked for a ditty about the message from space from an Alien race that was presented as a picture puzzle or perhaps it was instead no puzzle, but a daunting threat caused by a dying sun.

They were soon jogging to the ditty, and he was asked several times why he had suggested the words.

Bram refused to answer and replied that he had dreamt the answer in his sleep.

Pat had wondered what Bram's tossing and turning had been about and now she knew that he had spent a good part of the night working on the message.

Bram led the team into the cafeteria and suggested they all have breakfast and then relax until Linda let them know that their new team members were all in the auditorium. He would then test the new members for their ability to discern the changes in the message tones. Then he would have the team establish symbols for each of the sounds. Once they were organized, he would have them listen to the Alien message from the beginning. Once their new members had listened to the entire message, he would call a break and then everyone would listen to the tutorial and then go through the message once more.

He said that he hoped to decipher the message by the end of the following day.

Pat asked if he planned to share what he thought the message said.

Bram shook his head and said he did not plan to until they had figured out the body of the message. He hoped to learn the alien numbering system and their alphabet and then he would be willing to make suggestions on the translation of the message based on what was appearing on the white board.

Linda walked into the cafeteria and let them know that she had assembled the one Vietnamese couple, the four persons that knew Mandarin and the four that knew Cantonese.

Bram stood and head out toward the auditorium. Bob and Thomas jump up and assumed their body guarding positions.

Bram was always surprised at how his bodyguards were always at the ready.

He entered the auditorium and thanked the ten people sitting around the table for having responded to his request on such a short notice. He made the point that it was a historic opportunity and if they contributed to solving the Alien message, they would all be remembered in the history books.

He then explained that he would like them to listen to the message that everyone else had listened to and then put their take of the message in each section on the white board that corresponded to the section of the message.

The ten sat and listened to the message. They talked among themselves and then they let Linda know what to write in the section of the block.

Bram was satisfied with the fact that they all agreed that the message seemed to have the progression that he and the rest had identified.

At the end of message string, he listened to them discuss the fact that there seemed to be many characters to the message. Bram cut short a discussion of how many characters existed when it was apparent that the range the group was arguing about was from one hundred ten to one hundred eighteen characters.

He pointed at the wall clock and suggested they have the lunch that had been brought in. He then asked Linda to let the rest of the participants know that lunch was served, and they should return and spend a few moments with the new translation team members.

During lunch he explained to Erica that Marcus had been able to retrieve what he hoped was the tutorial that would help them decode the message. He asked her to explain this to the group and then take them through the very beginning of the message.

He asked Linda to capture questions, but that discussion about the question would wait until the end of the tutorial.

He explained that he wanted to focus on the tutorial and did not want to try to do that and lead the group.

He suggested that Erica keep the question-and-answer session short and focus on pulling out what each member had learned.

The Q&A session was brief.

The main request was to listen again to the tutorial but go through it very slowly because several of the team felt that they had figured out that there was a section that taught the number scale and there seemed to be parts where the alphabet was being explained.

The Vietnamese husband and wife team was certain that they had picked up on the alphabet portion.

The eight Chinese that understood Mandarin and Cantonese shared that they had to stop themselves from trying to use the pictorials that came to their minds when they listened to parts of the tutorial. They wanted to go slowly through those sections and see if they could break the pictorial code.

Bram suggested that they stop for the day and start the next morning and slowly go through the tutorial again and work on learning how to count and use the sounds used to count and apply that to the rest of the tutorial message.

Pat knew that Bram had an idea of the basic content of the message and that by the next morning he might have learned both the counting system and the alphabet. She was mentally preparing to sleep next to a person that would mumble to himself throughout the night. She had come to realize that Bram talked to and answered himself when he was working through a problem during his sleep.

Pat agreed with Bram when he suggested they walk home.

Pat always enjoyed the walk. The view of lake beyond the adjoining fruit farm was inspiring, the chatter between their bodyguards amusing and Bram's attempt to stay in the present was always interesting. He would periodically point out some view or comment on something that had occurred during the day to her and then he would return to his musings. She figured he was plotting how he was going to solve the problem he was working on.

This walk was no different and by the time they walked into the basement entrance to their house Bram came back to the present and suggested they relax for a short time before going into the study.

That night was as Pat had anticipated. She positioned herself slightly away from Bram and fell asleep.

She was surprised to find the bed empty when she awoke at four.

She got ready for the day and then went downstairs where she found Bram in his study on his computer.

She left and returned with two cups of coffee. She sat and watched as his fingers seemed to dance across the keys like a virtuoso playing a piano. She did not bother to try to engage instead she returned to the kitchen that now had all four of their bodyguards preparing their breakfast.

Zoe asked her where her other half happened to be.

Pat shared that she had lost him in the office where his computer had kidnapped him.

Castor and Donna made their entrance and asked the same question and then said they would love a cup of coffee.

Donna asked if there was a ransom that had been demanded to release Bram. The chatter took off in that direction and they all sat down in the dining area.

Pat knew that Bram would emerge as soon as he was finished with what he was doing or if it was getting close to the time when the morning session was to begin. Bram might be in his own world, but he always was early to any scheduled interaction in the normal world.

This time it was the normal world schedule that pulled him off his computer.

The Message

Bram walked out of his office and was greeted by all his bodyguards. He walked over to Pat and gave her a hug and kiss and thanked her for the cup of coffee.

He then said he would eat his breakfast when they arrived at the Fold site auditorium. He laughed when they all replied that they would be ready for their second breakfast by that time.

He nodded and said he appreciated their patience with his periodic upsets of their day's schedule.

On their jog in to work, he proposed a new limerick to jog to.

One, two, three, four an Alien counting lesson.
One, two three, four, count, count, One, two, three, four.
A, B, C, D, an Alien message.
A, B, C, D, learn, learn, A, B, C, D.
1234, 1234, ABCD, ABCD, Alien kindergarten, 1234,
ABCD
Let's do it. Let's say it.
Let's do it all once more.

Pat knew then that Bram had solved the message and she knew she would have to wait as he guided the decoding team on their learning journey.

Bram looked at Pat and let her know that he felt certain that he had made a breakthrough and thanked her for being patient with him.

Pat once again felt that surge of personal euphoria for having found such a dynamic and interesting soul mate. She reached up and touched his cheek as they continued the jog and singing the ditty.

Chapter 9: Solution

Bram enjoyed the jogging limerick. He however, kept thinking about what the message implied. He wanted the team to work through the message and come up with their interpretation. He felt strongly about the fact that the team would clarify any points that he might have missed. He felt confident on his understanding of the numbering system, but he had several interpretations of the visual parts of the alien language.

He was right on time, and everyone was at the table and most had a cup of coffee. He noted that Mallica and Elizabeth, Zuri and her parents had not yet arrived. He wondered what might be keeping them. Elizabeth was one that was usually early.

Orlando burst through the auditorium door and shouted that the "Star" had arrived then came weaving down the aisle toward the stage as he pushed the wheelchair in a weaving drunken like path. Jina and the rest were all smiles as they followed.

It was clear to Bram that something positive had occurred.

He waited until they were all on stage and then asked Zuri why she had kept Orlando away for so long.

Zuri smiled and said that Elizabeth had Dr. Sewal explain that he had set up a program that he hoped would improve her condition. But what had kept them was that he had received her motorized wheelchair and wanted to show her what it could do. She went on to explain that it was a beautiful maroon color and that it had features that would open up much of the world for her. She explained that chair would go up and down, would tilt at all angles. It had the ability to climb stairs, but she said she would want to try that out herself before being comfortable with that feature. She added that the umbrella feature was one that she was sure she would be able to put to use at the Fold facility. Then she added that she would be able to come in with Bram in the mornings and most likely be able to set a fast pace for the jog in.

Orlando pretended to wipe a tear away and said that he was about to lose his favorite job and would most likely be assigned to gate guard duty.

Bram played along and commented that the Corp would likely have to send him back to bootcamp for re-indoctrination before he was good for anything else.

He then walked over to Zuri and gave her a hug and quietly told her how pleased he was with the fact that she was getting the new chair.

He then looked around and declared that it was time to decode the message.

Zuri looked at him, nodded and then asked if he had already done it and he was just testing the rest of them for their ability to do so.

Bram had wanted to keep that information from the group, but he knew better than to deny that he had been able to do so. He replied that he had the basic message but there were some gaps that needed filling and he wanted to solidify the alphabet. He pointed out that the visual elements were challenging, and he needed help there.

He said that he was not going to directly share what he knew until the team took a cut, but he reassured them that he would contribute to the decodifying by keeping it on track. He made the point that he was remaining open to better interpretation or translation of the language.

It took them all longer than Bram had anticipated and three days later in the late afternoon the message was displayed on the white board and there was one huge file on one computer that was shown on one of three large screens that had been set up on the auditorium stage.

The whiteboard showing the visual message was now standing in the middle of the three large screens. The screens displayed three time lapse pictures of the solar system where the sun was dying and expanding.

The Message

The first visual showed the planet and the sun as it was at the beginning. Below the image of the planet and sun was an image that most closely resembled a skinny whale, with gill like openings behind very large forward looking eyes and almost halfway back two long arm like appendages came out the sides.

In the second visual the sun was twice as large, and the figure below was bottom side up and there was the number that equated to roughly one billion.

In the third visual the sun had encompassed the planet and the visual was shown as a pile of ashes.

Bram congratulated everyone on having contributed to solving the meaning of the message but also in having clarified both the numbering and the letter systems.

Earth had a numbering system based mainly on ten which corresponded to number of digits on each of the human appendages.

It turned out that the aliens had a numbering system based on the eight digits on the appendages that functioned like hands. They had a thumb like appendage and three fingers.

The numbering system seemed to have the same features as the one on Earth in the sense that it featured raising numbers by powers. Bram felt that they had the equivalent of a grade school understanding, but it was all that was necessary at the moment.

The alphabet with its visual elements was daunting. It was what had given the team the most problem. Bram felt that the Asian members made a huge contribution in extrapolating their own alphabets and visual languages and adjusting them to a world where there was no land but only water.

The late Friday discussion on the stage was about the difficulty in translating between English or any Earth language and what the group was now calling the Water World language. The Vietnamese couple commented that they had a phone AP that translated Vietnamese to English or any chosen language and vice versa. Why not have one to do it for the Water World language.

Bram replied that he was going to visit with folks in the IT department to see if any of them had that talent to program such and AP or could connect with someone that did.

Erica volunteered to contact the developers of the Vietnamese translation AP and see if they could re-apply it with some modifications and if they could do it quickly.

Bram told her that doing so would be great and if they had a local talent that could then own its maintenance and improvement, they would have a perfect match for a much-needed capability.

Elizabeth took the opportunity to announce that Zuri would be going to the Mayo Clinic in Minnesota for most of the coming month. While there she would be thoroughly evaluated by Dr. Sewal, and his team and a treatment program designed.

The Message

She would get her chair fitted and get trained on its use. She finished by saying that the entire Juma family would be staying there and enjoying weekends at various vacation spots that Bram had graciously asked her to arrange.

Bram asked Zuri if he could use her office while she was gone.

Zuri knew immediately what he was talking about and replied that her office was a good place for him to talk to Einstein about what to do and how to connect with the Aliens and that maybe Einstein could help him solve the problem with the Fold equations.

He thanked her and thanked Elizabeth for having so graciously arranged for the vacation spots. He had never asked her to do any such thing, but it was her way of letting him know that she had spared no expense in the arrangements that she had made.

He thought about the fact that he had a secret code with three separate women in the room: Pat, Elizabeth, and Zuri. He thought maybe he would ask the AP writer to make an Ap for each of them.

After the meeting ended, he immediately called the IT department and asked if someone there was into writing Aps. He was pleased to learn that there were programmers that belonged to an online AP writing network and who were currently writing some APs for the department of defense.

He set up a meeting with them and let Erica know about the meeting that he had scheduled a week out.

Erica thanked him and said she would see about getting the writer of the Vietnamese translation AP to be available that Friday as well. She said it would depend on where that developer lived.

Bram thanked her and asked if she were up to a three-pancake breakfast on Sunday.

On Sunday morning, Pat was at the range, bacon, and sausage sizzling in the black iron skillet with which she had a ying-yang affair. She loved the way it cooked the food, and she hated cleaning it and it was way too heavy, but it was her favorite because it held it heat and made it easy to make the pancakes.

She welcomed Erica in and let her know that Bram was in the study being guarded by Bob and Thomas.

Erica thanked her for letting her know but said she had dreamt about the pancakes and was going to stay in the kitchen and learn how to make them the way Pat did.

She wanted to make better friends with Pat who seemed a little reserved with her. She was not sure why since Pat had never been around her in her previous life as the witch of the Fold program. She still thanked the time when Bram had let her know that he was not interested in her role or any role dealing with the business side and that he really wanted the freedom to create the concepts and technology that would continually improve the program.

The Message

She marveled at what he had done and now he had the world on the verge of communicating with an Alien race and that might also have the technology to help them.

She realized now how cold and calculating she had been only a few years ago and how unhappy she had been and how happy she now was.

Pat let her know that the pancakes would be rolling out in about five minutes and asked her to set the table for eight.

Erica was about to ask who the eight persons might be when Orlando came in.

Orlando was in a good mood. He said that he had just put his princess and her parents on an early morning flight. He had thanked Bram for the breakfast invite and was looking forward to two eggs over easy, sausage links, buttered toast, coffee and one of the jelly filled rolls from the box of donuts that he had purchased on the way back from the airport.

He was surprised to see Erica, but he figured breakfast was a good time to get better acquainted. He was about to put the box of donuts on the table, but Erica handed him a serving platter and suggested they put them on display to make sure that there would be no leftovers.

He liked the idea and was about to pick out the donuts and rolls when Erica waved two plastic glove in front of him and made a joke about not knowing where a Marine might have had their hands.

He laughed and said that the line was, "the Navy guys washed their hands before not after touching treasured parts, whereas Marines just spit on theirs and rub them together before touching anything."

Erica replied that she definitely wanted him to wear gloves before touching the food.

Zoe had been listening to the exchange and agreed that gloves were required.

Pat asked Zoe to get Bram to the breakfast table and handed Erica a platter with half a dozen pancakes and a dozen sausages.

She then pointed at Orlando and said that his order was next, and he should get ready.

She was about to sit down when Castor and Donna entered the kitchen from the basement. She took out two plates, asked what they wanted and had them sit down.

She looked at the gathering and realized that no matter what meal they had at their home, the table was almost always full.

It reminded her that it closely matched the meals at her home when she was growing up. Her parents both worked, and the family was probably considered to be in the lower end of middle class but on Friday nights and on the weekends her house was the place where all the kids gathered for breakfast, lunch, and dinner. She remembered her mother saying that there was always enough food for good friends.

She was standing and enjoying looking at the group in the dining area when Bram quietly spoke to her as he went by to refresh his coffee. "Isn't it great to have a group of friends gathered around the table and enjoying each other's company."

She followed him back and sat down beside him. She then reached out for a roll but had Orlando slap her wrist and with his gloved hand asked which roll or donut she desired.

Chapter 10: Einstein Solution

Next morning on the jog into work Bram was quiet. He had figured out how he planned to evaluate the impact of each equation transition. He would ask Linda to set up a meeting with Marcus, Remi, and Lori with the objective of getting them to prepare for the various tests that he planned.

He was going to utilize the fact that a Folded object currently returned to its original position. This was somehow a feature of his current equation set. He was going to attach two bubbles with this programing to a larger one that would utilize his newly modified equation. If the larger one began to move on its own, it would pull the two smaller observation bubbles along with it. Once the larger one had about five minutes to move, the program in the large bubble would shut down. If it had traveled along the Fold wormhole the two smaller ones would then return to their original position and then they would time out and return to their positions in the launch hangar.

In this manner he would test the impact of each part of the Fold equation.

Orlando took note of Bram's silence and started the ditty,

"Silent leader, Silent Leader
Oh, so quiet on this day.
A poor bubble is bound to pay.
Yes, bound to pay!
Yes, bound to pay!
Pay, Pay, Pay
For the leaders desire to play
Bound to pay for the leader's silence today
Step aside, step aside,
Don't you dare get in the way."

The entire group took up the chant.

The ditty came through to Bram who smiled, shook his head to clear out his contemplations, and joined in.

The Marine guards along the way had gotten use to them coming by with a new ditty almost every morning and they always joined in for the period that they were within ear shot.

This morning Bram was going to start his day in his office. He would take a few minutes and share his thinking with Einstein and then go out to the lab and share his final plan there.

Linda was at her desk and greeted him.

He stopped long enough to ask her to call Lori, Marcus, Remi, and Erica and set up a meeting in the lab for nine.

He then went into his office and locked the door. He then turned on the electric water pitcher and prepared his teacup.

When he opened the door to the small door in the bookcase, Einstein came out and after sniffing his hand got into the palm.

He took Einstein over to his desk and placed him on the large glass that covered the entire desk and had a picture of the Milky Way below it. This was a picture that was permanently etched in his mind. He had learned that it was but one of perhaps billions of galaxies spread throughout the universe, but this was where at the edge, his solar system traveled.

Once he had his cup of tea in hand he slowly explained the plan to Einstein as he gave him little crumbs of a cookie. It seemed to him that Einstein always stopped to listen to the plan for the equation transition and would nod his head up and down in approval. That approval always earned him another crumb. The deciding test of Einstein's understanding was when Bram asked if he had missed anything, and Einstein shook his head in the negative. Bram gave him the remainder of the cookie and thanked him for listening and told him what a smart mouse he was.

Linda gave him his ten-minute warning.

Bram printed out copies of his equation test plan. It included sending out twelve bubbles in the next three days. It they all returned, then he would only need to modify six bubbles.

Lori and Erica were in a full animated discussion that Bram understood was about the great work that the lab had done and how the lab members would be able to train the personnel in the company being considered to mass produce them.

The room went quiet as soon as he was spotted.

He let them know the objective of the meeting, paused for a moment as the four read through the paper he had handed them. He then verbally described his test plan and asked how long it would take to prepare the bubbles.

Remi asked if Bram had the new program for the two lead bubbles and if he did, the Bubbles could be ready in two days.

Bram smiled and said that Thursday morning would be a perfect day to run the tests and that by Friday afternoon he would know if he had a chance at creating a Wormhole Bubble.

Lori commented that they had the two large bubbles that were to replace Wheel One and Wheel Two ready and they could be modified to become the first two Wormhole Spaceships. She asked if she and any other volunteers could figure out names for these ships.

Bram chuckled and commented that she was, "getting the cart before the horse."

Erica said she wanted to be on the naming team, and she was sure every Wheel member and probably every member on the Fold facility would want in. She suggested making it a contest that everyone could participate in.

Bram shook his head and said that he was open to doing so, but first he had to create the equation that resulted in the wormhole capability and then he and Remy had to provide the battery power needed to ensure the ability to go along the wormhole and then return to the hangar launch site.

Erica suggested that she work with Linda to set up the contest so they would be ready when he successfully created the first wormhole.

Bram smiled and said that it was great to be working with such positive team members and wished that he could be as certain as they that he would solve the problem of creating motion for a bubble.

Remi stood up and commented that he was going out with his team to select the six bubbles and get them to start the modifications. Lori said she was going with him and followed Remi out of the lab.

Bram realized that Erica had stayed behind and seemed to be waiting until the lab members followed their bosses out the door.

Once the room was empty, Erica said that she had located the lead programmer of the Vietnamese to English translation AP. She said he was currently creating and testing various improvements of how pilots communicated with their sophisticated supersonic planes. She had set up a meeting the following day to see if he could create a Waterworld to English AP. She apologized about making the meeting appointment without contacting him first, but it all happened dynamically, and she did not want spend weeks trying to schedule the meeting.

Bram said the timing was perfect since he would be sitting idly by waiting for the bubbles to be modified. He suggested including the members of the translation team that was on site and if possible, including Zuri and her parents.

Erica agreed that the full contingent would be invited but the meeting time would remain fixed.

Lori intercepted him on the way back to his office and asked if he were going to request a bubble that could hold a member of the Waterworld.

Bram stopped walking and was silent for a moment. He then commented that one Waterworld being was about as large as an Earth Whale Shark. The human bubbles were designed to hold a team of twelve. So, the Waterworld bubble would need to be at least large enough to hold twelve of aliens. He said she should figure out the dimensions of such a bubble and let him know who could construct one.

Lori stood looking at him in disbelief. She shook her head and mumbled that she was sorry she had asked.

Bram agreed that it was a daunting task that they might undertake. He suggested she find out the largest sphere that could economically be produced and then suggest options.

Pat met him at Linda's desk and said that she had ordered a mixed salad in for lunch, and it was waiting for him at his desk.

Bram gave her a hug and thanked her. He said that he needed to decompress from a full morning.

Pat asked about his test plan and what else he had done in the morning.

Bram stood and got Einstein and handed him to Pat. He then suggested they call Zuri and her parents to share what he had accomplished during the morning.

Pat said that it was a good idea.

The Message

Bram called and asked if Zuri had a few moments for him to share what he had accomplished with Einstein's help.

Zuri gave a small laugh and said she would send her wheelchair driving instructor away for a short time. She went on to say that her morning had been spent on learning to use her wheelchair and she hoped his morning had been spent on learning how to move a bubble through space.

Bram told her he hoped she was having more fun than he had so far on this day.

She replied that running into walls and almost tumbling down some stairs had scared her, but she was otherwise having a great time learning how to use her new motorized chair.

Bram then shared how Einstein had approved how each equation transition was going to be tested. He approved of using the tiniest of motion change to ensure that the bubble didn't jump across the universe but only a few feet.

He then commented on having two normal bubbles being towed by the wormhole bubble so that he could retrieve all of them and continue testing the effects of the various equation sections.

Close to the end of the call Bram shared that there was a naming contest being held to pick a name for the wormhole vessels. He asked what the first prize should be.

Zuri suggested that he offer a bullet proof fishing boat to the winner and a gun mounted drone to the second and a common grenade launcher to the third-place winner.

Jina commented that she was shocked at the suggestions of her daughter.

Pat spoke up and said that she hoped that she would at least get third prize. It would make her feel much better equipped to go fishing.

Bram closed the call by sharing that on the following day there would be a meeting with the programmer of the translation AP to see if he was willing to program an Alien to English AP for the Fold effort, and they were all invited.

He said to expect a call from Linda who would share the specifics of the meeting. He went on to let them know that attendance was optional.

Chapter 11: Reverse

ᘓram spent the last part of the day reviewing the work that had been done and had resulted in the Fold program being in a position that would allow it to potentially provide aid to an alien civilization that was several million light years away.

He wondered why a civilization that had learned to use the Fold to send out a distress signal had not also developed the ability to build the equivalent of his Wheels or the Bramlets. He speculated that a water world civilization made up of whale like inhabitants might not pursue the type of buildings and structures that the much smaller animal that was human would. They might also not have faced the multitude of predators and weather challenges that humans had to overcome.

He was certain that interaction with them would be one of learning and of developing new technical capabilities.

He knew that a new habitable water world would need to be found.

The Fold capability would be central to that search. The ability for a Fold vehicle to move along a selected trajectory would be invaluable in the search. He thought about the power needs of a Fold vehicle and knew that he needed another breakthrough in that arena.

He decided that he would see if Zuri would take on the project of coming up with a new power system for the Dynamic Wormhole Bubble. He hoped that she would look across the energy field and check out the claims of a breakthrough in the nuclear industry.

He had read about the breakthrough in China where they claimed to be able to create an energy source as powerful as the sun. He doubted it would be available in time to make a difference.

On the way home he told Pat about getting Zuri to tackle the power problem. He was surprised when she said that Zuri needed to get away from the Fold project and experience as normal a childhood, as a child, of her intellect and her disabilities would allow. She suggested asking Zuri's mother to tackle that assignment and have her use Zuri as a resource.

Bram thought about the fact that he had failed to see Zuri as a child but had focused on her superior mind.

He thanked Pat for having pointed out what he had failed to grasp and that now seemed so obvious.

He made the point that he was sure that Zuri would still have a problem of having a normal childhood since she would end up in some university as one of the younger or perhaps the youngest student.

Pat agreed and commented that Elizabeth had found a program for genius students. That university had a program that focused on merging the genius students, the advanced courses and also arranging social events that brought them together. Elizabeth had volunteered that she would attend the university with Zuri and attend several of the classes that she did.

Bram asked if Jina was planning to stay with the Fold project.

Pat said that Elizabeth had convinced her that she should continue to reside at the Fold housing complex and that Zuri would come home often and she could continue her role as a resource in the mathematical aspects of the Fold effort.

He then said that he was now thinking of offering Zuri's modified office to Mallika.

Pat gave a light laugh and said that she thought Mallika would love to have such a luxurious office that was larger than his, but she suggested that he make the office the center of communication about the message and about his bubble redesign testing. She made the point that it would provide a large area for information to be displayed. She suggested he invest in several additional large display screens.

He said that he would take her suggestion and get Linda to arrange the office to seat folks comfortably for design and translation activities.

Their conversation had transpired as they left work and rode to their house. Zoe and Eric had the guard duty. Zoe asked what Orlando would do while Zuri went to school.

Pat replied that he had decided to get his bachelor's degree. He planned to be Zuri's bodyguard during the day and take evening classes. She shared that he had put in a request to get a second Marine assigned to also guard Zuri. If that was approved, they would alternate times to allow him to attend classes during the day.

Zoe said that she hoped his request would be approved and then she added that she hoped that college did not dull his sense of humor.

Bram added, "Or his keen ability to come up with witty ditties."

Pat gave Bram a poke in the ribs and said that he should leave the witty ditties to others and concentrate on his simple Fold equation.

That night he had a dream where the bubble was going so fast through the wormhole that it left this universe and entered another. He kept trying to put it into reverse, but that section of the equation failed to activate.

Pat shook Bram awake and said that it was two in the morning and asked him if he knew where he was.

Bram embraced her and thanked her for rescuing him from the next universe. He said that he had found which equation had an error in it. He was not yet sure what the error was, but he would pursue it until he had found it.

Pat said she was happy for him to stay in her universe, but she was going back to sleep.

Bram gave her a kiss on the forehead and then focused on the black and the void of space and was soon asleep.

The next morning, he asked Linda if she was aware of Zuri going off to school. Linda nodded and said that she hoped he wasn't mad about her pushing for that.

Bram said he was not and that he had overlooked the fact that Zuri was still a child and socially not as developed as her super brain. He thanked her for pushing for that opportunity for Zuri and as a reward he was going to give her extra work.

Linda was used to Bram's dry humor and asked what her punishment was going to be.

He asked her to follow him to Zuri's office where he shared what he had in mind.

Linda said that it was a great idea and that she thought getting the architect that had set up the office to come in and see what he might suggest would be the next step.

Bram agreed that it was the way to proceed, and she should do it. He told her that he wanted to focus on the Fold equation for the rest of the day and did not want to be disturbed. He let her know that he had a lunch date with Pat at high noon and she should make sure he made it.

Linda said she would follow up and update him on what was happening with Zuri's office and that she would make sure he was not late for lunch.

Bram went into his office and got Einstein out and sat down and explained to him that he thought he had found the problem with the Fold equation that had been haunting him for months.

He asked Einstein if he had known that the problem was in the equation that provided the capability to go in reverse.

When Einstein seemed to nod in the affirmative.

Bram scratched him behind the ear and told him he needed to go and get voice lessons so he could talk so he could communicate what he knew.

He then got on his computer and pulled up the part of the Fold equation that dealt with the reverse feature and almost immediately he realized that one part that incremented in value only incremented upward. This meant that as it traveled in one direction it would increment up but when he wanted to go in reverse.

The equation needed to increment downward, and it needed enough power to negate the other sections of the equation that went in the opposite direction.

He studied how he could modify it so it would decrease in value and pull the bubble backward along the worm hole.

He soon realized that the parts of the equation that were pulling the bubble forward had to be turned off.

He wrote a reverse function program that provided a loop that would increment in the down direction until it got to zero value.

He wondered what would happen if it kept going into the negative and decided that would be one of the tests he would do after he verified he could get the wormhole bubble back to its original position.

Linda's voice on the speaker let him know it was time for him to break for lunch.

He looked at Einstein that was sitting next to the keyboard and told him that he was a genius and then put him back into his kingdom and closed the small door and put the books in front of it.

Pat waved to him from a table close to the windows of the cafeteria that had a view of Columbia River. She asked how the review of the equation had gone.

Bram told her that Einstein had solved the problem. He had written a program that he would try out that afternoon if he could get a bubble.

Pat reassured him that he could have any size bubble he wanted.

Erica walked over to their table and asked if she could join them. Once she had taken her seat, she commented that finding a company to quickly produce the bubbles was more of a challenge than she anticipated.

Bram asked if she had considered funding the establishment of a local bubble building company. She could hire one of the local entrepreneurs to run the business and then she would be able to have direct influence and more control over the production of high-quality bubbles.

Erica asked if he had someone in mind.

Bram suggested she check out Luke Stetson to see if he had the skill to manage a startup business. He was sure that his parents would provide great guidance on how to run such a business. He pointed out that Luke already had been checked out by the FBI and it would most likely be rather easy to get him a top-secret clearance.

Erica commented that her lunch tasted better than usual and that she would have to see about coming to lunch with Pat as often as possible.

Pat told her that she personally had bribed Linda to make sure she got Bram out of his office to eat lunch with her. She was sure that Linda would be open to Erica's bribes and all she had to do was hire her brother and she could have a tailor made lunch time reminder.

Bram gave a small laugh and said that he was not that hard to have lunch with it all depended on when exactly they wanted to have lunch. He said he had to turn off his mind to be able to focus on food unless it was preceded or followed by gunfire. Then food was the first thing he thought about.

Erica got up and said that she was going to check out the availability of labor, materials and a building that could be secured. She wondered if that huge fruit barn that was within sight of the housing area might be available for the right price.

Bram said that was a great idea. It was close enough that the Marine perimeter could be extended, and protection could be provided.

Pat made the point that the power needed was also very near. The one item they needed to make sure of was that there were enough workers to staff the operation.

Bram suggested using the folks already making the bubbles as the startup personnel and ask them to recruit dependable local folks who wanted a great place to work.

Erica replied that she was now getting excited about doing something locally. She was going to get together with the Stetsons and see what came of it.

Bram suggested enrolling Lacy in that endeavor. He said that she had worked wonders in getting things organized for him in her previous role.

Pat excused herself and said she was going to give Remi a heads up about Bram's next request for additional bubbles to play with.

Bram added that she should tell Remi that he would need two sets of a two-bubble arrangement.

Bram returned to his office and focused on creating two computer control versions of how to activate reverse for the wormhole bubble. He had just accomplished this when Linda came up on the speaker phone and let him know that her sister was insisting that she see him.

Bram intuitively knew that she was coming because Erica had contacted her. He just hoped the two were not having a problem. He opened his office door and was greeted by a beaming smile on Lacy's face.

After giving him a hug, she handed him a pint of his favorite peach ice cream with extra cream. Then she thanked him for thinking of Luke and giving him the opportunity of a lifetime. She shared that Luke had earned a business management degree but had returned home only to find that it did little to help him locally. He had offers in other parts of the country, but she said that Luke wanted to stay near his family.

Bram could tell that Lacy was experiencing an emotional high because she had to stop and wipe tears from her eyes. He asked her why she thought he had anything to do with the good fortune that had come Luke's way.

Lacy replied, "because Erica had let her know it was your idea." She went on to let him know that Erica had become one of his staunchest supporters.

Bram gave a small laugh and replied that he had suggested Luke because he was a great shot and drove an immaculate black fishing boat.

"Yes and you gifted our family enough money that everyone will be looked after for years to come because we do such a great job setting up exciting gun battle oriented fishing trips," Lacy joked back.

She then extended an offer from her mother and father to host a celebration dinner, but they wanted to use his dining room for it.

Bram replied that he would love to have them do so and he was counting on her to make up the invitation list.

He then said that he had to go to the lab to set up two experiments and that she should get busy planning the celebration dinner.

Pat, Lori, and Remi all walked over to Bram as he entered the Lab.

He looked around and saw that everyone in the lab had stopped what they were doing and were looking at him.

He joked that he was just stopping in to see if everyone was working hard enough.

Lori replied that they were worn out trying to adhere to his sweat shop management style. And they were all waiting to see if the two twin bubble set ups would satisfy him and keep him from imposing any additional restrictions on the workers in the lab.

She led him to the two large enclosures that held the two sets of one larger bubble and a smaller one tethered behind it.

Bram looked at the two then turned and put his computer down on one of the stainless-steel lab tables and transferred his two programs into the waiting bubble computers.

He asked that the first bubble be named Pat and the second bubble be named Lori. He looked at Remi and said that if they got bubble Pat and bubble Lori back then they would be renamed; Remi and Bramer and be sent out again.

He asked that bubbles Pat and Lori be taken out to the launch area and sent out to the coordinates he had programed in.

He said that if they came back in the next hour, then he would like bubble Remi to be sent out once the batteries in the Bramlets were recharged.

Lori turned to the rest of the folks and declared it was launch time and they all knew their part.

She then asked when bubble Bramer was to be sent out.

Bram watched as the Lab transformed into a beehive of activities.

He then let Lori know that Bramer would possibly never come back so he was delaying sending it out until the wormhole portion of the program was well underway. He shared that bubble Bramer would be going into what seemed to be negative space and that he had no idea what that meant or what would happen.

Pat took him by the arm and said that her role was to get him out of the way until it was time to launch. She suggested staying close by and he should relax and enjoy a cup of coffee or tea.

Bram suggested they sit at the back of the launch control room.

Pat asked him what made him think about such a thing as negative space.

Bram replied that when he had written the equation that pulled the bubble back from its forward path he had taken it into the negative values, and equation program had continued to function. However, since he had no idea what that would mean, he was going to experiment to learn what it meant physically.

He said that if he went negative beyond the zero point, he did not think the Fold would bring the bubbles back to the hangar landing area. He wondered where the Fold would end up on its return from the negative area.

Pat said that she was sure he would find out and that what he found would most likely be as astounding as creating a wormhole spaceship that could traverse the universe.

<u>Chapter 12: The Price of Progress</u>

The experiment went as Bram had expected. The Pat Bubble had to be deactivated and brought back as programed. The Lori Bubble had been programed so the pull part of the equation was decoupled and only the reversed equation was functional. It worked as expected.

He now knew how to set up the program so that it would function as desired and be controlled by both the computer and by a human.

He kept thinking about the negative test that he anticipated would take him into a totally new space environment but resisted the temptation to run that test.

The Remi bubble had been sent out with the enhanced design without the pullback bubble attached and was scheduled to return exactly at the end of the workday.

He had just heated the water for a cup of tea when Linda announced Erica's desire to update him.

Erica came in all smiles and said that she was looking forward to a pancake breakfast on Sunday.

Bram knew that she had good news. He asked if she wanted a cup of tea.

Erica said it was one of her better Friday's. She said that it seemed that getting the small bubble production situated in the fruit barn had provided a breakthrough for her. She credited Lacy with having helped in convincing the farm owners that a new building at the other end of the field would functionally improve their logistics of both selling apples locally and make handling distribution trucks more efficient.

Erica said that when she offered to pay the cost of the change, the deal was accepted immediately. She bought the parcel of land the barn and entrance were on and got agreement to a fence around it.

She stopped for a moment as she sipped her tea. Then she gave a small laugh and said that when she shared what she was doing with the aerospace leaders, the builders of the space wheels immediately offered to produce the large bubbles and would locate it in the same hanger where they had produced Wheel One and Two.

They had offered to help in securing the labor and had given reassurances that they would help staff the Dallas site with persons from both Seattle and Portland.

She went on and said that she and Luke had walked around the Fruit Barn and had decided that it was a perfect building for their needs. They were meeting with the architect on Monday to determine what needed to happen before production was moved into the Fruit Barn.

Then she asked what he thought of naming the new company, Fruit Barn Productions, LLC, and naming Luke as the President.

Bram leaned back in his chair and said that she had just broken his record for speed. He went on and congratulated her on making things happen fast and that he liked everything that he had heard.

He then said that she could have extra syrup for her Sunday morning pancakes.

She said that she was really looking forward to the pancakes and wondered whether she could invite three Stetson family members to breakfast as well.

"Well," Bram answered, "that would cost one trout for each of you."

The meeting ended as Linda let him know that he had five minutes until the Remi bubble was due back from its run.

He and Erica walked to the control room to watch the return.

The entire Lab team was still there, and Erica let them know that she had a great Friday end of the day message that would make their weekend that she would share right after they got Remi back into its position in the Lab.

Pat looked at Bram and asked who would be coming to breakfast on Sunday.

Bram rattled off the names. Then he went quiet as the Remi bubble appeared. He waited until the recovery team had moved it to the lab area and then he went out to inspect it.

Both he and Remi were standing in front of the viewing barrier and looking at the plant that was wilted and was apparently dead.

Bram knew that he had an additional problem to solve before he would be able to have humans traveling in a wormhole bubble.

He looked at Remi and said that it was good that he had suggested sending something live on his bubble's journey.

He asked if Remi liked pancakes and invited him to Sunday's breakfast.

Pat knew that because of the dead plant she would be sitting with Bram enjoying a book as he talked to himself with his eyes closed as he contemplated how to overcome his new problem.

Bram turned to her and asked what she thought the plants had died of.

Pat, Erica, and Lori all stepped up to take a look at the plant. They all agreed that the plant seemed to have died of natural causes. They conjectured that maybe a lack of water but most likely it had died of a natural cause such as old age.

Bram suspected that it had to do with time, and he needed to examine the Fold equation and see how it worked relative to time's passing.

He asked Remi to set up a precision mechanical clock with a backup that could be attached to a computer program.

Pat pointed to the door and said that it was time to go home and enjoy the weekend.

Bram saw that Erica had turned to join them and they all left the Lab together.

On the ride home Zoe asked whether he had heard about the ditty that Castor and Donna were working on about the wormhole that was going to eat Pat, but Bram saved her fat. The Wormhole tasted Lori and spat her back. Bram sent out Remi and his plant and it was shriveled dead when it got back.

Bram said that the Monday jog in would be an interesting one since they had the weekend to work on it and he was sure that they would share it with Orlando and give him a chance to smooth it out.

Once he got to the house he went up and took a shower and then retreated into his office.

Pat stopped by the kitchen and found out that everyone had decided on pizza and cheese nachos. The compound kitchen staff would deliver it as soon as it was ready. Mike said that they had agreed on three different kinds of pizza and had ordered enough for everyone.

Thomas said that the beer, wine, or soft drinks were in the fridge.

Pat grabbed two lights and headed back to the office.

She listened as Zoe was explaining that the Black-Eyed Susan plant that Remi had sent out was his favorite flower. She had asked Linda to order a new plant to replace it so that Bram could try again on Monday. She said she was all in favor of his success in keeping it alive on the next trial run and she would keep getting them delivered until he succeeded.

Pat sat down next to Bram who had listened, but she knew that he was already into his equation review and would not come back to them until he had found where time needed to be managed and manipulated. She was totally content to sit by him and read.

The next morning after a workout in the basement gym, she and Zoe were sitting at the kitchen table getting ready to indulge in some tea with a cookie or a sweet roll when the doorbell rang.

Zoe jumped up and said she had it. At the same time Thomas stepped out of the office.

Pat was surprised at their reactions, but she appreciated their vigilance. She heard Jina's voice and got up to greet her.

She invited her to share a cup of tea or coffee and a sweet roll.

Jina sat down at the table and then shared that it was hard for her to come back to the Fold facility and leave Zuri. She said that it was the first time she and Nuro had been away from Zuri for more than a day.

Pat said that she was sure it was hard, but that Zuri needed a chance to become independent and she pointed out that Zuri would have two people that would make sure that she would receive the best education and also do it in a safe environment.

Pat joked that Orlando would have the whole campus jogging and reciting ditties as they did.

Jina laughed and said that he already had two or three young men join him as he took Zuri to her first class. She said that she was sure that Orlando would change the atmosphere of the staid campus and would probably be the best recruiter of Marine Corp officers that the Marine Corp could ask for.

Pat said that she should send a message to Major General Tilson letting him know her impression of Orlando. She let Jina know that Orlando had requested a second Marine be assigned to guard Zuri so that he would have enough time to get a degree while he was at the university.

Jina said that she would do so as soon as she got home. Orlando was one of Zuri's favorite friends and the most connected to her on a personal level.

Zoe chuckled and said that Orlando connected with everyone on a personal level and was a favorite of everyone.

Jina then commented that Elizabeth was like the Grand Mother that she had always wanted Zuri to have. Elizabeth was already having a big impact on the social life of all the people that were somehow disabled but even more she had already made connections with the social life of what she called, "the spoiled socializers," and had set up events that included the disabled people.

Pat commented that Elizabeth was an extremely talented manipulator of the social and political scene and would make a huge positive difference for Zuri.

Pat then made the point that Jina and Nuro would need to focus on their own social development and prepare themselves for an independent Zuri. It would be a different Zuri than either of them or anyone who currently knew her would be expecting.

Jina put down her teacup and said that she had just enjoyed the best tea and cookie that she had ever eaten. She said she wished Nuro would have come with her.

Pat invited them to Sunday breakfast and then she would be able to talk to Nuro as she weakened him with buttered pancakes covered in maple syrup.

Jina said she would love to come to Sunday breakfast.

After Jina left, Zoe complimented Pat on how she handled Jina's feelings about missing Zuri. She said that she would keep that advice in mind for when her daughter went away to college.

Pat went into the study and saw Bram working away on his computer. He looked at her and smiled but then his eyes went back to the lap top screen.

Bram realized that he had just used up some of his emotional bank account, but he was more worried about killing the very person that held the account he just had drawn down.

He found that every one of the Fold equations had fixed time markers in them. He would need to make them all variables that only incremented at the pace of Earth time.

He marked every equation that had a time factor and then shut down his computer.

He decided to make a deposit with his favorite banker.

Pat was just getting ready to go for a walk and was surprised but very pleased when Bram came out of the office and asked what she wanted to do.

When they got outdoors, Bram was surprised at what a beautiful day it was. He had been in his office since early in the morning. He followed alongside of Pat as she said that they should go play some pool and maybe some ping pong and then grab something to eat from the snack bar, sit by the pool, and relax.

Melinda their neighborhood event organizer came over and said that it was great to see them. She said it was great that the Fold program was making such great progress. She asked if the expansion to the Fruit barn area meant that they would be getting more housing.

Bram shook his head and said he had no idea and that she should ask Erica what was planned. He said that even Erica might not have gotten that far yet in her planning. He commented that the part of the Fold project she was inquiring about would move slower than the news about its successes.

He and Pat started a walked around the perimeter of the of the compound but gave in to the request by the Marine guards to come back in toward the center because they were open targets out where they were walking.

Bram decided that at breakfast on Sunday he was going to ask Lacy how the Fold Offense Team was doing. He was sure that Lacy would have news of some sort to share.

Pat found the Sunday breakfast to be one that had several interesting aspects.

Jena brought up the fact that she and Nuro missed Zuri and that it was their first time to be away from her. Everyone reinforced Pat's earlier advice.

Soon after that, Erica shared the progress on bubble production and site expansion. She stopped when asked about housing and how it would impact the neighborhood and said that those aspects had yet to be addressed and now it would be on her radar screen.

Lacy then shared the fact that the Fold Offense had indeed been scoring against their opponents. She said that she was pursuing the money and had been able to freeze or seize several hundred million dollars that were in offshore accounts.

The offense had also identified several wealthy donors that had given money to several groups that had attacked the Fold compound or their members at the fishing outings. She was suing them in civil court and tying them up legally so that they would not have time to participate in actions against the Fold program.

She shared that currently her biggest worry was the smaller radical groups that resided in the northeastern part of the country. They could take radical action on their own. She had formed a surveillance group that was currently using thirty camera drones to monitor the groups they had identified. She was negotiating with the NIS to get them to track the online and phone activities of the more active and radical groups.

Bram thanked both Lacy and Erica for their work.

Linda pointed, to her brother, Luke and asked him whether he had any interesting news. Luke began by saying that his life was taking a big turn. The Fold bubble production barn was to be owned by his company that he was calling Fruit Farm Products LLC. He commented that the details of how he would, over time become the sole owner of the facility was being worked out. He said it would initially grow to a two hundred employ company.

He ended by thanking them all for such an opportunity.

Bram looked at Zoe and asked her what her opinion was about Luke getting such a break.

Zoe and Eric both shared the fact that they could think of nothing better to happen to person who had shielded her from a sniper during the last gun battle by standing in front of her and taking a bullet for her, than what was happening to Luke.

Zoe closed by saying she had dibs on being in his boat for the next fishing trip.

Bram thanked everyone for sharing and let them know that he had to get into his office and fix the mess he had as a Fold equation to ensure they all had a working future.

He heard the entire group say, "A very successful mess."

He got up and was pleased that the breakfast session continued. He noted that Pat was the one that was guiding the conversation. She knew that he enjoyed social interaction, but his threshold was much lower than most for social discussions that were almost always circular in nature.

He was off to make sure that he was not going to kill his willing explorers.

<u>Chapter 13: The Meaning of Time</u>

Bram entered his study and fired up his laptop. He was consumed with the thought of how time was a thread that ran through the fabric of the entire Fold tapestry. He had to figure out whether the time that the computer was using was Earth time or if it was the time that was passing as the Fold vessel traveled the wormhole. If it was external time then a lifetime might pass in a flash. He had to make sure that the time the passenger in the bubble experienced was based on the Earth clock time spent in the bubble.

He had to determine which time his Fold Wormhole bubble program was integrating?

The question on his mind was, how could he maintain the use of Earth time during a Fold wormhole trip?

Simple questions that could only be answered through trial-and-error physical tests.

He was sure that he would kill several more plants before he figured it out.

Even the reverse equation had a time thread. He figured if he didn't kill everything going in one direction, he might do it in the reverse direction.

He was glad that he had been lucky when he wrote the Fold equation, and it had no motion associated with it. Otherwise, his first Folds may have ended in death for all the Wheel personnel.

That thought sent a shiver down his back.

He took note that Zoe was uncharacteristically quiet and not playing her usual game of teasing him when he was deep in thought. He figured that he must be telegraphing his concern about what he had found wrong on the last run of the wormhole experiment.

He thought about the request he had sent Remi about getting the bubble ready for a Monday afternoon test. He stopped and sent him a text to let him know that the next test would be later in the week and Remi should not come in early on Monday to get the bubble ready to go.

He then told Zoe not to be so serious and that he would only be killing a Blacked Eye Susan on each of his failures to conquer father time.

Zoe nodded and said that she would order as many of them as he would need to figure out how to manage time. She wondered whether this affected the Fold team's ability to help the Aliens who had sent their message.

Bram replied that the response to the Aliens certainly would have to wait until he had solved the current time problem. He pointed out that the Aliens were not expecting a message from Earth and currently Earth did not have the capability to send a Fold message. He pointed out that currently each bubble had to return so they could get the information that had been collected. Even the Alien message had come back as a recording on the bubble's computer.

Zoe asked if a bubble could be Folded close to the alien's home world and the message beamed to them in a normal manner from there.

Bram smiled and said he liked the way she was thinking, and he had Marcus sending out probes so the space coordinates of the alien planet could be determined. Marcus would first send trial bubbles to make sure they sent the message to the right planet and that the bubble would not end up like Bramlet One with a boulder sharing the same space.

Zoe thanked him for sharing what Marcus was doing and said that perhaps if that was the way they delivered the reply perhaps they could ask the Aliens to share how they were able to send Fold messages.

Bram said that he liked brave bodyguards that were also smart, and he would keep her suggestion at the top of the list.

He suggested she engage Mallica who he had asked to see if she could learn how the message had been sent. He offered that a great question that would hook her was to ask if the message was made up of quarks that repeatedly Folded and whether the quarks might be transmitted like radio waves that were transmitted through Earth's atmosphere or whether up and down quarks might be used in some sort of up and down quark combinations that might periodically create hadrons as a way to transmit a Folded message through space.

Zoe smiled and said it was going to be all she could do to repeat the question that he had just suggested. She said that she had been recording his suggestion and would at least memorize it. She wondered if he had already asked that question of Mallika.

Bram replied that he had not.

He then smiled and said that when Mallika asked her how she had thought about such a question, Zoe should tell her that she had been taught that at the FBI academy.

Zoe laughed and said she was sure that Mallica would then figure out where she had really been fed that question.

He told her to ask the question anyway.

Bram looked at Eric and asked that he capture Mallica's face when Zoe asked the question. He said that he was sure that it would be one that the entire team would like to see, and Orlando would surely be able to make a jogging ditty that they would all enjoy from the interaction.

The Message

Pat, book in hand, had been standing in the doorway of the study listening and volunteered to go ahead of the two of them and have Mallica distracted with a few of her own simple questions. She laughed and said that her current surprised look was a shadow of what she thought Mallica's would be.

Bram took his laptop and sat down on the twin recliner and said he was ready for his reading partner.

Monday morning the jog to the work area was again rather quiet and no ditties were being sung.

Bram figured that everyone had heard about the shriveled plant, and he wondered how far up the chain of command the problem had been communicated. He was sure that Jefferey knew, and he was sure he would not send it any farther up until the two of them talked. He figured he had until Wednesday to figure it out or to describe the path he was following to figure out how to solve the problem.

The one thing Bram would not do was to send out any human on any Fold until he solved the problem with time. He kept thinking how lucky they had been to have had stationary Folds that locked in on a specific coordinate and how glad he was that Marcus had insisted, on what at the time he had thought were exceedingly accurate coordinates.

He mumbled something about luck and was surprised when Pat quietly told him that luck had nothing to do with the success of the Fold program. She said that it was skill, fortitude, tenacity and as Zuri had describe it, his unusual non-linear brain.

The next day, before going to his office, Bram went to the lab. He felt a need to explain to Remi about how embedded the impact of time was in the Fold equation and that until he had followed every embedded path there would be no scheduled Folds and warned Remi that Zoe had ordered a dozen Black Eyed Susan's that would need care and watering.

He was pleased with Remi's reply that he should take all the time needed to solve the Fold equation problem and that until then he had all the time needed to water plants.

Remi said that he was also engaged in helping set up the Fruit Production plant and getting it up and running. He smiled as he commented that "time" was of no concern to him.

Bram left the lab and headed for his office.

Linda greeted him and let him know that he would have a standing room only dinner on the coming Sunday.

She let him know that because of the number of folks that had accepted her invitation, she had moved the dinner to the community shelter.

She said that Zuri was planning to attend as well.

Bram replied that the celebration might be premature since he did not have a Fold worm hole that humans could use.

Linda said that he had until Sunday evening to solve that problem but as far as everyone was concerned, they were sure that he would.

Bram asked that he not be interrupted but that he did want to be at the cafeteria at noon.

He went into his office and sent a note to Zuri letting her know that he was working on the problem of Fold wormhole time, and he would review it with her on the weekend if she wanted to get an update.

Almost immediately he received a reply saying that he would have fifteen minutes at breakfast at his house on Sunday morning if she could have pancakes, sausage and two over easy eggs. She said that things were going great for her, but she really missed their morning meetings.

He sent back an emoji check mark and a smiley face.

He then got Einstein out and explained the problem to him as he fed him cookie crumbs and told him that if he didn't supply the solution, he might be sent out in the next wormhole experiment. He chuckled as Einstein shook his head in the negative.

He said that he was just kidding.

Then he chuckled again when he thought about talking to a mouse.

He spent the next two hours working through the first equation string. He was modifying the equation so that he could control the time with a mechanical clock that put out a signal every one sixtieth of a second. This was a dramatic slowdown in time that before had moved at the computer speed of microseconds, but it created a time frame that he could easily track and control.

He would see if he could locate a more precise mechanical clock if the approach worked. He began linking each time-based equation to the clock. It was a simple but tediously slow reprograming process where each step needed testing to make sure the program still functioned. He realized that it would take him two full days with a couple more hours in the evening to get through the entire string of Fold equations.

Then he would want to review everything with Mallica, and he decided he should also add two IT specialist to make sure the program was fully operational.

He would have Remi prepare the Fold Wormhole bubbles for a Friday morning trial. Then he would spend the day running a series of tests that hopefully let him tune a functional, working control equation.

He would get Linda to supply some bait fish and some meal worms to test the ride with several living riders when the first flower came back alive.

When he got the ten-minute warning, he went out to Linda's desk and asked her to make the arrangements with the people and to provide the bait fish and meal worm.

Linda laughed about supplying the fish and meal worms and asked if she could throw in some crickets.

Bram said he was leaving it up to her since he might kill all of them. He then headed for the cafeteria.

The Message

Pat had set up the contest to see who could come up with the best snipped about Bram's Fold wormhole time problem. The lab group got so excited that Lori declared the morning a half day off and they all concentrated in coming up with hand drawn posters about time.

Pat had put up the posters around the cafeteria that the lab group and the wheel teams had made.

She had also asked Chef D'Carluca to prepare one of Bram's favorite meals.

Bram stopped as he entered the cafeteria. He scanned the signs and the sayings about time.

"Time will do all – of us in."

"Only a Bram can control time."

"We are spending time waiting for Bram to give us a Fold wormhole ride."

"Wasted time cannot be recovered."

"Time cannot be stopped or reversed, unless you are a Bram."

He took note of cartoon characters and the famous one of a character with a long nose looking over the wall that said, "Bram will sniff out time, he just needs to get over the Fold wall."

He asked Pat if she had supplied the colored felt tips and asked if any work got done during the morning.

Pat replied she didn't think so because Lori had given the entire lab the morning off and made it into a contest.

Bram asked how the winners would be determined.

Pat said that everyone had three votes and they could distribute their votes any way they wished.

Linda and Lacy came in carrying their entries and asked if it was too late to compete.

Linda had a fishbowl with fish crying, a cricket with the words "why me" coming out of his mouth and a worm saying it was either a ride through a wormhole or a fishhook in his back.

Lacy had a picture of a camera drone flying down a worm hole shooting at the words, "time only gets one chance before getting "Bramed down."

Bram told Pat that he was putting one vote on Lacy's and one on Linda's entries and one on the nose over the wall.

Chef D'Carluca came out and looked around and did a mock shout about the mess that the Lab folks had created. Then laughed and put in his votes on the three posters that he liked.

He placed a Spaghetti alla Marinara in front of Bram and said that was all he could prepare in the "Time" he had available. And then laughed at his own joke.

Bram sat and listened as various folks came over and put in their votes with Pat. It seemed clear to him that the number one was going to be the nose. He wondered who had drawn it but decided to wait and be surprised by who it turned out to be.

Linda's entry seemed to be getting a large number of votes as well.

He asked Pat what the prizes were and was surprised that they were significant ones.

He asked who was paying for the prizes and laughed when Pat said not to worry it was coming from the Fold technical budget that was huge and bottomless. It was his budget, and the prizes were a full year's college scholarship, a gift of five thousand dollars to the food bank and three thousand dollars to the Dallas park budget to be spent on putting in a new hiking trail.

When he asked how they had come up with the prizes, Pat said that they had been ones that some of the lab folks had been wanting to gift.

He shook his head and said that he needed to get back to work and that she should somehow capture all of what was going on and put it out on the community network.

Pat liked the reaction that Bram had to the poster contest. She knew that the issue about time was Bram's current crisis, and she knew how significant it was by the amount of tossing and turning that she slept next to.

She hoped that he would solve the problem as fast as possible. She had not shared the fact that the folks at NASA, Jeffery's team and the folks at their large bubble production site were participating in the contest as well.

Bram decided to take a walk around the building to get some exercise before sitting himself down to continue the tedious task of modifying the equations.

He stopped and complimented Linda on her poster entry.

Linda let him know that she had contacted everyone, and they were ready for the review of the equation on Thursday afternoon and Remi would have the wormhole express ready to go on Friday.

That evening he learned that the contest ended at noon the following day and he was expected to hand out the awards.

He asked how he came to be the one to hand out the awards.

Pat laughed and said that it was his budget that was giving the awards and he was the only one authorized to use the money as he saw fit.

He replied that he was associating with a devious person.

Chapter 14: The Fish Bait Solution

When Bram walked into a full cafeteria for Tuesday's lunch, Pat guided him to the podium that was set up by the windows where three easels held the winning posters that were covered by cafeteria tablecloths.

He was asked about his poster choices but said that he couldn't remember which ones he had chosen and that they had all been good.

Pat knew that Bram never forgot, and she liked the fact that he was being diplomatic in trying to keep everyone happy.

She asked Bram for a layman's explanation of how the solution to the time problem with the Fold equations was coming.

He began with the fact that he needed more "time" and that they had not given him enough "time" to get through all the parts of the equation that dealt with "time."

He shared that the basic problem was that if he were to send a baby through the wormhole and across the galaxy with the current set of controls, the baby would comeback as dust.

He said that he was looking for some volunteers to send out to test his current solutions. He asked for any Fold Wormhole passenger volunteers to raise their hands. He then paused and waited. He laughed and said that he had so far only killed a flower but on Friday he would be sending out three fish, three meal worms and three crickets and hoped to get them back alive because Linda had threatened not to let her father take him fishing if he killed the bait.

He then asked, "Who wants to volunteer to take the ride after they comeback alive."

No one raised their hands!

Ya! I wouldn't want to go next either since all of them might be returning the day before their death.

So then, I will send three newly born mice and see if they return as baby mice.

He asked if there would be any volunteers if that worked. He was greeted by silence.

No. Wow, you all are a hard group.

I guess I will have to send out Wilbur the pig to see if he returns as a pig and not as cooked bacon.

He then asked, "If I am successful with Wilbur will I get any volunteers?"

Pat stepped out and said she would volunteer. The rest of the Wheel team members all shouted that so would they.

He thanked them and then said that it was "Time" to hand out the awards.

The Message

Pat explained that they would work up from third prize to the first prize. She stepped over to the first stand and pulled off the cover. It was a poster with a stick character with a voice bubble that had "Only a Bram can control time."

Once the winner came up to claim the cashier's check for three thousand dollars, Pat then went to the number two poster and revealed a drawing of a person with his finger on the hour arm and the saying, "Time cannot be stopped or reversed, unless you are a Bram."

Bram was pleased to see Lacy come forward to claim the five-thousand-dollar prize.

When Pat uncovered the first prize poster, the cafeteria erupted with a cheer. It was clear that it was the favorite for many people.

It was of a character with a long nose looking over the wall saying, "Bram will sniff out time, he just needs be able to get over the Fold wall."

When Zoe came forward to claim the prize, Bram broke into laughter. She had periodically tweaked his nose when he was deep in thought to see if he knew what was going on.

Zoe held up the certificate awarding her a one-year scholarship and said that she was going to become a mathematician so that she could help Bram solve his equation problems or maybe she would just go into the fifth dimension and disappear.

She received a round of applause and someone shouted she should choose the fifth dimension and that it was less of a challenge then working for Bram.

Bram complimented all three for having won and went on to thank everyone for contributing to the Fold program.

He was pleased with the enthusiasm in the room. It provided him with the desire to successfully solve the time problem.

Erica came over to the table where Pat and he were eating lunch and complimented Pat on creating such a motivating event. She said that she had never been part of an organization that had as much energy and fun.

Bram smiled and said that she was now leading one and should enjoy it as much as he did.

She chuckled and said that Jeffery had threatened to promote her so he could have her job.

Bram nodded and said that Jefferey needed to move up so that he had more control of what was on the political horizon. He made the point that communicating with an alien race that looked more like a whale and inhabited a water world was going to be a huge political challenge.

He then excused himself and said that he had to get back to follow the thread of time through the Fold equation.

Erica asked Pat if Bram was moving too fast and maybe taking too many chances.

The Message

Pat looked at her and said that, coming from her, it was a strange question because Erica had been with the Fold program from its beginning.

Erica nodded and said that Pat was right. She then asked if Pat was really willing to go out when Bram cleared people for the first wormhole Fold.

Pat smiled and said that she knew that Bram would not let anyone Fold anywhere until he was certain that it was safe.

She let Erica know that he looked back at all the previous Folds and kept saying that he had been lucky. She went on to say that he had tested his stationary Fold equation starting in the desert with apples, cherries, and candy. Then he had moved the effort out to a location near Seattle where he moved heavier and heavier weights until the power company stopped rebuilding the power station he kept blowing up, but he had worked his way up in weight to the point that he could Fold enough weight that he moved on to building the transports for people.

He built the bubbles that became wheels in shape because he envisioned months and perhaps years of the Fold personnel being on long term missions.

On the first Wheel fold from Seattle to Dalles he almost lost power when Wheel One Folded. He stopped everything until he could make sure he had enough reliable power before he would let Wheel Two-Fold.

I asked him what would have happened if the power had failed during either of the Folds.

He shook his head and said that he had no idea.

That is when he decided to send out smaller bubbles that only carried sensors and a control computer that was storage and had a built in return program that it triggered after a given time.

When Bramlet One came back with a boulder embedded in it, he insisted that before the Wheels would again be launched, the coordinates of the Fold location would be checked out with a host of bubbles to make sure it was clear of any objects.

He then limited the first Fold to be out to the Moon to make sure that distance did not affect the Fold capability.

Pat paused and looked at Erica and repeated her question about Bram moving too fast.

She went on and said that Bram moved very fast and that the Fold program had outpaced and outperformed any developmental program she was aware of.

Pat then spewed out a series of questions.

Did he move fast, Yes.

Did he ensure the safety of everyone involved, Yes.

Did he constantly worry about making a critical mistake, Yes.

Did he move too fast, No!"

She concluded by saying, "He just moves at Bram speed and time."

Erica nodded and said that she had asked a stupid question. She said that she had come to trust Bram to always do the right thing.

Pat agreed and she said they should check with Linda to see how many pigs and of what size he had asked her to get.

They walked out together and went to Linda's desk.

Pat asked how many pigs Bram had asked her to get.

Linda crinkled her eyes and asked how they knew about the pig request.

Erica gave a laugh and said that they had bet with each other that he would ask to get three pigs each one bigger than the first one.

Linda replied that he had indeed asked for three pigs. The sizes were to be one hundred fifty, three hundred and five hundred pounds and he wanted them clean and ready to Fold on Friday afternoon. Linda said that he had told her she could skip getting them trained to be bubble pilots.

Pat smiled and said that Linda might have time to actually train the pigs since all they had to learn to do was to push a button.

Linda replied that Pat was the experienced pilot so maybe she could teach the pigs to push the button.

Erica said that she would leave it up to them to decide who would teach the pigs and turned to go to her office.

Pat asked Linda to give Bram a ten-minute warning when it was time to go home. She said he would continue what he was working on, in the comfort of his recliner where they sat together every evening.

Linda said that she would.

On the way home, Pat asked how far Bram had gotten with his Fold equation modification.

Bram said that he was about halfway through one version of the changes he was planning and that subsequent versions would be modifications to learn how to control the source of time being used and learn the effect of integrating time and distance. He said that the subsequent versions would be easy to do.

He commented that he was going to see if the two IT reviewers would do the subsequent versions so he could focus on sending out the various plants and animals. He said that the plants would be at the most risk, then the fish, worms and crickets would be the next at risk. If they survived, he would then send newly born mice to see that they did not age in their round trip. Finally, he would send out the three pigs one at a time to make sure that size did not matter.

Pat asked when he thought he would be executing the Fold wormhole missions.

Bram said that if everything went according to plan, they would begin after lunch on Friday and end by five in the afternoon. If he killed the flowers, then he would need to reschedule the remainder of the trials until he quit killing flowers.

When they were comfortably sitting in their recliner, Pat said that she would sit quietly.

The Message

Bram gave her a hug and thanked her for having made Monday a great day that had boosted his energy level and had broadened his Fold Wormhole validation process. He admitted that he had added the mice and the pigs after the cafeteria speech.

Pat watched Bram slowly going back down his equation wormhole. She worried that he would mentally wear himself out.

The next day when they arrived at work, she asked him to take hourly breaks and share his progress with Mallica or anyone else that he thought would be useful to keep in the loop.

She was pleased when he agreed to do it twice a day and at lunch.

She stopped by Linda's desk and asked her to give Bram a call at ten and three to make sure he got out of his office to go to whoever's office he was going to share progress with.

She kept track for the next three days to make sure Bram didn't get consumed with the Fold equation.

Every evening she would sit by him on their shared reclining lounge and make sure that he got up and took an evening walk and talked to her.

She sensed that he knew what she was doing, and she took his quiet participation as approval.

On Thursday afternoon, she sat in the back of the viewing room and observed the review process. It was clear to her that only Mallica understood the basics of the Fold equation.

The two IT resources, though very capable programmers who understood how to write the program code for the Fold equation, were otherwise overwhelmed. They made several suggestions to improve the performance of the programing that Bram had done.

Bram thanked them and said that he would like them to make those changes immediately after the review and have the program ready to try on Friday morning.

Pat noticed how the two IT resources perked up and became more engaged. She was always impressed with how Bram could motivate and turn up the enthusiasm level as he turned up the level of work of those around him.

Bram suggested a ditty on the early Friday morning jog from the house to the compound that let Pat know that he was feeling confident.

Castor and Donna started the ditty, and then they were jogging singing:

> "The Birds and The Bees, have nothing.
> Nothing over the fishes,
> Nothing over the worms,
> Nothing over the crickets.
> The Birds and The Bees, have nothing.
> Nothing over pigs one, two or three.
> Nothing over pigs one, two or three.
> All will Fold.   All will Fold.
> And live to be, live to be.
> Very, very old
> Pigs one, two, and three."

The Message

By the time they got to the door where they normally entered the building, Pat could hear the entire compound reverberating with the ditty that had been taken up by the Marine's guarding the compound.

It was clear to her that everyone had noticed that the ditty that had been missing for days was back. It was a message to all that things were back to normal.

Pat realized that somehow, the entire organization watched how Bram was acting and absorbed his mood.

She knew firsthand how his persona affected her but then she was the one that was in love with him. She smiled and guessed that in a way so was everyone else.

Pat was in the back of what had been Zuri's office. The room was in the process of being renovated into a more theater like atmosphere. Comfortable seats were arranged so everyone had a clear view of the screens. They were the original screens and behind them the wall mounted screens were in the process of being installed.

Linda was sitting next to her, and Pat told her that the room was going to be a super place to meet.

The room filled to the point that there was standing room only.

Bram entered and sat at the seat that was in the center and that had been kept open for him. He thanked everyone for coming and then turned to look at Linda, smiled and asked her why she had let the room exceed the rated capacity. He asked if she had provided enough refreshments to tide everyone over for the next four hours of lecture.

The room went deathly silent.

Linda smiled and replied that she would have let more people in, but these were the only ones willing to listen to him go through his boring equations and she had also run out of funds to provide more refreshments.

Pat watched as the exchange had cause everyone to smile. They knew that Bram was joking, and that Linda was readily returning his volley.

Bram looked around the room and welcomed everyone. He said he was just kidding about the four hours and that his update would take no more than the next thirty minutes and that afterwards they were welcome to spend time at the refreshment cart in the hallway to make sure that Linda had not wasted any funds.

He then turned to the two IT resources, introduced them, and ask them if they had been able to get the Fold programing complete and ready to go.

They responded that they had indeed made the changes and they had tested it to make sure all the sections worked as intended.

Bram thanked them and then he activated the screen to show the test plan for the day. He had put a big question mark in red after the line that said,

"First Wormhole Fold returns with living plants?"
Yes →send out the fish, worms, and crickets.

No →go get a beer to cry.
"Second Wormhole Fold returns with living fish, worms, and crickets"
Yes →send out the baby mice.
"Third Wormhole Fold returns with living baby mice"
Yes →send out pig one, pig two, and pig three
The mice and the pigs live to grow old.
The Fold team gets to live bold.

Pat marveled at the simplicity of the test plan. She knew that Bram had a ton of tests and detailed analysis that would happen, but the essence of the day was up on the screen in seven short lines.

Bram asked if there were any questions.

Someone asked if the pigs went out one at a time.

Another asked if there would be a total of six Folds.

A third person asked how long each Fold would be.

Bram replied yes to the first two question.

He then said that he would be increasing the Fold duration after fold number two, but all the folds would be of very short durations because he did not know how fast or how far a vessel in a Fold wormhole would go.

He said that the data coming back from each wormhole Fold would allow him to learn about the motion inside of the Fold wormhole. He pointed out that most likely the information coming back would keep all of them busy for the foreseeable future.

Bram looked around and said that unless there were more questions the update was over, and the action was now going to be out at the lab and the launch area.

He pointed to the clock and said that the update time had only taken sixteen minutes and that all the extra time could be spent enjoying the refreshments that Linda had spent most of his budget on.

He asked the two IT folks to follow him to the Lab where they would program the bubble for the first Wormhole Fold.

Chapter 15: One Step Above

It seemed to Bram that the entire site personnel were following him toward the Lab. He stopped at the Lab entrance and let everyone know that only the folks working on the Fold Wormhole Bubble would be allowed in the Lab. He asked the two IT folks to set themselves up in Lori's office. He then turned and walked back to where Remi was already getting the first plant ready. They had agreed to measure the soil moisture, take a picture of the leaves and they had measured the main plant stem diameter and its height. These were their control measures.

Bram watched as Remi secured the plant and sealed the bubble. Then they extracted air from the bubble and sent it to the chem lab to have it analyzed.

Remi signaled the lab personnel that were dressed to move the sealed bubble in its launch enclosure, to the launch area.

Bram then followed Remi out to the launch control room.

Pat had arranged for Linda to press the launch button as part of their continuing teasing of each other about teaching pigs to fly.

Pat said that she knew of a city where they had a flying pig contest that had selected the best flying pig entry and that the winner had won a years' worth of sausage. She said that first contest had later turned into a yearly Flying Pig Marathon.

Bram interrupted the exchange and said that Linda should count down from three and hit the launch button.

The launch of a bubble was always anticlimactic because there was no noise. Only the disappearance of the bubble let one know that the launch had taken place.

Bram knew that he could have had the bubble return in less than a minute but he had set the return timer to ten minutes so the lab folks could turn around the analysis of the air that had been extracted from the bubble.

He took the time to explain that on every return there would be at least a thirty-minute period for initial analysis and then another thirty minutes if the Fold equation required tweaking.

He asked Linda to have the launches displayed throughout the facility on the information screens and suggested that everyone should follow their regular work routine.

He and Remi returned to the lab and discussed what they would do if there was any issue with the returning plant.

Bram pointed to the next plant and said it would be the next victim and they would follow the same process as before until the returning plant reading was the same as when it left.

Remi heard the call that return was one minute away.

The Message

They walked to the control room. They observed the return of the bubble and followed the crew rolling the containment to the lab.

Remi took a sample of air with an internal container and then opened the bubble and took the control measures. The soil was almost dry. The main stem was smaller, and the plant seemed to be drooping.

Bram was relieved that it had come back old but alive. He knew that he was on the right track and that he needed to refine the way time was being integrated. He let Remi know that in roughly an hour they would send out the bubble again with the next plant using a control program with some minor adjustments to the integration of time.

He excused himself and said he was going to ask the IT resources to make the modifications and then have them load the bubble's computer with the modified program.

The third flower plant to go out came back with all measures the same as when it was sent out.

Bram then asked that the fish, worms, and crickets be sent out.

They survived with seemingly no major issues.

The baby mice returned with their eyes open, and Bram once again adjusted the equation. He sent out the next set of three baby mice. They returned with their eyes still closed and seemingly had not aged but the lab workup that was to follow would be the definitive measure.

Bram now knew that he had the equation within the tolerance that he felt it was safe for the pigs.

The workday was almost over when the final pig was to be sent out. He had the time integration loop bias refined by a factor of one thousand. The refinement was made by changing the bias on the time equation and the numerical size of the change was now out to twelve digits.

There seemed to be no changes in any of the pigs, but Bram had asked the physical health lab folks to evaluate the health metrics of the pigs in detail. They said that they would need additional time for detailed analysis but said their initial readings indicated no impact from the ride.

Bram asked if they could get the analysis done by the following Wednesday and was pleased that it could be done if the Lab worked over the weekend.

He thanked them and suggested that after Wednesday they take the next week off and then prepare to analyze the human specimens that would go out next.

Bram looked at the three pigs, each in a controlled, clean environmental containment where they would be kept until they were moved to long a term farm where NASA kept all their experimental animals. He knew that the pigs, the worms, and the fish, would all live full lives and be studied for years to come. He was not sure what was to come of the two surviving Marigolds.

He thought about all the people that had gone through a Fold and knew that they too would be part of a lifelong health impact study.

He wondered what his legacy would be in the impact he was having and wondered how those individuals would remember him.

He walked out of his office a few minutes after five. He had taken the time to review his progress with Einstein and check with him what else he should do.

He credited his review with Einstein with reminding him that he had to check on the progress of how they would send back a message to the Aliens. He explained to Einstein that he had been so focused on solving the issues with the Fold Wormhole equation that he had not thought about the Aliens. He thanked Einstein for the reminder and put him back to his residence.

Bram felt he had gotten an insight how a message could be sent via the Fold process but first he wanted to review Mallica's progress in determining how the message had been sent by the Aliens via the Fold process.

He invited Mallica for breakfast on Sunday and was pleased to have her accept.

Linda gave him his normal ten-minute heads up and he packed up and walked out of the office just as she was getting ready to leave.

Thomas and Bob were standing by and led the way to the van.

Pat was already in her seat and after Bob got in the back seat, Bram got in and gave Pat a kiss.

Thomas shut the door and got into the driver's seat. After passing through the compound exit gate, he asked who they would have the pleasure of having for breakfast on Sunday.

Bram replied that he thought there might only be Mallica. He said that if Thomas had someone in mind, he should invite them.

Thomas replied that he had no one in mind and it really didn't matter who all would end up at Breakfast since it was Bob's turn to cook.

Bob thanked Thomas for his concern and said he was ready to feed anyone that sat at the table.

Bram reflected on the fact that his FBI and Marine bodyguards had become people that he considered his friends. He then gave a mental laugh at the fact that they were also the people that he spent the most time with. Socializing outside of the Fold personnel was almost nonexistent.

He would need to push for the Fold members to go on vacations away from the compound area.

He turned to Pat and asked where she would want to go on vacation.

She was surprised by the question. She thought for a moment and said that she would like to hike the mountains in Norway and stay in cabins along the trail and she would love to paddle board one of the fjords somewhere along the way.

Bram smiled and said that they could spend weekends there. They could travel by bubble and be there almost instantaneously.

Pat gave a small frown and commented that she had not thought about the impact the bubble technology was going to have on the travel industry.

Bram nodded and said that he had such a discussion with Jeffery and suggested that he develop a transition plan that could be presented to the President when the time came. He acknowledged it would have a dramatic impact on the world economy, on operations like NASA and all the transport and delivery businesses.

He foresaw a period of upheaval like the car industry had cause during its growth. He felt that the Fold impact would be a faster and more dramatic period of change that was more like the change the internet and the phone technology was having.

Bob commented that he had already been worried about having and raising children and now his worries had gone up astronomically.

Pat looked over her shoulder and laughingly said that he should use the Fold technology to search the world for his one and only so that he could worry about having children.

Bob nodded and agreed.

Bram had listened to the exchange and the request that Pat had made brought the idea of setting up a Fold travel agency for the people of the Fold community. He would bring that up with Linda to see if there was someone in the current community that could become a travel agent. As soon as he had that thought, Melissa's name popped up. She was always arranging the entertainment and other activities for the Fold community. She was a very good lab analyst, but she seemed to be better at getting the community to gather and enjoy themselves. She seemed to be the perfect person. He envisioned her coming up with the destinations and Marcus determining the specific coordinates for the vacation Folds. They would have to set up the destination end so that the Fold traffic was invisible.

At breakfast on Sunday, Mallica thanked Bram for inviting her then asked if the invite had to do with the Alien message.

Just as Bram was going to admit that was the primary reason, Orlando made his appearance and asked if he was in time for breakfast.

Mallica jumped up and gave him a hug and asked who was watching the other woman in his life that he guarded.

Orlando replied that a new Marine guard had been added to the protection assignment and her appearance gave him the opportunity to return to the Fold community for a couple of days.

He made a joke about them needing his wit to send back an uplifting message to the Aliens. Maybe he could come up with a ditty that would put a humor into the reply.

The Message

Bram thanked him for such dedication and asked what he was thinking of having for breakfast. He was pleased that Orlando had arrived before he had answered Mallica. He watched as the two of them chatted and discussed what they would do for the time he was visiting.

Bram knew he had to find out Mallica's progress and then he could let her have time off with Orlando.

Meanwhile he would work through how he was going to generate neutrinos, the most abundant particles that had mass. He knew that the potassium in a banana generated them but that would be too weak of a source. He needed a stronger potassium source. He immediately thought of potassium chloride, KCl, a naturally occurring potassium salt used as a fertilizer. It would be inexpensive, and he could build a transmitter that would concentrate the neutrinos and then set up a pulse modulator so he could control the formation as the neutrinos were Folded into a message that used the Alien alphabet.

He laughed to himself about using such a cheap source material to create the world's first Fold message transmitter.

It was clear that everyone at the table had heard him laugh, since they stopped and looked at him and Pat asked what was amusing him.

He apologized and said that he would let them know after they all were done with breakfast.

He was pulled back into his focus on neutrinos and speculated that the Aliens were using them as well since the message had passed through the bubble and its construction with no discernible damage. He knew that neutrinos could readily pass through almost all ordinary matter. Top scientists had speculated about using them as a way of sending messages through the Earth or the Moon. Such an ability would greatly enhance the exploration of both bodies.

Since neutrinos had been discovered in the late seventies, he wondered why this capability had not been exploited and developed.

He would ask Erica to investigate to see if any progress in that field had been made. If there was an organization or group that had made significant progress, he might be able to accelerate the creation of the neutrino transmitter.

Pat had kept quiet as she watched Bram slowly and somewhat mechanically eat his breakfast. It was clear to her that he was deep in the development of something. She speculated, since he had invited Mallica who had been looking into how the Aliens were able to Fold their message that it had something to do with sending a response to the Aliens.

When she saw that everyone was through with breakfast, she asked Bram to let them know what he had laughed about.

Bram stopped and looked around the table.

He asked Mallica to give them an update on the progress she was making to determine what particle the Aliens were Folding to make their message.

Mallica took a sip of her coffee and then said that it was little, she thought it was smaller than an electron, but she was not sure what particle it happened to be or how it would be Folded. She went on to say that she had come to the end of her analysis and other than what she had just shared, she figured she had come out empty handed.

Bram nodded and said that she had just confirmed for him that he was on the right track and said that made her research useful and valuable.

He went on to explain that he had laughed about the fact that he was contemplating using common fertilizer to create the world's first Fold message transmitter out of material one step above sh--t.

This caused the whole table to burst into laughter.

Pat said that was probably all they all needed to know and that she would leave the details up to him.

Bram looked over to Mallica and told her that she was through with her assignment and that she should take time off with Orlando. He smiled and said that the price for such time off generosity was for Orlando to come up with a Tuesday morning ditty for the team to jog to on their way into work.

Orlando replied that he would have that done before lunch and he would stay until the Wednesday jog to lead them in singing the ditty.

Bram laughed and said that it was time to go to the site entertainment facility and play pool or ping pong and maybe get a dip in the pool before lunch.

Chapter 16: Leak

Bram was up and ready to begin work on constructing a neutrino generator. He went to the kitchen for his normal morning coffee before jogging to work.

He was surprised that Orlando and Mallica were at the kitchen table. He asked what was up.

Orlando smiled and said that he was going to lead the team in and get them into rhythm singing a ditty about the Aliens that he had promised to think up. He jokingly said that he had made it simple but was sure it would inspire Bram and speed his development of the Neutrino transmitter.

He then shared the ditty and said that he wanted the team to wake up all the Marines in the compound.

> Hurrah! Hurrah!
>> An Alien's call.
>> A red sun,
> Hot bun,
>> No fun
> The message received, perceived.
>> Bram's Aha!
>> Can give them an answer.
> Hurrah! Hurrah!

> Frogs in hot water
> Bram's Aha
> Message transmitted.
> Were sure they'll get it.
> Hurrah! Hurrah!

Bram was surprised at its simplicity. Then he said it was time to go and wake up the Marines at the compound.

By the time they got to the hanger entrance, they had every Marine in the compound repeating the simple ditty.

Bram invited Mallica and Orlando to have breakfast with he and Pat.

Castro, Donna, Zoe, and Eric sat at the next table. They all complimented Orlando for keeping it simple.

They were all relaxed and chatting about what the next steps would be when what seemed to be a major earthquake hit and was followed by a huge explosion.

Bram was surprised when Lacy came on over the intercom and told everyone that a major attack on the compound was underway. She asked everyone to take cover but to stay in place.

He found himself under the table and realized that his bodyguards had pushed multiple turned over tables around them and had taken defensive positions.

He heard Orlando, comment to Castor that he would rather be fishing and that out on the water they had been able to return fire.

Lacy came back on the intercom and announced that Major Sharp and the Marine contingent had complete control of the compound and the attackers were being taken out.

She said that her team had taken out the mortars located at the river's edge and had destroyed a personal carrier and a tank coming from the direction of the power plant. She said that the bubbles were in hot pursuit of several hundred retreating armed persons running for their vehicles and her team was showing no mercy.

It was clear that Lacy was using the bubble technology that seemed to be armed with missiles and other weaponry.

Orlando commented that Lacy and her team seemed to be swift and deadly and the only ones seeing any action. He wondered where she had gotten her weapons.

Bram commented that he had asked her to develop a Fold offense. He was surprised at the speed and the impact that her team was having.

Lacy came on again and let them know that all the escape vehicles were destroyed and that at least a third of the attackers were dead.

She went on to say that the person who had provided the funding for the attack was no longer around to fund another one and that the main leaders of the attack were also no longer in the picture.

Bram wondered where Lacy had gotten the authorization for such lethal action.

Major Sharp came on and announced that all the attackers were captured or dead. He went on to say that the hanger had suffered major damage and Wheel One was now in pieces after taking a direct hit in the mortar attack.

He announced that he and Lacy would hold a debriefing session at noon in the auditorium.

Bram asked Donna and Castor to go and find out if they could go to the hangar.

He suggested to Orlando and Mallica that they return to the housing area and let folks there know that none of the personnel at the compound had been hurt but no one should come to work until they got the OK from Major Sharp.

He asked Pat to go with him to his office and have a cup of tea. He was going to ask Linda to get the inside information from Lacy.

As they walked out of the Cafeteria, Bob and Thomas met them and said that they had received a message that the raid had been triggered by a message coming from inside the compound and they all were to go to Zuri's old office until Bram's office could be checked for explosives and cleared.

Bram invited Linda to come with them as he was getting ready to go to Zuri's old office.

Once they were all comfortable in what now was the Viewing Room. Bram asked Linda to see if Lacy could come and share the inside information.

He then asked if she could put in an order with the cafeteria for coffee, and other refreshments.

The Message

Once everyone was settled, he said that he would like them to participate in creating the response message to the Alien request for help.

He asked Pat to lead the effort.

Pat nodded and said that she no longer had a Wheel to command, and she needed to find a new skill that would keep her employed.

Bram knew that the destruction of Wheel One would have a sobering effect on Pat.

He had not told her, but he was sure that she was aware that he had been thinking of repurposing the materials of both Wheel One and Wheel Two since their original design was to have enabled a crew to stay out for extended periods of time and that no longer seemed necessary.

Pat had the group composing a reply message when Lacy entered.

The room went silent.

Lacy nodded and walked over to where Pat was standing.

She then looked over to Bram and said that her team had to wait until they were attacked before she had been authorized to act.

The authorization had been cleared to the very top of the military command and to the very top of the political hierarchy, the President.

Once the first mortar hit, her team took out all the mortars and the personnel at the mortar sites using their armed bubbles. They then turned toward the electrical power plant where a tank and personnel carrier backed by about three hundred armed fighters had been spotted. They eliminated the tank and the personnel carrier and then began to mow down the fighters.

She stopped for a moment. She went on to say that she and her team had discussed how they would respond if the site was ever attacked. They had decided that not only the attackers, but the backers of the attack would all be treated equally.

The local financial backer that had come to the area where the mortars were located had been killed. The remote financial backer in Seattle had a gas explosion at his home that killed him.

She stopped again and then said that the Fold organization had an offense that was second to none and it took no prisoners. She made the point that it was more difficult than defense because it required the setting of priorities and actions organized and planned in detail. It required discipline and the need to avoid distractions. It required a hard hand. She commented that the offense she had designed was lethal and meant to discourage future attempts.

She apologized for being a second off in the first part of the Fold's offensive action. By the time, the first mortar shell hit the hanger, all the mortars and the people using them had been eliminated.

Her team had hesitated for only a fraction of second and that hesitation had given the attackers just enough time to drop the first mortar into its barrel. They had nothing in place to stop that mortar round.

Bram thanked Lacy for having developed a defense that turned into offense at a moment's notice and that she had used what was available to her in a unique and deadly way.

He shook his head and commented that each time science made a technological leap forward, humans figured out how to use it as a weapon.

He commented that this time a seemingly sweet but deadly woman had developed the weapon.

Lacy nodded and replied, that her mother had always advised her to make the most of what she had on hand. She looked at Bram, smiled and said that he had given her the most powerful hand that anyone could have to play, and she had made sure she was allowed to play it.

Pat asked where Lacy had obtained the weapons that were mounted on the bubbles.

Lacy said that General Tilson had connected her with a General in the army who had made all the latest small missiles, grenade launchers and small machine guns available and that her team had modified the bubbles that Remi had provided so that each could hold multiple weapons and carry the needed ammunition.

She volunteered to tour the team through the section of the Fruit Farm facility that was off limits to all but her team members.

She then excused herself and said that she needed to get back to her team and Major Sharp to assess the situation.

Bram thanked her for taking the time to get them in the know.

He then suggested they take a break, and then Pat should continue leading them through composing the response to the Alien message.

A knock on the door caused the break discussion to end immediately.

Zoe cautiously opened the door. Erica was standing in front of two armed Marines. She walked in and commented that it had taken orders from the General to allow her to come the compound.

She looked around and smiled and then said, "and what do I find but everyone chatting, having coffee and rolls and enjoying themselves."

She walked over and poured herself a coffee and took a jelly roll.

Pat commented that everyone in the room should take their seats and they would get back to composing the reply to the Alien message. She pointed to Erica and asked if she was going to join in.

The Message

When it was closing in on noon, Bram knew that the reply was as done as it could be until the moment it could be sent. He thanked everyone for contributing and suggested that they see if the cafeteria was serving and that afterward they could go and listen to the details associated with the attack.

After lunch they all went to the auditorium. General Tilson was introduced by Linda who had been recruited to formally introduce him, Major Sharp, and Lacy.

A camera crew was at the top of the auditorium's sloping floor ready to record the presentation.

It was clear to him that the video would be used to update both the military brass and the political leaders. He knew that Lacy's performance would up the pressure to produce bubbles and use the Fold technology to improve the military capability of the country.

He resigned himself to the fact that he would have little influence over that process.

He was surprised to find out that the Marines guarding the compound had not fired a shot. The fire power had all come from the use of the bubbles by Lacy's team. Her team had killed almost one hundred of the attackers, destroyed ten mortars, one personnel carrier, one tank and more than thirty trucks and RV's.

Major Sharp commented that the Marines had close to two hundred persons being held as prisoners.

The General commented that some of those that had been killed were prominent local figures and one was known to have been financing the folks making the attack.

Bram asked what was driving the effort to stop the Fold program.

General Tilson replied that there was a political side and an economic one. It was similar to the demise of public transport via trains and busses as the auto industry pushed the individual automobile. In the case of the Fold technology, it was most likely many factors that involved transportation, military power, and current investment strategies.

He looked over to Lacy and asked what she had determined from her interaction with the many organizations she had contacted.

Lacy stood up and said that she had encountered economic fear and she felt it by far was the biggest factor.

The folks she had engaged with feared that a technology change as dramatic as the Fold capability could cause a global economic collapse. Somehow a few very wealthy individuals had learned the basics of the Fold technology and they were actively funding the efforts to delay or end it all together.

Bram asked how widespread this concern or fear was.

Lacy said that it was less than a handful of individuals, but these individuals had billions to spend on whatever concerned them.

The Message

Bram stopped asking questions but knew that he would be working to learn how he could counter those individuals that were willing to use their fortunes to hold back progress.

He was surprised also by those at the lower economic levels of society had enough concern or hate to give up their lives to support some individual's misguided belief. He thought about the carnage that Lacy had unleashed using the very technology that they thought they had a chance to stop.

The folks in opposition were unaware that the "ship had already sailed," or said another way, "the train had left the station." Bram knew that he had discovered a technology that would change many things around the world.

Bram returned to his office where Linda asked if her sister was mean enough for the role, he had promoted her to.

He nodded and said that she was as tough as the toughest member in the Stetson family, and she was in the right role, and she needed to be given a grander title and a raise.

He then asked that he not be interrupted for the next couple of hours.

The morning events had disrupted the work he had been focused on. He had turned his attention to developing the means of creating actual hardware that would enable the transmission of Fold based messages.

Bram envisioned several modifications that would allow him to control the transmission from the magnetron that created the Fold action.

The learnings from having translated the Alien Fold based message and how they had most likely been able to create it gave him fresh insight on how the magnetron could be physically manipulated to create Fold pulses.

He figured out that he had to synchronize the release of the neutrinos that would merge with the Fold pulses in such a fashion as to create a message the Aliens could read.

Remi wondered why Bram had asked him to come to his office. He stopped at Linda's desk and asked if she knew what the meeting was about. She said that Bram must have gotten a breakthrough of some kind because he had asked not to be disturbed.

He followed Linda into Bram's office.

Bram got up and pointed to the two lounge chairs and asked if Remi wanted tea, coffee, or a soft drink.

Remi replied he would go for a soft drink and walked over to the small refrigerator on the counter to see what kinds were available. He selected a citrus based drink. Then sat down. He was a little nervous since he had spent the morning with Bram, and nothing had been mentioned about meeting later.

Bram knew that he had created an apprehensive atmosphere. He had done it intentionally because he was going to ask Remi to change his current role. He was going to ask Remi to become the Fold Hardware Manufacturing Director.

He had laughed at himself as he sought to invent titles for different members of his team.

The Message

The title was of no importance to him but the fact that Remi had been a key part of getting the Fold hardware rapidly developed and constructed was important.

He asked if Remi was ready to be promoted.

Remi replied that he did not know of a role in the current organization that he would want to be promoted into.

Bram nodded and agreed that currently there was no role that suited Remi's superb capabilities, but that situation was about to change.

He then described the role that he had in mind. Remi was to lead a team that would produce hardware that would enable the manufacture of a magnetron that had variably controlled physical chambers, a neutrino generator that had controls that would synchronize with the magnetron pulses and the power systems that would support the two.

Bram went on to say that there were also physical production improvements that the Fold program needed for the continued improvement of the current Fold effort.

Remi would be responsible for selecting the members of his team. He stressed that Remi should select the folks that would contribute the most and that pay increases would be part of their participation.

Remi asked about Lori.

Bram replied that Lori would take on a bigger role in the Fruit Farm Production facility and that she was not in consideration for the role he was being offered.

Remi smiled and thanked him for the opportunity, and said he was anxious to get started.

Bram said that he should start by getting a facility designed and put in place next to the Fruit Farm Facility but in the short term he wanted to have him produce the first modified magnetron and neutrino generator in the current lab with the team that he would select.

He should also select a company that could produce the two pieces of hardware and if they worked out those companies could be absorbed or enhanced but the production should be done at the new Plant Production Facility.

Remi said he would see how fast his team could come up with what Bram was asking for.

He then said that he wanted Bram to be part of reviewing the design of the new facility.

Bram agreed that he would love to have input to the design of the new facility but that he needed to continue to focus on the design of the hardware so they would have a robust product.

Chapter 17: Inside Spy

*O*n the following morning, Linda let him know that Lacy and General Tilson had requested a meeting with him. They would come to his office at ten to discuss internal security at the Fold complex.

Bram asked if they had indicated anything more than that and got a "No." He then asked Linda to give him a five-minute warning and that he planned on working on the design of the hardware to generate a Fold signal.

It seemed that he had just explained his concept to Einstein and had taken a moment to take a sip of tea when Linda gave him the warning.

He put Einstein back into his kingdom and sat down and sipped his tea.

Linda knocked on the door and led the General and Lacy into the room.

Bram noted the look on the General's face and figured that they had come to deliver a message that they were not sure how he would respond to. He thought about the times he had railed against the security being put up around the compound and thought about how right it had been. He was just not use to the actions some bad people were willing to take.

Lacy began by saying they had two important and critical items to discuss with him. One was the fact that they were sure there was a spy inside the Fold organization and the second was a modification of Bram's Living arrangement.

The General went on to say that he would cover the changes that he was planning to take to increase the protection being provided to the Fold organization. He went on to share the fact that a Marine unit would be using the Fold technology to scan the area around the compound on a twenty-four by seven basis. This unit would be located remotely. They would take over as soon as Lacy set up the system and trained them.

Then he stopped for a moment and asked if he could have a cup of coffee.

Bram nodded and said that he needed one as well since he figured the next part of the discussion was going to focus on him. He asked what Lacy would like.

She replied, "black."

After Bram had served the coffee, he sat down and said that he was ready for the next part.

The Message

Lacy once again opened the conversation. She said that the General was insisting that the security around him needed to be beefed up.

Bram gave a small laugh and asked how much more security could possibly be added.

The General snorted and said that Bram was only on the first level of security and that he was only being moved one rung up the ladder.

He then said that he was going to address four areas where security would be increased.

One was at work.

A second area was at home.

A third area was the journey to work.

And the final area was in the area of rest and relaxation.

Bram smiled and said he wondered what moving up two levels of security would mean.

The General replied that he didn't want to know but it was much worse than the time Bram had spent in the desert. He then went on and said that he would cover each area in the order that he had stated them.

He looked around the office and said that the outside of the office would get a protective layer that would be able to withstand a small rocket. This would be a total encasement.

His bodyguards would be augmented. Two would be in the office and an additional two would be outside the door. He understood Bram needed his privacy and a bullet proof wall would be put up a few feet inside the door and the inside guards would be on the door side.

Bram looked at the space between his desk and the door and asked if his desk could be rotated so that it would face the windows.

Lacy replied that she would have Linda rearrange the office the way he desired.

The General then went on to say that his office would be guarded twenty-four seven and have an early morning bomb sweep before he was allowed to enter.

Lacy asked if Bram was OK with what was going to happen.

Bram shook his head and said that he was leaving security to those who knew something about security, and he would focus on doing something easy like Folding time and space.

He thought back about how he had railed against being put out in the desert for protection and how much his attitude had changed since then, after multiple attacks.

The General said he knew this was hard on Bram who he saw as a warm hearted but a naive liberal. He said he had a son just like him but not quite as smart.

The General then said the next part was about the modifications to the house.

The Message

A safe room was going to be added in the basement. Zoe's current bedroom located directly above would become his bedroom. He would be able to get directly to the safe room via a pole much like that of a fire fighter's pole but modified to have lowering and raising capabilities. He said that he would have preferred a full elevator but that would have wiped out the kitchen area whereas the proposed arrangement only took over the pantry area. The bedroom walls would receive an armored layer that would add additional protection.

The General stopped and walked over to the coffee pot and poured himself another cup. He turned and said that the next change would affect Bram's home office. It would be moved to the basement and would be totally encased in armor, but it would look exactly as the one he was currently in. The only inconvenience he could see was that getting to the study would require going down the stairs. Two people could use the safe room pole to go up to the bedroom.

The dining area would be expanded but the kitchen table space would be used to provide a kitchen worktable and the kitchen rearranged so that the pantry area could be moved.

Lacy asked if Bram agreed to get the changes made.

Bram smiled and replied that he was sure that he was being informed about the changes that had already been decided upon.

Lacy nodded and said that she didn't see another way of protecting him unless they built a very large bubble and put it over his house and that would just make it a bigger target.

She was about to apologize when Bram put up his hand and reminded her that one did not apologize for doing the right thing.

The General then said that they were to the social part of the changes. He had suggested that coming to work should change to being brought to work in an armored vehicle, but Lacy had insisted that you would reject that proposal. She suggested several routes that could be used to jog to work each morning with the route being randomly chosen each morning but called in to the observation group that would ensure no one was in the area. And that the ride back to the house would be in an armored van that looked the same as the current armored van but fortified.

Bram thanked Lacy for having protected the one part that set his mood for the day. He had made that jog, rain or shine or snow and felt it was a needed part of his existence.

The General added that he had listened carefully to Lacy. She had earned the respect of not only the Marine Corp but had received kudos from every group that had dealt with her.

He went on to say that he was almost through. The last part was that walks in the community would be given double security. He asked that for even impromptu walks that the observation group be notified. They would scan the area and monitor for any drones or missiles. In addition, the FBI protection would be augmented with four Marines.

For outings outside of the Fold area, the security would be beefed up in a similar manner. The details for them would be worked out at the time of the outing.

Lacy spoke up and said that she had suggested that any outing location should be guarded as appropriate. Everything was to be put into position ahead of time and anyone going there would be conventionally taken there but you and Pat should be delivered using Fold technology.

She asked him how he was reacting to what she and he General had decided needed to be done about his security.

Bram was silent for a moment. He was thinking through the changes and realized that the two of them had been very thorough about his safety.

He saw some continued weak security spots during his workday. Based on the attack, the additional Marine guards would seem like a normal addition.

He thanked both of them for having thought of almost everything, but he did have one request.

He waited a moment to create an anticipatory atmosphere. He wanted the room to lighten up.

He asked if Lacy could get a tailor to make a custom shirt with a target with a bullseye on the back of the shirt and he wanted a hat that had a flat top and a bullseye target on it as well.

That caused the General to guffa and comment that he had just lost a twenty to Lacy who had bet that he would do something like he had done. He ceremoniously pulled out his wallet and handed Lacy a crisp twenty-dollar bill.

Lacy accepted the twenty and commented that she knew her boss and she knew that he would understand that the changes were needed.

Bram said that he was inviting them both to a Sunday breakfast so they could share all the changes in detail with the folks that lived with him and those that were close team players.

Both of them accepted and said that by the end of the week they hoped to be able to have all the changes documented and most would be in place.

The General added that the changes would not be reflected in the documents being stored in compound data bases but would be held back at headquarters. The old drawings would remain as they were.

Lacy then got serious and said that they were now to the part where Bram would be the key player. They needed to find out who the internal spy or spies were. She said that it was an area that had her stumped as how to proceed. She was going to closely monitor people around Bram wherever he was and then see if there was someone that stood out.

Bram said that he agreed with the monitoring.

He then added that she should look closely at the IT folks or folks that had access to the data bases. She should then look at the messages that had gone outside of the Fold firewall. They would be coded messages.

He then said that she should see who had taken extra vacations or had purchased items that seemed to indicate spending more than would be expected from someone with their salary. They should also investigate the bank accounts of the select few that would no doubt surface and also see about accounts that were larger than expected. He added that they might have outside accounts in other banks or offshore.

Lacy had been writing what he said down. She looked up and commented that she did not want to be hunted by him.

She said that she wondered if they could play a game of leaking information in the cafeteria to see where the leak went.

Bram said that was a good idea, but he should not be the person doing the leaking. It should be Pat and Linda talking at lunch, or she and Pat, or Erica, or Mallica. He added that he had only named women because he was betting on the spy being a male and naïve enough to think he was superior.

Lacy added that she also did not want to play poker with him.

The General wondered if any one of the Marines might be a spy.

Bram responded that there was little doubt that there were spies in the Marine Corp. They would leak the military aspects about the Fold compound. Given the most recent attack and the accuracy of the first mortar hit, he felt that would be the leak from a military mind and he should put his people on the list.

Lacy reinforced that by sharing the fact that the initial inspection of the targets for the mortars that were not fired had coordinates for the location of the second wheel, the lab area, the cafeteria, and his office. She commented that to her it certainly spoke of a military mind.

The General agreed and reiterated that he would have his people examine all those assigned to the Fold compound. He said he now felt certain that he had a spy in his command.

Lacy said that she had what she needed and that she would share her plan with him when she had it detailed. She planned to seek out the spy or spies and would include all personnel at the compound.

Bram thanked both of them for being thorough and for looking out for his wellbeing as well as for everyone at the Fold compound.

Lacy stopped and said she had almost forgotten to share an important announcement that she wanted to share with him first.

She smiled and said that she had accepted the proposal of marriage.

Bram congratulated her and then asked when she had found time for romance let alone snagging a husband.

Lacy said that on one of her many trips she had met him at a boring evening dinner hosted by John Morgan, NASA's director. Jeffery had introduced her to one of his organization's lawyers and financial advisor. His name is Raymond Daedlus. So, if I hyphenate my last name, my initials will be LSD.

The Message

Bram laughed and said that it was great news and having LSD around always brightened his day.

The General congratulated Lacy and then said it was time for him to get busy and get the people back at headquarters to check out the Marines assigned to him. He made the point that someone back at headquarters would contact her.

He would deliver the spy to her if there was one assigned to him.

Bram walked out with them to Linda's desk. The extra Marine guards were already in position. He asked Bob and Thomas who had the protection assignment for the day to come into his office.

Bob commented that the General had let them know about the additional added protection.

Bram shared the protection changes and that he had asked Lacy to breakfast on Sunday to explain in detail all of the structural changes to the house.

He then said that it was lunch time and that he was not sure how security was going to be managed but they should do the usual and let the Marine contingent do as they were ordered to do.

Linda asked if he wanted Sunday's breakfast catered and that her family was eager to do it so they could all enjoy Lacy's good fortune.

She shared that Lacy's partner to be, would be part of the breakfast and if they had dinner catered they would be there as well. She figured that lunch should be by the pool area and as relaxing as possible.

Bram said that he looked forward to a calm, relaxing Sunday where the Stetson family members pampered him. He asked if Lacy's partner to be had all the right clearances to attend.

Linda said she would make sure and let him know tomorrow.

The next morning Bram was surprised that Orlando was at the kitchen table having coffee.

Orlando let him know that the General had requested that he stay until the new protection protocol could be implemented and the internal spies apprehended.

Bram commented on his use of multiple spies.

Orlando replied that the General thought there was a Marine spy and Lacy thought there was as spy on the Fold civilian side.

He volunteered that he had enrolled all of the Marines that he trusted and had been with him long before there was a Fold effort to help find the Marine traitor. He said he had to get them to pledge that they would not injure or kill him but turn him over to him or to the General.

Bram thanked Orlando for staying and that he looked forward to his ditties.

Orlando said that he had a simple one for this morning's jog in. He commented that the jog would be on a new route and would be a little longer.

Bram put his cup into the sink and said it was time to get to work.

Pat had been listening to the exchange and also thanked Orlando. She commented that she had been worried about jogging into work, but she knew Bram used it to get ready to dive into the depths of his mind. Having alternate routes was important but having extra marine guards made it feel safe.

Orlando let her know that he had personally selected the additional Marines who he had been in battle with and who he trusted to have his back.

Ron Mueller

Chapter 18: Discovered

The increased security was noticeable to Bram. Two additional Marines were in front and two brought up the rear. The ditty singing seemed to have been augmented and it resounded across the terrain.

Bram now looked directly out of his office windows and had a great view of the river to his left and the Dalles power plant to his right. The distant snow-covered peak of Mt Adam's was at the center of his view. He thought the new office arrangement was better than the previous one.

The privacy bullet proof wall was installed and comfortable chairs where his two FBI bodyguards sat positioned facing the door.

He asked that they move the chairs to his side of the wall and face into the room. He felt uneasy having them in a position that would be deadly should a rocket grenade be used to blow in the door.

The bookcase and the refreshment area remained unchanged.

Given that he had no choice, he felt relieved that he liked the outcome.

The modification and security changes at the house was happening at a rapid pace. Work began when Bram left for work, and it stopped when he returned. The safe room was the first change to get put in. Then work went up through the house.

By the weekend, the two-person elevator from the basement to the bedroom was complete. The additional armor for the walls was next and was scheduled to be completed the following week. The remainder of the modification would take several more weeks.

The work was all being done by military personnel in a very disciplined manner focused on minimal living disruption.

Bram appreciated the attempt to minimize his personal life.

The office layout in the basement was almost a duplicate of the one on the first floor, but it was a little more spacious and it was built inside what could only be described as a huge vault.

He asked Pat to manage the basement office construction to meet her standards. She had more lights put in and made sure the ventilation was quiet.

Moving their books and drawings to the basement was done by a group of Marines that were supervised by Castor.

The location for the catered meals on Sunday was changed from the house to the community recreation center. The changes to the kitchen and dining areas were being done over the weekend and into the beginning of the following week.

The Message

Bram and everyone else in the house would take the following weeks meals at the main cafeteria while the kitchen and dining area was modified.

Bram asked his FBI body guards to be the reviewers and approvers of the kitchen area changes.

He focused his effort on developing the hardware that needed to be developed to create the ability to send Fold based messages.

By Sunday he felt that he and Remi were close to having a prototype that could be used to send a simple message. They were going to send a bubble to the far side of the moon and send it a message. It would then transmit it back using conventional technology.

Generating the message required the bulk of the power and the return signal was similar to the light that a mirror reflected and required just a fraction of the power.

He was aware that Lacy and the General had spent the week focused on identifying the spies. He planned to ask about their progress after Sunday's breakfast.

Linda had shielded Bram at work from the contractors by having him use the Viewing Room to get him away from the construction noise in his office.

Bram spent most of his time working with Remi in the Lab building the prototype Fold message transmitter. They came to the realization that they were creating a dramatically miniaturized version of the bubbles. These miniatures were being sent out in something similar to morse code.

It changed Bram's perception of folding the bubbles across the distances that they had done so far. It was like sending out one letter of the alphabet and then bringing it back. The Fold message transmitter was a machine gun version of Folding one bubble. The bubbles were the neutrinos, millions of times smaller, than a Fold bubble with humans or equipment, but in reality, it was just still a physical bubble that got Folded. When the machine gun was modulated to give it dit, dot and dash capability a rapid-fire Fold message could be created.

Designing the control system to enable creating a comprehensive Fold message using the Alien alphabet was a task that Bram was currently in the middle of.

He asked Erica to get the most powerful computer that was available as rapidly as possible. He stated that timing was critical, and that cost was secondary and of a much lower concern.

Meanwhile he had worked out a way to utilize a half a dozen top end desk top computers, but he needed something close to a supercomputer to have the control speed that would allow faster coding.

He and Remi had celebrated their success, at rapidly building the prototype, with a glass of wine. They were both looking forward to sharing their progress with everyone at the Sunday breakfast.

The Message

Lacy was having the opposite result. She had slogged through the records of all the folks working on the Fold project. She did a quick once over of all the records, but nothing popped up. There were no obvious spy standouts and she had not expected there to be any, but the review got her oriented for the more detailed examination.

She then organized her small team of three people that she had personally scrutinized and vetted and assigned them to go into the details of each individual.

She had worked with Erica to arrange CIA and NEC support for her team as they delved into each individual being investigating. She asked Erica to stress the need for speed in finding the spy.

Personal phone use was a more difficult issue and she learned that when she narrowed her spy list to just a few people. She asked the NEC if they would be able to get the phone logs and know what was being said.

She personally reviewed all the outgoing e-mail messages and noted the message recipients.

By the end of the week, she was down to three potential spy candidates, but she was not confident that any of the three was the spy.

She was frustrated and emotionally on a low as she left work for the weekend.

She shared her frustration with Linda, who said that she was sure that if she shared her progress on Sunday that someone would give her a nugget that would help her identify the spy.

During the same time, the General had each of the Marines assigned to the Fold project scrutinized by the specialists at the Pentagon. He concluded that the person that was identified had not been very smart about covering his tracks. It turned out his assignments had included being a guard at events where the two Wheels were located as well as being a gate guard and a perimeter guard.

The General thanked the Pentagon personnel for their quick response and asked them to trace all communications that the Marine had and who he had contacted. He said he was more interested to learn who else might be involved.

The General went into the weekend with the feeling of anticipation about who the Marine was working with. He was now sure that the direct hit of Wheel one was due to coordinates that the Marine had shared with someone on the outside. He expected to find another Marine, most likely higher in rank and somehow connected with the people that had attacked the Fold compound. He figured the next one up the ladder would not be the one that would have connections to the right civilian groups.

He was sure the Marine on the base was just the spotter and that someone higher up was a pure traitor.

The Message

Linda had observed each of the close team members and knew that the attack had affected all of them. Until the moment of the attack, she had felt that she was working in the most secure place possible. The ability for a major attack to be mounted against the heavily guarded compound surprised her.

She was surprised by everyone's unique response.

Bram seemed to brush it off and then dig deeper into the current technical problem.

Pat became more involved in the details of providing Bram security.

Lacy had enlisted her as she worked around the clock digging through people's personal lives trying to find the internal spy. And she knew that Lacy was very frustrated by not making any headway.

The General became invisible but when she saw him in the cafeteria it was clear to her that he had made progress.

The security changes for Bram's office became her primary focus and she pushed the architect and the contractors on getting the changes done rapidly. She had insisted that the work went on twenty-four seven so that Bram could settle into his office and concentrate on his project.

She was glad that Bram was spending his time in the Lab with Remi. It let her deal with the work in the office.

She went into the weekend looking forward to spending time with her parents as they catered the meals for the entire weekend. She had made that arrangement when Pat had shared the condition of the modifications that was going on at her home.

Bram was surprised when Rita Stetson greeted him for breakfast on Saturday morning and served him his normal two soft boiled eggs, sausage, toast, and a cup of coffee.

He recalled that Pat had mentioned it to him the previous evening, but he had not paid attention. He looked back into the kitchen and realized that it was all being rearranged and was not useable.

He asked about Ted and Rita said that he was out in the truck doing the cooking but planned to come in to say good morning and to see what Bram wanted for lunch and dinner.

Bram really did not have anything special in mind. He asked Pat what she had in mind.

Pat said that she wanted to keep the meals light and save herself for the meals the next day. She thought that at lunch a mixed salad with Salmon would be great and for dinner a small steak with mashed potatoes and steamed broccoli would be fine. She added that apple pie with ice cream would make a great desert.

Bram said he would take the same.

Orlando came in with Mallica and said that rumor had it that breakfast was free, and he had come to collect.

Bram chuckled and replied that the price had just doubled.

Orlando then said that Zuri had come home for the weekend and would be joining everyone on Sunday.

She wanted to show off her new wheelchair and had suggested they all take a walk after lunch.

Bram said that he was happy that she had come home and was looking forward to the walk. He asked Orlando about security for the walk.

Orlando replied that security was in place twenty-four seven and his guards would enjoy the walk as much as anyone. He made the point that sitting, and waiting was the really boring part of a security detail.

Bram replied that he was used to having his security firing their weapons as the bad guys tried to get him.

Orlando continued the banter by saying that the battles only happened when the fish learned that he was fishing and notified the bad guys to take out the smart guy with the hook in the water.

Linda had come in with breakfast for Orlando and Mallica and burst out laughing as she took in the banter.

She added that they had it wrong and that the bad guys only attacked because they had not been invited to feast on the Stetson catered meal.

She continued by pointing at Bram and saying that she had witnessed him fighting the bad guys off to save the last piece of desert for himself.

Rita chuckled and added that now she knew why her two daughters had chosen to live at the compound versus staying at home. They had both caught the Bram flue and had lost their minds.

She went on to say that she hoped that Lacy's choice of someone to be her husband was resilient enough to withstand the whirlwind social scene that he was getting himself into.

Bram asked whether Ray had yet arrived.

Linda replied that he was arriving that afternoon. Lacy was meeting him at the airport. She said that the General had insisted that Lacy be taken to the airport in one of the armored vans and that four Marines would provide security. Two would go with her to meet Ray at the luggage area and would be in their parade uniforms but armed. Two would stay with the van and pick everyone up at curb side.

Bram nodded and said that he was pleased that the General had done that.

Orlando added that the General had issued a standing order that the people that he had listed would always have a security detail when leaving the Fold area.

He looked at Bram and said that the General would have assigned a tank to be part of that order for him but said that the highways in the area couldn't take the pounding. As it was Bram's protection was twice that of everyone else and it included a helicopter gunship overhead.

Bram said he would talk with the General about his protection. He said that so far all he needed were two top notch Marine's that knew how to shoot.

Orlando laughed and asked where he was keeping those two Marines.

Bram replied that one of them was mooching a free breakfast off of him and the other was likely sleeping while on guard duty outside the house.

Rita looked at Pat and asked if the back and forth ever stopped.

Pat replied that only when the two of them were not in the same room.

The highlight of the day was the walk with Zuri. It was clear to Pat that Zuri had already begun to grow socially and to have increased confidence in her own mobility.

Zuri put on a show of how she could manipulate her powered wheelchair and commented that it went faster than most bike riders.

She looked around and said that it was hard to see around Orlando and past all the Marine and other bodyguards. She said that she had been asked to interview two more Marine's that were being assigned to guard her.

Orlando agreed and said that the ones she was interviewing were so she would have time to tutor him and help him get his BS degree.

Zuri chuckled and said that he already had all the BS that he needed, anymore and he would earn a Master's in BS.

Bram agreed that there were too many guards and he turned to show the back of his shirt that had a target with a red bullseye that said, "This is the Spot." He then took out the hat he had been carrying in his back pocket and put it on and bowed to Zuri so she could see the target on the Flat top.

Zuri broke down laughing. She said that now it was clear why so many guards were needed.

Bram enjoyed seeing Zuri with such a cheerful outlook.

He noticed that Linda had tears in her eyes and knew that she felt the same. Linda had been her nurse and had nurtured Zuri's intellect for more than a year and had constantly pushed to have Zuri evaluated to see if she was the genius that Linda had thought she was.

The walk ended at the recreation center, and everyone picked out what they wanted to do for the rest of the day.

Bram relaxed and watched as Orlando played ping pong with Zuri.

Mallica commented that seeing a macho Marine like Orlando be such a great companion to Zuri made her want to have kids that he could raise.

Bram asked when that would happen.

Mallica replied that it would happen as soon as he quit working her so hard.

Bram knew that Mallica had taken up learning how to write in the Alien language. It was a rather intense effort that he understood because she was constantly reviewing her progress with him. He in turn was learning the language with her. He figured that the two of them would be able to send back a reply that was written in Alienese.

He said that she better pick a different criteria because he was sure she would do her work so well that the reward would be to do even more of it.

The next morning, Zoe intercepted Bram as he was getting ready to go down to the recreation center for breakfast. She handed him a cup of coffee and let him know that they would go down to the recreation center for breakfast as soon as the bodyguard contingent was ready.

Pat gave Bram a good morning hug and asked what he was in a hurry about.

Bram replied that he had dreamed the solution of how to optimize the hardware and wanted to discuss it with Remi.

Pat chuckled and said that she was sure Remi was not going to be waiting for him at the recreation center.

Bram nodded and sat down at the table and waited for everyone to gather and be ready to go down to get breakfast. He decided that a chat with Ted about another fishing trip was what he would do until everyone arrived for breakfast.

He was looking forward to hear from both Lacy and the General on how their spy search was going.

He hoped that Erica had found the computer he wanted.

A few moments later he was being escorted to the Rec center by his small army.

Pat accepted her breakfast order and was slowly working her way through her three pancakes smothered in maple syrup with two over easy eggs on top.

She had been surprised that Bram had asked for the same but chose strawberry preserve to smother his pancakes with.

It was clear to her that he was controlling himself and that he was watching Lacy, the General and Erica.

She noted that Orlando was sitting on one side of Zuri and Linda was sitting on the other side. Mallica, Nuro and Jina were sitting on the other side of the table.

Lacy was sitting with Raymond, her husband to be. Luke and Cedric were at their table.

Rita and Marial were doing the serving and Ted was overseeing the cooking.

The General, Erica, Remi and Lori were sitting at a table that was almost in the center of the breakfast party.

Marcus and his family were at a table of their own.

The conversation was lively, and it was clear that it was not about work.

Linda had watched the breakfast activity and when it was clear that everyone was sipping their beverage, she said that Bram would like to have everyone take a moment to share how their week had gone.

She looked at Bram and asked him to take over.

Bram thanked her.

He looked over to Lacy's table and said that he was pleased to introduce Raymond Daedlus. A person of pure talent and intellect who Lacy said she had decided to wed in hopes that he would guide the Fold organization in solving the paradigmatic challenge in sending a reply to the Aliens.

He waited until the applause subsided and then he said that he was going to ask for updates from three persons but before calling on them he was going to give them the responses that he felt they should be sharing with the group.

He pointed to Erica and said. "Erica is going to share with us how she found and redirected a supercomputer to be delivered to the Fold project in the coming week. I can confidently say that because I am proof that nothing stops Erica when she is on a quest."

He then Pointed at the General and said, "The General has identified his man, but he is not satisfied with a foot soldier but is hunting the big cheese. He will keep the little guy on the hook until the big, mouthed bass strikes and then the General will reel them both in."

He then pointed to Lacy and said that she was struggling to find the person she was after. She was down to just two, but he suspected that neither of them was the person she sought. He said that because he knew the person who she was seeking. He knew who the spy was.

He then said that they should hear from each of the three in the reverse order that he had introduced them.

Lacy stood up and said that Bram should just tell her who the spy was because the two people that she currently had on the list did not seem to meet the criteria. One was financially draining all his savings to bailout his son from a gambling debt and the other had bought a pleasure yacht that turned into a hole to pour all his money into, and he was now on the verge of having it repossessed. She said that they were both going to get counseling and they would either change their ways or they would lose their jobs. She looked at Bram and told him that she had no clue as to who the internal spy might be.

Bram thanked her for her update. He volunteered that he would like to get involved with the person who was trying to bailout his son and that he would see if he and Erica could be of help.

He then shared that his mind had been relentless at going through every meeting, every trip to the cafeteria, and every meeting in search of a recurring person who didn't seem out of place but who was always present in an inconspicuous way.

He was relieved when he finally found that person because it freed his mind from what had become cumbrous to manage and was eating too much of his time.

He said he would give her the name and she should check out that person's communication and finances. She might be able to tap into the General's connection and get help as well.

He just wanted to make sure that she did not send out her gunship bubble to take the spy out.

He said he would give her the name when the two of them got a private moment.

He then looked at the General and asked how close his guess had been.

The General smiled and said that he was indeed using the Marine spy as fish bait. There was no way for that person to get away but what he was after were the contacts that he expected to find up the chain of command. He shared that he was after a big catch and the bait would stay on the hook as long as he served a purpose.

He looked at Lacy and said he would be glad to help in checking out her bait fish and that they should see who that person was linked to.

Bram thanked the General and then looked at Erica and asked her to share the good news and let them know who she had alienated in repurposing their computer to the Fold program.

Erica stood up and said that Bram had hit the bull's eye. She had a team at NASA that had tried to stop her from the repurposing of their supercomputer. They had tried to use their connections to stop her but had found that her connections went higher than theirs.

She was sure she was the least popular person on their do not like list, but the computer would physically arrive during the following week and be installed at the Fold's computer center and would be ready the following week.

She said that she had learned long ago to support Bram or get out of his way. She had decided then to become his ice breaker and open the path he needed to be opened.

Bram thanked Erica and said that he was now on the hook to work out the kinks in his Fold Message transmitter system so he would be ready when the computer was ready.

He then shared that he and Remi were working kinks out of the hardware that would be controlled by the supercomputer. The goal was to make the hardware respond at the speed of a supercomputer.

They would then be able to compose the content of the messages and Fold them. He pointed out that to be able to achieve that speed the hardware had to be designed with no physically moving parts.

Pat said that breakfast was over, and she needed to enjoy her tea and just socialize. It was time to end the business part of breakfast and get on with the fun part.

Bram sat down and thanked her for stopping him from going any deeper into what he was doing.

Chapter 19: Whisper

When Bram came in, Lacy was chatting with Linda. He knew that she wanted to know who the civilian spy was and how he knew who it was. He asked for five minutes before they met.

He went in followed by Zoe and Eric. They sat down in the two chairs located behind the bullet proof shield and he took his seat in his desk that had been rotated ninety degrees and faced the windows. He invited them to help themselves to whatever snacks they would like as he poured himself a cup of coffee.

He had learned to accept his close in bodyguards and now he had two additional marine guards out by Linda's desk.

He had been surprised to learn that his office was ready. It had been re-arranged and painted. It smelled like a new office. He would have to tell the General that his construction crew had done a marvelous job.

He buzzed Linda and said he was ready for Lacy and Pat.

Pat had stayed with Lacy because Bram had asked her to. He said she would understand when he explained what he had in mind.

Pat helped herself to a cup of coffee and then sat down. She knew that Bram had identified the internal spy and that he had a plan on how to find out who external to the Fold compound they were sending their information to.

Lacy grabbed a bottle of water from the small frig and then sat down in the chair next to Pat. She then looked at Bram, as she twisted the cap off the bottle, and asked how he knew who the civilian spy was.

Bram said that he had gone through all the scenes of group gatherings for the last few months and had identified the individual in most of them or who might be within hearing range. He said that it was a picture search like 'Where is Waldo? Only the question was "Who is the spy? And who is her master."

Lacy said that she knew he had photographic memory, but she had not realized that he could play it back like a movie.

Bram chuckled and said that the memories did not reel out in a linear fashion, but it was more random, that is why it had taken him so long and each scene was triggered by something in the previous scene.

Zoe asked if he could count how many times, she had tweaked his nose.

He said that of course he could, and he smiled and said he was instead going to spend his time and focus on how he would get even with her.

He then nodded to Lacy and said that the spy was a woman. Her name was Cynthia Norris a member in the IT department.

Lacy said that she had reviewed her record and there was nothing on record to connect her. Her bank account seemed balanced with her pay and her meager spending. There did not seem to be any outside bank accounts nor were there many private messages.

Bram said that made her a perfect spy. He suggested that Lacy expand the check to the accounts of other family members and other close friends. He was sure that she could get help from the FBI or DEA.

He went on to suggest that they concentrate on finding out to whom she was sending information.

Lacy asked what he had in mind.

He looked at Pat and smiled and told Lacy that she and Pat were going to go to the cafeteria for lunch and share a secret that if it was true, would-be worth billions of dollars. It would be significant enough to cause their spy to contact the person she was sending information to.

Pat is going to tell you in a voice just loud enough for Cynthia to hear that the Fold process when run backwards will decrease the age of the person who is in the Fold vehicle and that I am in the process of calibrating it so that a person would spend a few moments going backward in time and when that person stepped out of the Fold vehicle, they would be years younger than when they entered it.

Lacy laughed and said that was a great idea. She then asked if by any chance it was close to being true.

Bram shook his head and said that so far time seemed to be a one direction occurrence. He was going to play with a negative Fold in the near future and if he found that time acted differently, she could be a guinea pig.

Lacy said that she could easily get a real pig for him to use before she went out.

Linda buzzed in to let them know that time was up, and Remi had arrived.

Bram looked at Pat and Lacy and said they should make the leak as real as they could.

As they walked out, Pat said that she thought they could enhance the lunch scene by having Erica participate. She led the way to Erica's office to share the plan with her. Pat asked her to come into the cafeteria on cue so that the leak could happen twice.

She would first tell Lacy about Bram's discovery and then Erica could enter, and Pat would share the breakthrough again.

Pat said that she normally had lunch at twelve sharp and that she would go in by herself and then Lacy would join her.

The hour hand on the walk clock seemed to be stuck but the hand finally clicked over to twelve. Pat left the lab and headed for the cafeteria.

After selecting a large salad and a large, iced tea, she sat down at her usual table.

A moment later Lacy walked in and walked over to her table and asked if she could join her.

As if by magic, Cynthia walked in a moment later, got her food and sat a table away.

Lacy asked if it was true about the discovery that Bram had made.

Pat replied that she was really excited about the fact that he had found a way to turn back time. He had sent out a mouse and it had returned back as a pink baby mouse.

She said he was in the process of calibrating how to turn back time in a controlled fashion.

Erica came over with her tray and joined them.

Lacy asked if she had heard about Bram's latest breakthrough.

Erica replied that she had heard it had something to do with time.

Pat replied that it indeed had to do with time. She then repeated the line about calibrating the process of reducing a person's age.

The rest of the lunch time was talking about the great dinner they all had enjoyed out at pool side.

When Cynthia left, Lacy said that she was going to get with her team who would be monitoring Cynthia's out going connections. The DEA was handling phone calls and text messages and her team was monitoring the internet.

The internet connection was a surprise. It was a simple message to the Assistant Director of NASA! It said "breakthrough."

A few moments later a reply came through that said it was time for a progress review and Cynthia should come to NASA headquarters by Friday.

Lacy asked Linda to let Bram know that he had picked the right person and that she needed him to contact John Morgan, the director of NASA.

Bram asked Lacy to step into his office. Once he had learned who Cynthia was connected to, he said that he would make the call immediately and that she should plan to be at Cape Canaveral when the arrest was made and press the charge of spying.

John and he were well acquainted, and his call went through immediately. Bram made sure that John was alone and in his office. He then asked John to call on a secure line other than the one he normally used.

A few moments later John called back and said that he had gone several offices away to one of his security folks. He was alone and really curious about the desire to use a different line.

Bram explained about the information leaks at the Fold site and that one of the leaks went straight to the NASA Assistant Director. He said that the internal spy was a NASA junior employee who was coming with a message for the Assistant Director at his request and would be there for a Friday meeting.

He asked that a warrant be arranged that put the Assistant Director under arrest. He let John know that Lacy Stetson would be arriving the next day and would be there to assist in the arrest of the person traveling there from the Oregon Fold site.

John commented that he had heard about the attack on the compound and wondered if any of the NASA personnel had been involved in making that happen.

Bram replied that at the moment neither seemed to have a direct link to the attack but once they were in custody they would be questioned to see if there was some sort of indirect link.

John said he would be very surprised if his Assistant Director had links to an attack on the Fold site.

Bram replied that he would not be surprised because he was still looking for the source of the leak that had exposed the fact that the two wheels were in a hangar in the Seattle area and had almost caused a catastrophe that still haunted him.

John replied that he had not thought about that incident recently and if it were true then he had a major problem.

Bram replied that he had a major problem, and he should be looking at who would fill the Assistant Director role.

After Bram had hung up, he looked at Lacy and suggested that she take a little extra time in Florida. He suggested that maybe Jefferey, Raymond's boss would give him a few days off for him to join her.

Lacy smiled and said that she was going to call Jefferey and ask for that favor.

Remi had been sipping on a diet drink and had listened to the entire exchange as had Zoe and Eric.

He commented that life around Bram was better than being in a spy thriller movie that was full of gun battles, secret intrigues, unfounded love affairs and unforeseen twists. He said that around Bram all of it was real and not make believe and much more frightening.

Bram nodded and said that all he had ever wanted to do was to invent stuff and had never thought about how bad people around him would react to the good stuff he discovered and invented.

He looked at Remi and said that they needed to finish testing their current version of the Fold message transmitter and then get one designed to work with the supercomputer that Erica had reappropriated for them.

Zoe looked at Remi and said that Bram was able to move from being shot at, to shooting someone, to translating Alien and then working on the Fold equation all within a heartbeat.

She laughed and said he had even kept track of how many times she had tweaked his nose when he was in one of his deep trances.

Bram loved the exchange. It kept him from getting lost in his mind. He now needed to focus on how to modify the magnetron so that he could modulate it at the speed that the supercomputer operated.

He looked down at the picture of the Milky Way that was under the glass that covered his desk. It was his inspiration picture. He knew instinctively that he had to modulate the magnetron with a laser pulse that would hit a spiraled wall and generate different length pulses as it went along the spiral. Its curvature would be the curvature of a spiral galaxy. The different pulses generated by the laser bending as it moved to different points on the spiral could then be matched to the Alien alphabet.

He looked at Zoe and thanked her for having solved his problem and that he would go easy on the revenge that he figured out for her nose tweaking.

He then said that he was going to introduce them to Einstein with whom he always reviewed his finds and of whom he always asked for additional help in making improvements.

He walked to his bookcase and moved a set of books aside and got Einstein and brought him to his desk where he gave him a small piece of cookie.

He introduced each of them to Einstein and then shared his spiraled magnetron design concept with him.

He asked him what the spiral should be and then asked Remi to write down what Einstein agreed to.

He then asked Einstein if the spiral should be the Fibonacci sequence that starts with a zero, followed by a one, then by another one, and then by a series of steadily increasing numbers that followed the rule that each number is equal to the sum of the preceding two numbers.

He pointed at Einstein as his head nodded up and down and said that he had gotten positive confirmation.

He then asked if the laser should move one electron distance along the spiral to generate each unique magnetron pulse.

Once again Einstein seemed to nod in the affirmative.

He then asked if the laser power level should be increased to generate stronger pulses that could be differentiated from each other.

This time it was clear that Einstein was shaking his head in a negative response.

Bram stopped and thought for a minute and said that he agreed with him.

Then he asked if the laser beam frequency should be changed to enable additional signal generation.

Again, Einstein shook his head in the negative.

Bram then asked if the length of the spiral should be increased to make it possible to have all the signaling capability that might be required.

This time Einstein shook his head in the affirmative.

Bram looked at Remi and asked him if he had gotten it all down.

Remi nodded and said that it was hard for him to believe that Bram was using a mouse to make decisions about designs of the Fold Messaging system.

Bram chuckled and said that Einstein's batting average was one thousand and had been in the game from the earliest moment when the two met out on the desert on Einstein's boulder home.

Zoe asked how old that made Einstein.

Bram handed Einstein to her and asked her how old she though he was.

Zoe said that Einstein looked too young to have been around in the desert since that was more than four years ago.

Bram nodded and said that he had noticed the same thing about Einstein and the fact that Einstein seemed to be the same age as when the two first met on the boulder in the desert.

He said that he thought the Fold experience seemed to rejuvenate the animal that experienced the Fold. It did not necessarily turn back time, but it seemed to fix cell damage. So, his story about turning back time was not what the Fold process did but he was almost sure that it made the living entity experiencing it a healthier one.

Zoe looked at Eric and said that she now believed him when he had shared the fact that he had gone out feeling like he was coming down with a cold but when he got back, he felt great.

Bram nodded and said that he was going to set up a series of tests to verify that side effect of a Fold experience.

He then said that he wanted to keep Einstein's participation a secret. He said he did not want some mouser hunting Einstein down.

Zoe nodded and said that it would be hard to convince the FBI to assign mouse guards.

Remi said that if what he had written down that Einstein had agreed to worked, he would come in and stand guard of the genius mouse named after a genius.

Bram put Einstein back and said that it was about time that he took Einstein for a visit to his boulder in his desert home.

Linda called in and said that the supercomputer had arrived and was being set up in the computer lab.

He suggested they go to see what size a supercomputer was now days.

He was pleasantly surprised when Linh and Duong greeted them and led them to an area that was separated from all the other areas. They pointed to where technicians were connecting the computer to power and to the site internal internet.

The computer was about the size of Bram's office refrigerator. It was smaller than he had expected. Linh explained that they would be ready to program the computer that afternoon. She let him know that they would come to his office and connect his personal computer to the supercomputer so he would be able to operate it from wherever he happened to be.

Bram said that he would like Remi to also have access and he wanted access in the short term to be limited to just the two of them. He also wanted to make sure that only his Fold translation program was allowed to run on the supercomputer.

The Message

Duong commented that made the job of getting the computer online rather easy. He pointed out that it could do much more.

Bram said that he understood that it could, but until he had mastered getting the Fold Message Transmitter operational and working smoothly, he did not want the computer doing anything else.

Remi asked what Bram expected him to do with his access.

Bram replied that the two of them were going to pretend to be Marconi and Tesla and send messages to each other. They would test the new Magnetron that they would have the machinists make that afternoon. They would power up the magnetron with their current power sources and use their current transmitters.

Once they were sure everything worked, they would have a transmission bubble created that could be positioned close to the Alien galaxy.

He wanted to be able to transmit the Fold message to the bubble and then have the bubble retransmit it to the Aliens.

He said that would ensure a two-level security shield for the location of the Earth.

Remi asked why Bram was thinking of the two-level security system.

Bram replied that he was just being cautious because the messages he would send out would continue to travel for millions of years through the Folded Space and there was no way to know what other civilization would receive the message. He wanted to make sure that Earth did not shout out, "Here we are come and get us."

He said that he wanted to quietly whisper, "Welcome we are friendly but fierce. We embrace intelligence and grace. We help those in need. May we all live in peace.'

Remi said, "Wow, I am working for the Fold Peace Whisperer."

Chapter 20: Money Connection

Bram suggested they try the supercomputer on how well it could break into very secure systems and not be detected.

Remi laughed and commented that he had just gotten the impression of a Saint and almost immediately he was working for a sinner willing to break security systems to evaluate his supercomputer.

Bram responded that Lacy was off to make sure that she arrested the Fold civilian spy that was going to meet with the person she was spying for. He wanted to check out that person, who was the NASA Assistant Director, to see if he had any growing offshore bank account and he wanted to check if he was communicating with any specific individual associated with the attack on the Fold compound. He figured they might as well put the supercomputer through its paces and see if they could use it to find out this kind of information.

Remi said that he didn't know how to write the code for a hacking routine that could break through the security systems that would yield such information.

Bram replied that he had obtained a basic hacking routines that would be on steroids when running on a supercomputer. He said that he hoped they would do.

They began by searching the cash inflows, on specific dates, of offshore banks. After an hour they hit paydirt. Shortly after, they had the assistant director's account detail, and it was clear that he was putting in a substantial sum every month. It seemed he was providing someone with a big account the information they were seeking.

Bram then had the computer track the source of the money transfer. It surprised him when the very company that had helped build Wheel's One and Two was the source. Someone was paying to get inside information about the Fold program.

Bram speculated that the Assistant Director was simply trying to make himself wealthy by sharing information about the Fold progress.

He would have Lacy find out who the person was that was paying the money and with whom they were interacting. He figured that that person might be the one connected with the attacks and was most likely also motivated by greed.

He then declared that he was satisfied with the supercomputer's capability, and it was time to program it to become a magnetron modulator that would enable a continuous signal generation.

The Message

He wanted it to be controlled by the person who was generating the message. This meant creating a storage buffer to hold the message in queue and then merge it with the magnetron signal to a transmit routine that controlled the position of the laser. The computer would then manipulate the laser that would shoot into the spiraled magnetron to generate the Fold based message.

Remi asked what he should do.

Bram said that he should call Linh and Duong into the computer room, and he would explain what code he wanted them to write that would do what he had just described.

Then they would go to the cafeteria for lunch and afterwards they would finalize the physical design of the magnetron and get it machined and have it and the laser synchronized. He projected that by the end of the week they would be very close to having a system that would work at the speed and the precision that would let them generate a reply to the Aliens.

Remi commented that now he understood Erica's comment that being around him was at times like standing calmly and watching a huge tsunami approaching and feeling the wind blow your hair straight back but not being able to run for cover.

Bram commented that she was exaggerating as he put in a call to Marcus and Mallica. He asked them to meet him the following morning at his office so he could bring them up to speed and get them prepared to generate the reply to the Aliens and to determine where in the universe the bubble relay transmitter would be located.

After dinner as he and Pat were sitting in their twin recliners, he asked her how she felt. He was thinking about the effect that a fold had on each living thing that experienced the Fold.

Pat replied that she felt great.

Bram asked her whether she had any chronic problems that had disappeared.

Pat looked at him and asked him what was up. What had he discovered about the Fold process. Did it actually make people younger?

Bram replied that the fact that Einstein had remained healthy and seemingly looked like he did when the two of them had met in the desert had made him realize that the Fold process did have a positive effect on a living animal. He thought it might be more along the lines of curing or fixing the problems that a body might have. If that was the case the Fold process would be almost as coveted as if it reversed aging.

Pat said that she did not have any chronic problems, so she was not a good sample of the Fold effect.

Bram said that they would have to set up a series of experiments to determine the longer-term effects on humans.

Pat suggested that they start out with some damaged fruit and vegetables and see what happened. She volunteered to set up that investigation.

She said they could utilize the cats and dogs that various people owned and then bring in some pigs that had some sort of specific problem.

Bram thanked her for volunteering.

Zoe who had been quietly listening to the exchange said that she would volunteer to go after the pigs. She said that she had a scar on the back of her leg from a childhood bike accident that she would love to have removed.

Pat asked to see it.

Zoe pulled down her knee-high sock to show the scar.

Pat walked over and knelt and ran her hand down the back of Zoe's calf and said that there was no scar. She asked if it was on the other leg.

Zoe pulled the other sock down. She ran her hand down each leg.

Pat stood up and smiled. She commented that she had her answer even before she started the actual verification of the effect of experiencing a Fold. She would take the disappearance of Zoe's scar as the initial proof that experiencing a Fold was very beneficial.

Eric commented that he had thought the appearance of a healthy big toe, toenail had occurred because of the medicine that he had been putting on it but now he felt that his Fold experience was the most likely reason.

Bram suggested that Pat start by interviewing everyone that had experienced a Fold to see if there were additional bits of evidence before going into a full-scale series of experiments.

Pat made some notes to remind her to look for the Fold effect in external physically visible markers. She then put down a series of questions.

How about internal organs?

How about the mind?

How about bone structure? This question popped up when she thought of Zuri.

She decided to engage Amy to help her. She wondered who else might want to be a third person.

Bram looked at what Pat had written on her pad.

He said that if her investigation worked on bone structure, he would personally get involved to see that Zuri took as many Fold trips as possible.

He had been considering her to participate in a Fold wormhole journey. Such a journey currently was based on a series of sequential Folds, and it would be good to know how such a journey would affect Zuri before letting her take it.

The Message

Pat instinctively knew that her experiments would be verification experiments and she planned to execute the experiments as rapidly as possible. She knew instinctively that Bram was already designing the experiment for Zuri. She wanted to get there before he leaped frogged her.

Bram commented that he promised to wait until Pat had tested her pig, but he warned her that he was already dying to see Zuri walking defect free.

Pat said that she would go as fast as bubbles could Fold and return. She cautioned them that they should keep the conversation in the room a secret until she had done the confirmation tests.

Bram smiled and said that his nose got tweaked but no secrets had ever leaked out of his office.

The next day he and Remi worked with the senior machinist to get the magnetron internals formed to the specifications they had determined were needed. The machinist commented that he did not have the equipment to produce the magnetron to the accuracy that Bram wanted. He knew a Navy machine shop in San Diego that could. He went on to say that it would need to be made of the finest and hardest steel available and the magnetron would need to be in a temperature-controlled environment in order to maintain the accuracy Bram was asking for.

Bram asked him to take charge and make it happen.

The machinist, whose name Bram found out was Henry Wilkins, said he would contact the San Diego shop and see if they could expedite getting it made.

Bram said that would be great and he asked that Erica be involved because she was one person that could get it expedited.

At lunch he asked Pat how her experiments were going.

She said that she had gone through many of them and would do the pig the next day. The pig had been delivered and she had used a scalpel to make a cut along its front left leg. She said she had named the pig Zoe since Zoe had claimed to have a scar on her leg.

She let him know that she had recruited Linda who had volunteered that she had a burn scar from the exhaust of a motorcycle.

Bram laughed and said that he wanted his support back unharmed even if she still had her scar.

Pat replied that so far, his Fold equation had not done any living thing in.

Bram asked if turning plants into ash counted as doing a living thing in because he had done that.

Erica came over with her lunch tray and joined them. She looked to Bram and said that he had thrown her into the briar patch when he had the machinist engage her in expediting getting the magnetron machined as a priority. She had agreed to go to San Diego and be there at eight Monday morning to pick up the first of the six magnetrons she had ordered.

Bram looked at her in surprise and said that he had only requested one.

Erica laughed and said that she was aware of that but the smart-alecky officer in charge of the machinists said that specifying the material to use, "as the best material" was too general and that meant that there were about six materials that fit that description. So, she told him to make one out of each of the materials and send them up.

He said that he could not provide the transportation that was suitable to keep the magnetrons in a stable condition.

She went to Henry Wilkins and asked him to make the environmentally stable containers to transport the magnetrons.

She said she had arranged for two drivers to take them down in a comfortable conversion van. The General insisted that a lead van and a tail van would provide protection.

Bram shook his head and said he apologized and that he had only gotten her involved because she had come through with the supercomputer. He said that he would design an experiment to test each magnetron to see if the material made a significant difference.

After lunch, Bram said he was going to his office to make a call. He asked Remi to set up their message transmitter and to use the behind the moon coordinate and set up the receiver/repeater bubble.

Bram called the General and explained the situation. He asked him to contact someone in the Chain of Command in the Navy that would straighten out the Lieutenant in charge of the machine shop.

He let him know that Erica would arrive in a reasonable time. He pointed out that the drive down would take more than one day.

He then suggested that the Lieutenant extend an apology to Erica for his rude behavior.

The General said that he was well acquainted with the Base Commander and Erica would get an apology and she would travel down at a reasonable speed.

Bram thanked him and then let Linda know that he would spend the rest of the day in the Lab with Remi. He asked when Remi's office at the new lab building would be ready.

Linda said that the office was going to be ready on the following Tuesday, but the entire lab would not be done until the following week.

He then asked to see her burn scar on her leg.

She gave a little laugh and asked if Pat had mentioned that she had volunteered to be a guinea pig.

Bram said that indeed she had and that he had warned her to bring her back alive.

Linda said that if Pat killed the pig, she would decline being next.

Bram said that would be a wise choice.

He then asked Linda to contact Erica and let her know that the trip to San Diego would begin at eight Monday morning and the drive down and back should be done at a leisurely pace and that she should expect an apology from the Lieutenant in charge of the machine shop.

He then left for the Lab to meet with Remi for the rest of the day and then he would go home for the weekend.

The lab was busy. Remi had set up at the far end in an effort to stay out of the way of the bubbles that were getting launched and retrieved, examined, and then launched again. He noted that Pat was turning the experiments around in record time and that she was taking copious notes but was wearing a smile the entire time. He figured success was in the air and hoped it would extend to the experiment that he and Bram were about to try.

He felt a degree of tension that he had not expected. He thought about the Magnetrons that were getting machined in San Diego and knew if the experiment that they were about to conduct failed those magnetrons would most likely be worthless.

He watched as Bram entered the lab. For a moment the entire lab seemed to freeze and then, almost in the blink of the eye, it snapped back into action.

Bram was surprised at the bustle that was taking place in the Lab. He noted the people stop when he entered but Pat had them all back in action almost immediately.

She whispered that he scared people as she walked by.

Bram wondered why he would scare anyone. He walked over to where Remi had set up the computer with the message program. He asked if the bubble was ready.

Remi said everything was a go and the two bubble handlers were ready to be taken to the launch stand.

Bram said, "let's do it."

As the bubble was taken from the Lab, Remi asked what the first message would be.

Bram said that it was a saying that he had learned in his high school typing class that used all the letters of the Alphabet, "The quick brow fox jumped over the lazy dog's back."

Remi said that his professor had taught him that at coding school when he had complained about being a poor typist. He had practiced that until he could do it at sixty words per minute.

Bram stepped back from the computer and said Remi should Fold the repeater bubble into location and send the message five times and then see what they got back.

The launch as always was anticlimactic.

After a couple of minutes, Remi sent the message out five times.

A split second later,

The quick brow fox jumped over the lazy dogs back.
The quick brow fox jumped over the lazy dogs back.
The quick brow fox jumped over the lazy dogs back.
The quick brow fox jumped over the lazy dogs back.
The quick brow fox jumped over the lazy dogs back.

Appeared on the computer screen.

The Message

Remi pumped his fist and yelled out, "Yes!" Which caused everyone in the lab to stop.

Bram shouted out, "Success."

The lab resounded with the sound of applause.

Bram then typed a message in Alien and sent it out five times.

It too came back five times.

Remi asked what the message said, and Bram chuckled and replied that it was the same message in Alien that he had sent out.

It turned out that both he and Pat had been successful with their experiments and that evening as they sat in their twin recliners, they shared a glass of their favorite wine.

Ron Mueller

<u>Chapter 21: Magnetron Romance</u>

Saturday Bram got a call from Erica asking if she could be at Sunday breakfast at his place. He knew she wanted to know how he had been able to change the timing for her to go to San Diego. He assured her that she was welcome.

At breakfast on Sunday, Bram explained that he had asked the General to make a call to someone high enough in base hierarchy to take the Lieutenant in charge of the machine shop to the carpet for his rude behavior. He had no idea who the General knew or had contacted.

Erica said she got a call from the base commander, a Navy Admiral who evidently was an old friend of the General saying that she should take her time traveling down to his base and that she would be cordially greeted.

Not long after a Navy Captain that said he was the Lieutenant's superior called her and said he had the Lieutenant on the line.

The Lieutenant apologized for his rudeness and said that he was pleased to be able to produce the magnetrons she had requested. They would be ready when she arrived.

The Navy Captain had then invited her and her team to dinner at the base officer's club. He had also recommended an upscale hotel at which he could arrange a room at her request.

Bram said that was a great ending to a poor start with the San Diego base.

Erica agreed and thanked him for having taken action.

Pat commented that the cycle of events at the Flow compound had also gone from the very bottom to the very top. She shared that every one of her experiments was verifying the fact that a Fold experience was a positive event for both plants and vertebrates. She shared the fact that the pig that was delivered was in perfect shape and did not have a single scar. She had one of the techs cut the pig on the right front shoulder and another cut behind his snout. She would send the pig out on Monday morning and if he came back with no scar, then Linda would take the next trip out.

Bram said he was anticipating Monday's successes and once that was certain he would contact Elizabeth to arrange to have Zuri spend the next week making a series of Folds and they would see if the process would make a difference for her.

Orlando commented that if it did, he would be glad to lose his job.

Bram said that he could accompany Zuri on each of her Folds and maybe it would work on him, and he would be able make it through college and get a degree. He looked around the table and asked if they had ever met a Marine Sergeant smart enough to get a degree without some sort of help?

Orlando laughed and said that he hoped to get smart enough to compete with Bram and create a better Fold process.

Zoe said that she hoped that the Fold process would help her go from flat to having some round bumps.

Bram figured he would change the subject and asked who wanted to take a nostalgic trip back to the boulder where he had sat many a day as he worked to create the equation.

Amy had wondered why Pat had invited her for breakfast and Bram had just unveiled the reason. She said that she was definitely in.

Pat said she was in because she wanted to see that boulder and sit on it at five in the morning. Perhaps it would inspire her to help her decide what she should do next.

Orlando said that he was in. He wanted to see the desert that had somehow inspired Bram's non-linear mind create the Fold equation.

Erica said that she probably should go but she was not planning to make the trip. She commented that she was not the person she had been at that time, and she did not want to relive that part of her life.

Bram added that none of them was the person of that time and that the light of that time was now billions of miles away on its way across the universe.

On Monday morning, Orlando was in the lead as they jogged to work. He started to chant a ditty and soon had them all chanting along.

Fold, Fold, Fold
It's not about growing old.
It's about being bold.
Fold, Fold, Fold
Take a person from the chair.
Fold, Fold, Fold
Give her legs, give arms, give her hair,
Fold, Fold, Fold,
Lift her, Lift her.
Let's be bold.
Lift her, Lift her.
Let's be bold.

Once again, the entire compound echoed the ditty as the other Marines joined the chant.

Linda greeted him at the door and said that she had tears in her eyes as she heard the ditty.

Bram said that he too was touched and hoped that by the end of the day they were arranging to get Zuri back to Dalles so they could see if the Fold process would do what Orlando had so eloquently expressed.

Pat asked Linda to come with her to the lab so she could get ready. She said that they would send the pig out and depending on the condition the of the wounds they might send him out again until the scars disappeared.

Then Linda would be next and once again how many of the Fold cycles she would experience would depend on the condition of her scar.

Bram redirected his desire to be there when Linda returned and instead went to the IT department. He wanted to see if Linh and Duong had been able to make progress in creating the Fold Transmission control software and the queue buffer that would hold the message until it was time to transmit it.

Linh commented that they had worked over the weekend to create their first draft that they wanted to debug the code that day. She asked whether he had been able to create the hardware for the laser that would activate the signal in the magnetron and create the Fold transmission beam.

Bram said that he and Remi would be working throughout the day to upscale the design that they had successfully tested. He expected to have that model online the next day. He then expected to have the magnetron connected and tested in another day.

He suggested that on Friday morning they would send out their rebound bubble to test the entire system.

At eight am sharp, the van to take Erica to San Diego stopped at the front door of the apartment building. She had a small suitcase that she had decided to take when she found out that the trip would take more than one day.

She noted that the van that she was riding in was in the middle of two other black vans. She felt like a dignitary on tour.

She got in behind the passenger seat.

Henry was sitting on the left reclining bucket seat.

She noted that there were two marines in uniform in the front two seats and there was one sitting behind her.

She asked them their names and wrote them down so she could remember them.

The Marine in the passenger seat was a sergeant and the one in charge of the other Marines who were all privates. He explained that they had been ordered to do as she requested. He said that each of them in the van only carried their side arms. He then said that the two other vans had four Marines in full battle gear, and they carried additional firearms for the three of them. They did not anticipate any action, but they were prepared for almost any attack.

He pointed to the cooler and the five boxes on top of the cooler and said that Chef D'Carluca had sent breakfast sandwiches, coffee, and juice. He had filled the cooler with a variety of drinks and a mix of fruit.

The Sergeant relayed a message from the General that wished her a good trip.

She thanked him and said that she was looking forward to their trip and that he should look ahead for a good place to have lunch.

She asked if they could make San Francisco and spend the night there and then get an early start for San Diego and plan to arrive there in the early afternoon.

When the leader replied that it would be easy to arrange, Erica asked that he let folks know. She commented that the Navy brass in San Diego should get their schedule.

She then suggested that he be the one to select the mealtimes, stops and that he arrange the hotel stays at top-of-the-line hotels. It would be on her budget.

She grinned as she realized that the overall site budget was still in Bram's name. She had decided to leave it that way because his name seemed to open the bank every time they needed money.

The music varied between country western, to current pop artists and to jazz.

She fell asleep and only came awake when the Marine in front quietly let her know that they were at the California state line, and it was time for lunch.

During lunch, the Marine clarified that dinner would be in San Francisco and if she wanted to continue, they could continue as long as she desired.

She said that it would be good to make Long Beach so that on the following day they would get to San Diego in the late morning. She suggested spending one night in San Diego and then the following day heading back to Dallas.

The Marine said they would arrange a hotel at Long Beach where they could all stay.

They ordered a takeout for dinner and arrived in at the hotel in Long Beach as the evening turned into a dark night.

The evening was uneventful, and they were on the road early the next morning.

The rest of the trip was one of dozing, sleeping, and dozing some more.

She learned more about Henry and his family than she wanted to know.

She came wide awake when close to noon the following day they arrived at the Coronado Naval Base.

The guard greeted them and said that the Admiral was expecting them. He stepped back from the van and made a call and then after a "Yes Sir," he directed the driver to the Officer's mess where the Admiral was waiting to meet them.

Erica had not been expecting such a high-level reception. She was in one of her practical pant suits and was glad that it included a jacket that made it look more formal.

The Marine up front doing the driving commented that he had never escorted anyone that got received by an Admiral.

Erica replied that she had not expected to be met by an Admiral either.

The Admiral was standing at the front of the Officer's Club and had two additional officers with him.

He came down the steps and held his hand out for Erica and then after guiding her up the steps, he introduced her to a rather handsome, somewhat young-looking Naval Captain. She was told that he was in command of the department that was the home of the machinist department.

The Message

He then introduced the Lieutenant that was in charge of the machinist department. He commented that the two of them had talked with each other before and he hoped that all fences had been mended.

Erica smiled; she knew that the Lieutenant was in trouble. She replied that everything had worked out very well and she was pleased to have made the trip to pick up the magnetrons that the Lieutenant's machinists had skillfully made.

She said that the help of the Admiral's people were providing would help make world history and they all should enjoy the moment. She asked that their names be engraved on the six magnetrons.

She commented that she was sure they would all end up at the Smithsonian or some other comparable museum and their grandchildren would be pointing to the names and letting people know that their grandfathers had made them.

The Admiral then apologized and said that he had to attend to a video conference with his Navy bosses at the Pentagon, but he was leaving her in the care of Captain Sooner who was to make sure that she would get a great lunch and then he would ensure that everything was ready for her return trip.

The Admiral saluted her and then turned and walked off. The Lieutenant did the same thing after letting her know that his staff would have the magnetrons ready to go when she requested them.

Erica thanked him and then turned her attention to the Captain.

The Captain asked when she was planning to start her return journey.

Erica replied that after lunch she would like to take a quick tour of the base before going to pick up the magnetrons. She said that her Marine escorts deserved a good night's rest before starting back and that she was thinking to leave in the morning.

Captain Sooner said that a full tour would take the rest of the day. He suggested that he have his aid make reservations at the hotel of her choice and that they plan to have dinner at the Officers Club and then he would drop her of at the hotel.

Then in the morning she could pick up the Magnetrons and start the trip back to Dallas.

Erica thanked him and let him know that her team had already made the hotel reservations.

She said that she would enjoy spending the afternoon touring and that dinner at the club sounded great.

Captain Sooner had taken an immediate liking to Erica. She was very good looking and had great self-confidence. He was pleased with the response she had given to the Admiral. It had probably saved the Lieutenant's career. He felt that he had met the woman he had been looking for and the fact that she had come to him seemed to be a sign.

The Message

On being introduced, Erica had felt an immediate attraction she had not previously experienced when meeting other men. She checked the Captain's hand for the sign of a wedding ring and was glad to see none but before she went too far, she would make sure he was single. She had not expected to be going on a date but it was clear to her that the Captain had made arrangements so they could be alone and get to know each other better.

Henry had watched the interaction between the two and knew that he was going to be a third wheel. He enjoyed the tour of the base. The Captains historical information about the base was very interesting. He learned that it had been opened up as a US Destroyer Base in 1922.

Then it was expanded during World War Two when it was it became the US Repair Base. Then after the war it became the Naval Station San Diego in 1946. It became the Naval Base San Diego in 1990 and it now provided for nearly a third of the Navy's Pacific assets. The Coronado Naval Amphibious was added in 1943 by dredging Naval Station to increase its dept to allow larger ships to us it as a home base.

When it came time for dinner at the Officer's club, Henry said that he preferred going to the hotel and having a few beers with the Marines that were guarding them.

He was not surprised to hear the Captain volunteer to bring Erica to the hotel after dinner.

During the dinner, the Captain asked if Erica would like to relax and enjoy the piano bar and have a glass of wine or any drink that she would like. He said that if she was so inclined, he looked forward to a dance with her.

Erica was more than happy to be asked. She said that a glass of wine would be great.

The wine was great, and the dancing became somewhat romantic.

When they got to the Captain's car, Erica surprised herself by putting her hand behind the Captain's head and pulling him to her and giving him a kiss.

She was surprised by her action and not sure what to expect.

The fact that he responded by pulling her to him sealed the deal.

She felt a shiver run up her back and took in the moment. She knew that she was hooked.

When they got to the Hotel, she invited him up to her room for a night cap.

What followed was intimate and took her to a Shangri-La that she had never experienced.

The next morning, she sat on the bedside and relived the love making that the two had enjoyed. She hoped that it would blossom into a full romance. She was sure he was the one for her. Now she would see if he felt the same about her.

He had left early saying he would see her off but had a morning meeting he could not miss.

The Message

On the way to pick up the magnetrons she kept thinking about the great day, the evening dinner and the intimate love making she had enjoyed at the Coronado Naval base.

The Lieutenant met her van. He was now very accommodating, and the magnetrons were placed in the rear van.

He thanked her for having saved his butt.

Erica smiled and said that a very dear friend had told her that she should treat others as she wished to be treated. That simple adage had changed her life.

She said he should try it.

She was disappointed that the Captain was not there to see her off. She was just ready to get into the van when Captain Sooner's car pulled up alongside.

The Captain got out of the car and said that he was glad that he had not missed her departure and asked if in the very near future she would reciprocate and give him a tour of the Dallas site.

Erica resisted giving him a kiss but smiled and said that she would be very happy to give him the tour and that she would have the Fold Chef at the Dallas site prepare the meal of his choice and later they could enjoy a drink and have dessert at her apartment.

She then got into van and the Captain gave her a salute and said he would call her and let her know when he was planning to come up.

Chapter 22: Exploration Plan

Bram welcomed Erica back when she delivered the six magnetrons. He had each environmentally controlled box put into the six places in the lab that had been prepared for them.

He commented that rumor had it that she got the apology that she deserved from the Lieutenant that had given her a hard time. He then asked how the date with the Lieutenant's boss had turned out. He smiled and said that rumor also had it that this boss was planning to come to the Fold compound for a tour of the facility.

Erica's face turned red in anger at the thought that she was being spied on flared in her mind. She asked who had been spying on her and reporting it to him.

Bram chuckled and said that the rumor came from the very top of the military organization. It went from Admiral to General to him faster than she was able to travel back to Dallas.

He said that the General had the excuse that he wanted to update getting the magnetrons on site, but it became clear that what he really wanted to do was to talk about the Captain who had gone out with the most amazing woman that the Captain had ever met.

Bram then smiled and said that it seemed that the Captain was a favorite of the Admiral who asked him how things had gone and if the issue of how the magnetrons were handled had been resolved. The Admiral shared that the Captain was smitten by the charming woman that had come to pick up the magnetrons.

Erica lightened up and said that indeed she too had been smitten and she was looking forward to hosting the Captain when he came to visit.

She said that she never knew that the top brass gossiped.

Bram replied that they only gossiped about romance and never about military intel.

He complemented her on a successful trip and that he looked forward to meeting the Captain and hosting the two of them for a Sunday breakfast.

Erica then asked what he was going to do with six magnetrons.

Bram explained that he would set up all six for an extended trial to see if the material they were made of made any significant difference in the accuracy and reliability.

He shared the fact that the less precise magnetron that had been made at the Fold machine shop had functioned very well and he was going to verify if his very stretching specifications were needed.

He wondered if the expensive materials were actually required. He figured that would only be important if the magnetron ever went into mass production.

He jokingly asked if she wanted to become the Magnetron Guru or was, she through with magnetrons. He made the point that her first round with them had produced something better than gold.

Erica thanked him for offering but she replied that she was going to concentrate on her more boring role of managing the civilian side of the Fold site.

Bram excused himself and said he had to get to Marcus's office to review the Fold Wormhole exploration plan.

He felt like he had neglected the Fold Wormhole effort, but he knew that Marcus had been focused on it. He was confident that the review would verify that all was well in that area.

Marcus was nervous about the review. He had sent out more than one hundred scout bubbles to as many solar systems looking for a water world. Nothing promising had surfaced. There were countless galaxies and solar systems but finding a planet that was in the orbit that would allow it to be warm enough to have a surface of nothing, but water was a daunting task.

Once he found such a world, he would have to make sure that it was water in which life could exist and not so acid or base that it would dissolve objects that were in the water.

He wondered how he could improve his search algorithm.

Bram sensed Marcus's nervousness. He jokingly asked if Marcus had found a world to which Earth could send its prisoners.

Marcus caught the reference to how the British had managed both their political and criminal prisoners by sending them to Australia. He nodded and said that in fact he had found plenty such worlds, but ones covered in water seemed to be in short supply.

Bram's approach immediately put him at ease.

Bram asked which direction in the universe Marcus had been looking.

Marcus said that he had used a spherical pattern around the Alien's solar system.

Bram asked what the ratio of water worlds to desert to ice worlds might be.

Marcus shook his head and said he would have no clue.

Bram said he had no clue either, but he figured planets similar to Earth and the Aliens total water world that were located in an orbit that kept the planet warm enough for life to flourish were rare.

He suggested looking elsewhere in some other part of the universe.

The Message

He suggested Marcus reach out to the two lead agencies for astronomical research in the United States, NASA, the National Science Foundation NSF, the Department of Energy (DOE) and the Department of Defense (DOD) and check if there were potential water worlds that had been discovered or there were galaxies that were suspected to have water worlds.

At a minimum he should look in the opposite direction for water worlds.

Marcus agreed and said he would reach out to all of the organizations that had been suggested and he knew of several others that he would add to the list.

He said that he was sending out the scouts in mass to cut the search time.

Bram wished Marcus good luck in his search and said that finding a water world was the current priority and being able to let the Aliens know that a new home had been found would be the icing on the cake when Earth contacted them.

Mallica and her team had been focused on the return message to the Aliens and learning their language. She found that the four members with Asian heritage extremely helpful as she tried to learn the Alien language. The nature of that language seemed to be very musical. The team decided to listen to the vocalization of Earth's whales to get a sense of how the Aliens might sound since they would be communicating under water.

A synthesizer was added, and the message was adjusted and sounded much different than when humans vocalized the alphabet.

In her review with Bram, she was going to ask if he could play music with his Fold Message transmitter. If he could she wanted to add music to the part of the message that provided the Aliens with the description of Earthlings. She thought of Music as a magnificent counter to the terrible side of Earth's social behavior.

Bram picked up immediately on Mallica's sense of accomplishment. He knew that she and her team had been eating, sleeping, and living with the Alien language.

Linh and Duong had practiced their Alien on him as they programed the supercomputer. They were even practicing making it sound closer to what a whale would sound.

When she asked if he could make a magnetron to send out the sound of music, he replied that he would need to set up an experiment on the supercomputer and see what it could do.

He suggested that she work with Linh and Duong to program a simple test. If the current magnetron design proved successful then they could program the piece of music that the team selected as part of the message.

If the current magnetron design failed, then he would work with her and her team to design one that would do so.

Mallica thanked him and said that her team would give it a try as soon as he allocated some time in his tests of the Fold message transmitter.

Bram let her know that he had the control program to debug and test. Then he had six magnetrons to test and analyze before he was in position to test the ability to transmit music. He pointed out that if it could transmit music, it would in actuality be equivalent to a Fold radio transmitter.

He jokingly asked if she wanted to send a picture of herself as well, if so, he would need to add testing the ability to transmit video.

Mallica laughed and said that she would send a picture of the Mona Lisa and The Last Supper by Leonardo da Vinci and superimpose the music of The Messiah by Handel.

She then asked when he would have the Fold ability to send pictures developed.

Bram shook his head and replied that she had just given him several years of work that she wanted to have in a few days and that he would get back to her about the timing.

Before he left her office, he complimented her on creating an excellent team that was really into getting the communication right.

He then said, "have a good day," in Alien and enjoyed the look of amazement on Mallica's face.

So far, he only knew a few phrases that he had learned from Pat who was part of Mallica's team.

He knew that Mallica had daily language lessons for the team and that Pat was as excited as the everyone else on the team about their progress.

Linda observed Bram coming down the hall, at least she observed the small army coming down the hall. There were two fully armed Marines in the lead, then Bob and Thomas were next and then two fully armed Marines behind him.

She knew that Bram had learned to ignore all of them by concentrating on the schedule that she worked up with him for each day.

She was prepared to review the rest of the week and then detail tomorrow. The two of them always planned two weeks out and then focused on the next day.

They had learned to only make plans for four solid hours of what Bram called work and to leave the rest of the time as white space to be used by the immediate occurrences on that day. This gave him a good work plan with the flexibility he needed to keep up with the various parts of the Fold program.

She reflected on how involved he had gotten her into the Fold effort and how little of the regular support stuff she did that most supports would have been doing. She now understood why Lacy had been such an enthusiast and supporter of both Bram and the Fold project. She knew that she had become just as passionate as her sister.

The Message

The whole Stetson family were Fold and Bram supporters. They had all grown closer together and their entire family conversations had broadened and expanded to topics that before they would never have even imagined.

Bram arrived at his office and was relieved to be going in and leaving his Marine guards at the door. He followed Linda in and walked over and got himself a cup of coffee. He offered it to Bob, and Thomas as Linda took a bottle of water from the frig.

He enjoyed planning ahead. He knew that it was the time now to do so.

He asked Linda to put down the development of sending voice and video via the Fold process as items in his to do list.

She commented that he had a long to do list that seemed to ensure her long term employment.

Bram agreed and suggested they put in vacations, parties, fishing trips and other activities on the to do list to ensure that work, and play got an appropriate balance.

Erica was surprised when late in the afternoon she received a call from Captain Sooner. He asked if the coming Sunday was too soon to come for a visit of the Fold facility.

She responded that it would be contingent on him getting clearance for the Fold project and that she was not sure it would happen so quickly.

Captain Sooner said that he had asked his hierarchy that question and had received a go after the Admiral had checked with General Tilson.

Erica commented that the two men at the top seemed to know each other well. The Captain let her know that two had been classmates in the Academy.

She said she would be pleased to see him and that she would arrange accommodations at the Fold location.

She waited until close to the end of the workday before going to Bram's office to make sure about the weekend and the following weekend visit.

As the site leader it was her decision to make but she wanted to make sure that she did not encroach on the work that Bram was doing.

Linda knew that Erica had met Mr. Right and she wondered what she might want this late in the day.

Erica commented that she was there to see about getting an invite for a Sunday breakfast.

Linda buzzed Bram and announced Linda's arrival.

Bram wondered what was up and waited as Erica entered.

Erica smiled and said that she was coming in to give him the latest gossip that he could share when he went home. She then explained that her new flame had asked if he could come up on the weekend and she was checking on an invite to the Sunday morning breakfast.

Bram said that would be no problem but maybe she should consider spending the weekend at everyone's favorite mountain bed and breakfast. They could go hiking and enjoy river fishing.

Erica thanked him for the idea and said that she would see if she could get a room at the lodge. She was not sure about the fishing but as Mike, at the lodge would most likely comment, she had already caught her big fish.

Bram smiled and said he was glad to see her lighten up. He was glad that she had gone to San Diego to get the magnetrons.

Erika nodded and agreed that at the moment she was on a high that she hoped would last.

Bram said that if she wanted when he met this Captain, he would make sure to check on his intentions.

Erica laughed and thanked him but said she figured she could handle the Captain. She went on to say that she was really happy that she had made the move from the politics of her East Coast role to the West Coast Fold environment. It was such a breath of fresh air and a time of personal growth. Meeting the Captain was more than icing on the cake, it was a shooting star that she wanted to ride for the rest of her life.

Bram smiled and added that the Fold community was a great place for a love affair.

He then added that he was speaking for himself. He had gone from a hectic East Coast environment, then she had sent him to an undisclosed place in the desert from which he had escaped to find love on the West Coast.

Erika replied that she had not sent him into the desert. She said that he should blame that on Jeffery and she pointed out that he had met his soul mate in Houston, not on the West Coast. But she agreed about the hectic East Coast and about the much more relaxed West Coast.

Linda gave Bram the ten-minute signal and Bram asked if Erica wanted a ride home to her apartment.

Erica accepted and followed Bram out to the van.

She commented on the small army that was assigned to protect him.

Bram nodded and said that the people that had attacked the site and had personally tried to kill him were responsible.

Pat had been listening to the conversation and added that life with Bram had the flavor of sweet and sour. Life with him was sweet but the attacks had been intense and added the sour.

Bram commented that even with the Fold counter offense being led by Lacy, he figured that when the world learned about the contact with the Aliens there would be additional attacks from enemies that at this moment, they had no idea existed.

Chapter 23: The Replies

*T*hat evening Pat said that the Alien reply team Mallica was leading was ready for a final review and let Bram know that it would be great for him to participate with the team the next afternoon.

He agreed and would let Mallica know in the morning.

Bram felt the competing pull of all the efforts he had initiated. He had the best leaders, leading several projects but they all wanted his periodic involvement that he knew he had to provide.

He had launched efforts in composing a reply to the Alien message and had put Mallica in charge.

Then, he had focused on his other efforts.

He had launched an effort to see if the Fold process resulted in the improvement of a person's health and put Pat in charge. He got updates almost every day from her.

Linda had shared the success of having her burn scar on her leg disappear after two-Fold round trips. She commented that the pig only needed one trip to heal his new scars but hers had been a very bad scar and now there was no sign of it ever happening.

He immediately asked if Zuri had been asked to come home and Linda let him know that it had been arranged.

He continued going down his list of teams that had been launched.

He had launched an effort to develop the Fold Message Transmitter and he and Remi were working on that together. That effort was at the stage where in the next couple of days they would know if they could use it to reply to the Aliens.

He had launched an effort to create a Fold Wormhole that allowed forward and reverse movement through the fabric of the space-time continuum. He was the primary actor, but Marcus was providing the direction and the Fold time dilation that would take a bubble to his distant targets that he had selected to explore for water worlds.

Most people would consider each a major effort. Each effort had been launched with very tight time targets that most would have thought was impossible to achieve.

Bram was making sure they were all on track.

Now it seemed that they were all coming to a head at the same time. He smiled as he thought that it was his fault for having picked such great leaders, who were making their efforts successful. They were making it happen.

The next morning, he had Linda contact Mallica to find out when she was scheduling the message review. He asked her to let Mallica know that he would attend.

The Message

He asked her to work with Pat to get him on the final review she was having. He said that he was especially interested in the next steps for the studying the health effects that the Fold had on plant and animals.

He then said that on Thursday afternoon he and Remi would share how the Fold Message transmitter worked and they would demonstrate it by transmitting and receiving the message that Mallica's team had agreed on.

Then on Friday morning, he and Marcus would share the results of their Fold Wormhole experiments.

Linda asked who he would like to have in attendance for the Friday review.

He suggested that Jeffery, General Tilson, NASA's John Morgan, Elizabeth, Zuri, Lori, and Erica all be invited to participate in each session. He commented that he did not expect everyone to be able to make it and the invitation was to insure they had the opportunity if they desired to be involved.

Linda suggested that each review get videotaped and that she would arrange to have the videos professionally edited and then make them available to everyone that was part of the review or had been invited.

Bram agreed that would be a very good way to record and share the progress for each effort. He said he would like to put a forward on the recordings that recognized the exceptional work of the individuals and of all those involved in the Fold work.

Erica's Captain arrived early on Saturday. She had to meet him at the gate to get him into the compound. Then she took him on a walking tour of the Fold site.

She was not surprised about Gerald's reaction when he saw the USS Rainier, Wheel Two.

When she told him about the attack and the destruction of the USS Hood, Wheel One, he commented that The German Battleship Bismarck had sunk the British HMS Hood toward the end of WWII.

He was surprised when he learned of the response and the destruction of the attackers when Lacy used the Fold technology to route the attackers. He commented that the Fold technology would sunset all the ships that the US Navy had afloat.

Erica agreed and commented that the technology would change the world as much as the internet and the I-phone had done but it would be more drastic, and the transition would need to social and economic impact needed to go a bit slower to allow the physical structure of society to adapt.

The Captain agreed and said that he would need to look to his future to see what part he would play in empowering the Navy with the Fold technology.

Erica had chosen to end the tour of the Fold compound at the cafeteria. She had arranged with Chef D'Carluca to prepare a steak lunch with bleu cheese melted on top. She knew this was a favorite that Gerald had mentioned. She also knew that Bram had mentioned it was the best he had ever tasted.

The Message

Gerry, as he asked to be called, said that the cafeteria looked like a very large high-class restaurant and when he took a bite of the steak, he said that the food was better than the best restaurant that he had eaten in.

The Chef D'Carluca, who had been standing by to see what the reaction would be, thanked him and then looked at Erica and said that she had chosen well when she had chosen the Captain.

Gerry commented that so far the tour had exceeded anything that he had ever imagined. He said that his boss was told by the General to let me know to expect to be overwhelmed by what was going on and he said that what he had learned so far was more than overwhelming. It was mind altering.

Erica said that after lunch she was going to take him to the Viewing Room and bring him up to speed with all the projects that were going on in parallel and she commented that he would not be overwhelmed, he would literally enter a different world and realize that the Fold effort had opened up the Universe.

Before leaving the cafeteria, Erica went to Chef D'Carluca and placed an order for snacks to be brought to the Viewing Room.

Gerry asked about the snacks and how long they were going to be in the viewing room.

Erica said that it would be for at least four hours and that afterwards they would go to her apartment, and they would order dinner in.

Erica stopped the viewing after Bram's introduction and asked what he thought about it.

Gerry commented that Bram seemed like any ordinary guy that valued the people around him.

She shared how she had recruited him when NASA had identified the concepts that Bram was proposing as world changing. She took him through a brief history of how Bram single handedly changed the effort in which he was now the center. How he created the Fold technology. And how in a very short period established a program that had changed the personal lives of everyone currently working at the site.

She paused for a moment and then pointed out that, whether they knew it or not, he had changed the lives of everyone in the world.

She smiled and said that he had been a person who she at first thought naïve, then a person she thought wanted her job and then she realized he was a person who didn't want much for himself but enjoyed seeing others be happy and here she was one of his ardent supporters because he had made her happy.

Gerry looked at her and said that he was eager to meet this Bram Nielson, wonder man.

When the message from the Aliens was played and the review of the reply was played, Gerry asked whether Erica could serve him a double shot of whisky. He asked if it was all real and how long had the Fold team known about the existence of Aliens.

When Erica let him know that the team had known for two months and that they had all worked together for almost a month on learning what the message said.

She pointed out that it was Bram that had guided the team through the decoding of the message and that he had added Vietnamese and Chinese members to the team and their contribution had led to the breakthrough.

Gerry asked why Bram had selected them.

Erica shared that he had realized that the Alien alphabet seemed long and seemed to have a musical cadence. He learned that the Vietnamese had the longest alphabet in the world and the Chinese, Mandarin and Cantonese had the musical and visual elements. He felt that having such knowledge would make the difference and he had been right.

Gerry asked how he would know such a thing if he didn't know the Alien alphabet.

Erica laughed and said she really had no clue, and he should ask that of Bram at breakfast on the following day.

He looked surprised and asked about breakfast.

Erica let him know that the two of them were invited for breakfast at Bram's house. She told him that by the end of breakfast he would feel like he was part of the Fold team.

She then added that if he didn't, they would have to relook at their blossoming relationship.

Gerry's eyes widened and then said that he was now going to have a hard time sleeping with all the pressure he felt.

Erica smiled and said that she thought that might make the evening much more interesting.

Erica then took him through the review of the health effects of a Fold experience.

Gerry said that he needed to take a few Fold trips so that the pain in his back would disappear. He asked if the surprises would continue.

Erica said that indeed they would continue.

She then took him through the section on the Fold Message transmitter development.

Gerry thought for a minute and then asked how, if the Alien message was a Fold message had they been able to get it if Earth did not have a Fold receiver.

Erica said that like, the invention of rubber, and the invention of X-ray technology, luck had a lot to do with it. The message would never have reached the Earth for another few thousand years if ever. It had been captured by one of the scout bubbles sent out on a Fold reconnaissance and then later noticed during the analysis of the recording that had been captured.

Once Bram recognized that it seemed to be a message, he had to determine if it was recent and worth deciphering.

Once it had been deciphered, Bram decided that a Message Fold transmitter needed to be developed. The magnetrons that were produced in the shop in San Diego were part of that effort.

Gerry commented that it was hard to imagine all the efforts coming from one mind.

Erica replied that he would find it even harder when he met Bram, who appeared to be like any regular guy.

She then showed him the last clip on the Fold Wormhole effort.

Erica pointed out that Bram gave credit to everyone and individually praised their contribution. She commented that the sum of all their contributions would not have produced one breakthrough, but that Bram had listened to them and had provided the linkages that took their inputs and made breakthroughs with them.

Gerry thanked her for taking the time to show him the summary video of all the breakthroughs. Then he asked if there were any other surprises.

Erica said that yes there was one more that might happen if she could convince him to take a few extra days and go fishing with her.

"Wow, talk about a fork in the road," he commented and then asked why she was inviting him to go fishing.

She smiled and said that all lovers who had gone to this particular fishing location were now paired and that she figured they should give fishing a chance to do that for them.

Gerry took her in his arms and said that fishing sounded great to him and then kissed her.

Much later that night after he finally did fall asleep, he dreamt that a voice kept repeating that he should take the leap.

The next morning as they walked up to Bram's house, Gerry said that he felt a like an invader going to someone's home when he had never met anyone that lived there.

Erica chuckled and said that if she arrived without him she would be sent back to her apartment without breakfast. She said she was sure he would be well accepted, but he was going to have to endure a grilling like he had never experienced before.

Erica was correct. Bram was sitting at the dining room table. It was Eric's turn at the stove and Zoe's turn to serve. The conversation was about who was going to ask what of this "Captain" that Erica was bringing to breakfast.

Pat suggested that everyone take it easy and that a slow grilling was more effective than hitting him with a firehose of questions.

Zoe laughed and commented that the expert at making her catch had spoken and she would heed the advice.

Pat replied that she thought that everyone in the room had done well with their romances as well. She was pleased that Erica had found Mr. Right.

Linda and Lacy arrived before Erica and announced that she was right behind them, and everyone should get ready.

Bram stood up as Erica entered via the basement entrance and walked over to the "Captain" and let him know that everyone was eager to get to know him. He asked him what he preferred to be called.

He got the answer that the "Captain" preferred to be called Gerry by his friends, and he hoped that would be what everyone in the room called him.

Gerry added that Erica had blown him away showing him the summary that they had all appeared in, and she had given him a brief biography of each of them. He felt that they were all already friends. He went on to say that he was in awe of all of them.

Bram asked him for his breakfast order as he led him to the dining room table.

Gerry replied that he had been advised to try the pancakes smothered in maple syrup, two eggs on top, with sausage on the side.

Bram was quiet for during breakfast and just listened to the questions and the answers that Gerry gave. He envisioned a championship tennis match and couldn't help but to keep score.

He finally smiled and told Gerry that he had just won the singles Fold community Grand Slam Q & A Championship and that he could now officially be deemed a friend.

Gerry beamed a smile and replied that Bram as the line coach had been silent and wondered what question he might have.

Bram chuckled and replied that he was silent because Erika had warned him not to ask him what his intentions toward her were.

Erika laughed and said that it was hard to keep Bram away from his initial inclinations.

Bram innocently replied that the Captain had asked, and he had just replied honestly.

Pat decided this was a good time to ask Erika if a fishing outing was in the works.

Erika smiled and said that she had rented the same room that Pat had used in the past and that the two of them were leaving that afternoon. She commented that the General had assigned two of his Marines to protection duty for them, so she had rented three rooms.

She added that Mike and Mary had asked whether there was any talk of Bram and the rest of his small army planning anything soon.

They said that they had reinforced the new door of the cave with a one-inch-thick steel plate that had fifty through the door bolts to keep it from being blown off and were now prepared for his next visit. They felt they were now able to host Bram again.

Pat said that she was ready for another fishing trip and that they should convince Bram to take time off to celebrate the tremendous achievements that had happened in the last couple of months.

Bram took a sip of his coffee and asked who wanted to go for another boring fishing trip to the Rushing River.

All hands went up. Zoe added that they needed to let Orlando know so that he and Castor would both be present for the next attack.

The Message

Bram agreed that Orlando should be invited but he commented that attacks didn't happen every time he went fishing.

Erica asked Bram to share a time when he had gone fishing when an attack had not occurred.

Bram nodded and was silent.

Little did he know that his fishing attack experience would be extended and intensified.

The Sunday morning breakfast came to a late end.

Late that afternoon, Erica and Gerry were greeted by Mike and Mary who commented that she was becoming as guarded as Bram.

Erica laughed and said that she had only two armed guards and one of them was the driver and only had to rent three rooms. Bram would come only when his small army could reserve the whole bed and breakfast lodge.

The next day's early morning fishing was great they both caught some nice trout but had chosen to fish cast and release with no barbed hooks. The hike up the river was leisurely, the air was crisp, and the scenery kept them pointing and exclaiming at the wonderful interactions of the breaks in the forest, and parting of the trees that ran up the mountain side.

Mike and Mary interacted with them just enough to make it feel like they were with friends. Erica realized that this was how she felt with everyone she had met through Bram.

Then on the last day, after dinner, Gerry got down on his knee and asked whether she would hike with him for the rest of their lives.

Erica had not been expecting a proposal. She hesitated a minute and asked if he had a ring if she said yes.

Gerry held up a ring that he had woven from the tall saw grass, and it had a gold nugget, that he had found in the river, intricately mounted into the band.

Tears welled up in Erika's eyes. She wondered when he had the time to make the ring.

She knew her answer and held out her hand and said that "Yes she would love to hike with him for a lifetime."

Gerry carefully slipped the ring on her finger and then stood and the two of them kissed.

Mike and marry both raised their wine glasses and proposed a toast.

Chapter 24: Preparation

Bram had not expected Gerry to propose marriage during the fishing trip. When Erica told him, he congratulated her on the proposal and asked when the marriage would happen.

Her reply caught him by surprise when she said she had heard, that somewhere in his past, he had become an ordained minister and was legally able to perform the marriage ceremony. So, she was thinking that they could plan another fishing trip and he could make sure she landed the big one for life.

She smiled and said that from the journey from the desert to conferring Holy Matrimony was like a journey from the very depths to the very heights of heaven.

Bram nodded and said that so far it had been a great journey for both of them and it seemed that it would continue into the future. He said he was honored by her request and that they indeed should plan her fishing trip.

He pointed out that she had landed the big one on her own and he was just making it official for the Fold records.

Bram then asked about her engagement ring and how Gerry had been able to get one so quickly.

She smiled and opened up her purse and opened a ring case. She said that Gerry had found a gold nugget at the edge of the river and had seen it as a biblical sign. Since they were fishing, he decided to use a fishtail braid using the long river grass leaves growing on the riverbank above the spot where he had found the nugget. She pointed out the intricate way he had secured the nugget to the ring. She said that she had worn it home to her apartment but had put it into a ring case that she had for another ring. She said that the ring was a treasure that she would keep and show her children.

Bram examined the ring and asked how much the gold was worth.

Erica replied that it was worth her weight in gold and laughed and said it did not matter because it was priceless.

Bram asked what Gerry's degree was in and found out he had a degree in oceanography. He commented that it seemed that Gerry did indeed love the ocean. He asked whether he might be interested in a role on the Fold project in the near future.

When Erica asked in what capacity he would be hired, Bram said that as soon as they found a water world it would need to be analyzed and researched to make sure that it did not have intelligent life and that it was suitable as a new home for the Aliens.

He was already looking for someone to take the lead role. It might also be a role that would land the first human onto another planet.

Erica commented that it was a super opportunity. She would ask and see about his interest would be in such a role. She said that she knew at the moment, he was working through what he would do with his career. He had mentioned he did not want to be part of an old technology trying to hold on.

Bram told Erica to let him know and that now he had an appointment with Marcus in the viewing room where they were going to see about finding a water world. He pointed out that finding one was a million more times as difficult as finding a needle in a haystack.

Erica said she would let him know later about the timing of the fishing trip and the list of invitees. She commented that their close friends would be housed in the lodge, but she was not sure where else they could stay.

Bram said she should check with Pat because she had looked at several lodges in the area. He then got up and headed to the viewing room.

Marcus came rushing in just as Bram got the screens powered up.

He asked Marcus why he was rushing.

Marcus laughed and said he had been trying to beat him in.

Bram told him to relax and set up his computer so that he could lead the search for a water world.

He let Marcus know that he had asked Linda to order in the usual refreshment mix.

It arrived right on time as he finished speaking.

He suggested they get whatever they wanted before getting into the search.

Marcus said that he had picked three solar systems for them to review every morning for as long as it took for them to find a water world.

He said that he had also sent three bubbles into the Alien's solar system. He shared that he had positioned them behind a large moon, a small planet nearer the dying sun and one farther out than the orbit of the Alien planet. They would gather all the vital information about the Alien's planet and about the condition of the sun. He commented that he did not know when they would get around to analyze all the data the three bubbles would capture.

Bram commented that when they found a destination water world, he would assemble a team to do all the analysis.

Marcus said that sounded like a good plan. He commented, that when they finally got into regular contact with the Aliens, there would be work for lots of people. He was sure that the political arm would want to reach in and take control.

Bram agreed and said he was going to push on Jeffrey to get into position to guide his old friend the President in the politics of dealing with the Aliens. He would suggest that they first focus on providing the aid that would transport the giant Aliens to another water world.

He said that they had the technology to build the size of enclosure that would be required to Fold them from their current world to their destination water world. However, the power needed for the Folds of such large bubbles would need to be generated somewhere in their solar system.

He said that he envisioned either using their sun as the source of energy or to use nuclear fusion to generate the power needed. He pointed out that either option would require several years to get into place.

Marcus nodded in agreement and said that dealing with the Aliens was going to be a big challenge.

Bram looked at the screen and said it was time to start scanning the three solar system Marcus had selected.

By lunch time they had verified that there were no water worlds in those specific solar systems. Marcus said that the surveillance scouts would return at twelve sharp and get processed and made ready for the following morning's survey of the next three solar systems.

Bram said he was meeting with Remi and Pat to plan an upcoming trip to the Alien solar system. He shared that the current plan was for he and Pat and Daryl, Pat's back up, to make the first excursion and then most likely Amy and Harold, Amy's backup would make the second Fold.

Marcus said that he planned to review the solar system selection and add an additional three to the list. He said that he planned to stay six solar systems ahead so that they would be able to keep searching in a continuous pattern.

Bram said that sounded like a good plan, but he wanted to speed things up. He suggested that he use a hemispherical pattern in the sector of the universe that he had selected. If they did not find the water world in that portion of space, they should use a similar pattern aimed at a different sector in the universe.

He suggested that they figure out the characteristic metrics of what they were looking for and automate the data gathering so they could do more than a dozen planets a day.

They would only look more closely at those that met the required metrics that indicated a water world might be present.

Marcus said he liked the idea and would spend the afternoon developing the automation routine and get Remi to allocate some additional bubbles so that they could get that rolling.

He said that he had been as bored as Bram about searching in the manner that they had spent the morning doing.

Bram agreed and said that he was sure that he did not want to spend as much time as they had spent that morning unless there was a good prospect to look at.

Bram signaled that it was time to head for the cafeteria.

Mallica and Pat were sitting at their normal table.

Bram decided that a mixed salad would suffice. He had snacked and almost continuously fed Einstein during their look at the three solar systems. He felt he was on a sugar high.

Pat recognized the look on Bram's face and asked if he had figured out a better way to search for the water world.

Bram commented that once again she had signaled him that he should never play poker against her. She was too perceptive of a face and emotion reader.

He pointed to Marcus and said that Marcus had taken him through one of the most boring mornings that he had experienced for a long time.

Marcus gave out a long, ex-cu-u-u-use me, but who kept wanting to take a closer look.

Bram looked at Mallica and asked if Marcus had acted like that during his stay in the desert.

Mallica smiled and said that actually he had not because the two of them were so bored that both of them would have thought that looking at planets in distant galaxies would have been really exciting.

She said that at the moment that he had called to bring them to Dallas, they had been discussing if there was a cliff somewhere in the desert from which they could jump.

Bram bowed his head and said that he had been remiss, but that Pat had insisted that he deal with getting the two Wheels Fold from Seattle to Dallas before he was allowed to do anything else.

Pat said she had nothing to do with any decision making at that time and in fact she was afraid to talk to Bram. He seemed to be some sort of mad scientist that Amy had picked up each morning as he wandered through the desert.

Bram laughed and said that he really valued having such dear friends that thought so highly of him.

Pat let Bram know that she had spent the morning prepping Amy, Daryl, and Harold by reviewing all the work that had been done in preparation of replying to the Alien's call for help and in trying to find a new water world to which they could migrate.

She said that she had reserved the viewing room for their meeting.

Bram thanked her for setting up the meeting.

They all met in the Viewing Room and Pat took the lead to get the meeting started.

Bram shared the objectives of the meeting in the language of the Aliens.

He said he was ready to share a skeleton plan of a visit to the Alien planet's solar system and perhaps contact them. He was hoping to find a water world for them before they made contact.

The objective of the meeting was for them to think about such a Fold and to suggest activities or data gathering that should be included.

After that brief introduction he switched back to English and asked if there was anyone who had not understood what he had just said.

Daryl, and Harold raised their hands and said that they didn't even recognize the language in which he spoke.

Bram suggest that they join Mallica's class on learning the Alien language. He told them to take a crash course because he was going to insist that the bubble pilots know the language.

It was clear to Bram that neither of the two would make the first two trips. He mentally put Pat and Amy in the bubbles with him for those Folds.

He then asked Pat to lead the group through a brainstorming session of what the first two visits should cover.

That evening he asked Pat about the two backup pilots and what they had been doing.

Pat replied that the two spent their day waiting for the next Fold.

Bram asked if they had shown any interest in any of the work that was going on.

Pat replied that they always spent the morning in one of the huddle rooms on their computers and then they left early in the afternoon and went to their apartments.

Bram nodded and said that he was sending them back to NASA and they could do whatever astronauts did there as they waited for a ride out to space.

Pat said that was not going to look good on their records and being sent back would mean an end to their astronaut careers.

Bram asked what she would suggest he do.

Pat thought for a moment then she said he should give them the feedback about his disappointment in their lack of initiative and put them on probation for a three-month period.

He should assign them to work for Marcus to find a water world and they were to attend Mallica's language class and pass her second level language test by the end of their probation.

Bram said he liked the part about them finding the water worlds. It would free he and Marcus to get on with other work. He agreed to what she suggested, and he added that they would be required to jog in to work each morning with him.

Pat said that the last was a good idea and might be key in changing their attitude.

Bram said that their current behavior was a surprise to him, and he wanted to get to know them better so that he would be ready for the end of their probation period.

Pat commented that the social fabric of the Fold community seemed to be bubbling and changing.

The Message

Bram replied that love was in the air and weddings being planned and now there were two people needing motivation. He commented that perhaps he had initiated too many major projects and people were losing connection with the required speed at which that work was happening.

<u>Chapter 25: Water Worlds</u>

𝒜 week later at breakfast, Castor commented that whatever Bram had told Daryl and Harold had changed their behavior and attitude. They had been known to the Marines as freeloaders but were now seen as two hustlers that seemed to have changed their ways.

He asked what Bram had done to change their ways.

Bram smiled and said he had threatened to have them inducted into the Marine core to learn discipline and how to do hard work.

That brought a laugh from both Castor and Donna.

Donna commented that she doubted they would get through boot camp if they did enlist.

She followed Bram out and was pleased to see the two astronauts waiting with the other Marines.

Later that morning, Bram met with Marcus and asked how the two were doing.

Marcus said that having them do the searching for a water world had changed how fast the search was progressing. He had now searched through more than a hundred solar systems and had identified just one potential planet, but it was really cold, and the ocean had a layer of ice that covered more than ninety percent of the planet.

He commented that the two only stopped their monitoring to attend Mallica's Alien language classes.

At lunch Bram asked Mallica how the two were doing in her language class.

Mallica said that they were whizzing through and had already passed the first level class where they learned the Alien alphabet and how to count to one hundred.

Pat smiled and said that he had put the fear of getting sent away into them.

She commented that the two had been picked as backup pilots because they were among the smartest and most experienced of the astronauts, so she was not surprised that they were doing well in both language classes and in looking for water worlds.

They had both talked with her and Amy and apologized for their lax behavior. They had expressed their desire to make up for their past behavior and were using all of their capabilities to slog through the immense amount of data they were going through in the hunt for a water world.

Bram said that he was glad to have made a positive impact on their behavior. He hoped they were actually getting into being part of the team in an enthusiastic way.

Marcus came in and joined the group for lunch. He had a huge smile on his face and in an excited voice he said that there seemed to be several water worlds in the last set of solar systems.

Daryl and Harold came in a moment later and shouted that they had found what they were searching for and pumped their fists up and down.

Bram pointed to a table next to where he was sitting and called out to them and congratulated them.

He then gave each of them a high five as they came to the table.

He asked them how it felt to find the needle in the Universe's haystack.

Both of them said they were still on a high from having found three water worlds in sequence after reviewing more than two hundred solar systems.

They pointed at Marcus and in Alien they together said, "Slave Driver."

Bram replied to them in Alien that they were invited to breakfast on Sunday.

He chuckled when the two of them looked at Mallica and asked what Bram had just said.

They then replied that they would love to be at Bram's famous breakfast gathering.

Bram asked since when his breakfast had become famous.

Mallica replied that it was Pat that had made it famous with her maple syrup smothered three pancakes with two over easy eggs on top and sausage on the side.

She pointed out that Bram had leveraged Pat's famous breakfast and used it to convince his guests that the Fold project was the best place to have a breakfast that was out of this world.

Bram asked Marcus to update him on the find and when they would go to those planets and get a direct view of the planets.

Marcus replied that would be based on when Bram decided to make the journey. He suggested that they do one-Fold to each of the Planets on separate days so that they could review all the data that they would gather.

Bram said that was a great idea and he wanted to add multiple Folds to the same Planet. He added that one of the Folds would employ the Fold Wormhole capability so that he could evaluate the ability to use it to get in close to the surface of the planet in question.

Marcus said he was going to refine the coordinate calculations and program three bubbles to Fold to co-ordinates of one thousand miles from the surface of the planet. Once they took that Fold, he would be able to make a more accurate calculation for the next Fold to the same planet.

Bram agreed that was a good plan and said that he had the seats for each bubble already decided.

He then said that he wanted to set up a remote laboratory where samples from each water world could be brought for analysis. The remote laboratory should be in the largest bubble that they were currently producing, and it would be located out near the Alien planet. He suggested that they get a team together to define the tests for the samples they gathered and then equip the bubble with totally automated systems to carry out the testing. The only thing that would come back to Earth was the information.

He said he envisioned them Folding, sending a small bubble near the surface of the water where it would take a sample of the water and the air and then seal itself so the samples would not get contaminated. The bubble would then Fold to its location in the Lab where it would have its own section that was isolated from the other three samples. The samples for analysis would be extracted via a specially designed syringe.

The data from the analysis would then be transmitted to the analysists located at the Dallas Fold compound.

He commented that he wanted the sampling and subsequent analysis to be kept a secret by a limited number of people.

He suggested that Marcus, Remi, and himself determine the minimum people that would need to know. Even the lab people that gave them the parameters to be measured should not know about the samples being taken of the water world.

Marcus asked why Bram was putting such a high level of security in place.

Bram replied that when the world found out about the Aliens the Fold project would be under political attack and the turmoil was going to be significant.

When the world found out about giving aid to the Aliens there would be a bigger backlash.

If they found out about the capability to get samples from other planets the Fold project would be overrun.

He wanted to delay all information until the Aliens had the technology to move to the new planet. Then the turmoil and battles on Earth could go on and not endanger a species that was trying to survive the death of their star.

Marcus nodded and said, "top, top, super top secret." I got it and I agree. We have been attacked for a technology that only a few people are supposed to know about. The progress that we have made in the last few months makes the previous capability look like child's play. Even the top leaders still only know about that previous technology. There is no way they could imagine how far the Fold program has gone.

Bram said that when all the capabilities of the Fold program became public, they might want to be on a second Earth like world several light years away where they could hide and not be burned at the stake.

Marcus smiled and said that he had logged at least six worlds that were very much like earth and that they might want to set up another Bubble Lab so they could indeed make the escape that Bram had alluded to.

Bram nodded and said he was up for doing exactly that and they might as well at the same time as they set up the other Bubble labs.

That evening Pat asked why Bram had not shared who was going with him on the Folds.

He replied that he was going to make the final decision about who was on each Fold just before the Fold itself.

He let her know that she and Amy would be on the first and second Folds to each of the first two planets and that he would decide on having Daryl and Harold be backups on the two folds to the third planet.

Then she and Amy would be on the third Fold to each of the three planets.

Pat said she was surprised that he was giving she and Amy such a big piece of the Fold journeys.

Bram replied that the two of them were reaping the reward for the contribution that they had made and that their two backups were also getting rewarded for their more recent contributions.

By the weekend Bram had the lab bubble specifications defined and he and Remi had selected the bubbles and had the construction under way.

Once defined, Bram took the list of the necessary lab equipment to Erica and asked her to procure it as soon as possible.

She asked about the rush and then put up her hand and said that she would get what he was asking for as rapidly as possible.

She asked if by any chance there would be a seat available on one of the exploration trips.

Bram smiled and said that only qualified pilots would be going out with him. He then told her to get with Pat and get herself qualified.

Erika thanked him and said she would.

She then said that she wanted to change the subject to Fishing. She said that she had reserved the required number of rooms and had arranged to have the wedding in the field on the other side of the Rushing River opposite from the lodge.

She had asked Linda to check on everyone's schedule and had gotten the green light for the dates.

Bram said that he was looking forward to going fishing and that he would make sure she landed her big fish.

He then asked if she had checked with her Gerry about his interest in leading the analysis and preparation of delivering aid to the Aliens.

Erica nodded and said that he was super excited about the opportunity and wondered what the timeline would be for starting.

Bram replied that it could be as soon as after the honeymoon. "And where in the world would the honeymoon take place," he asked?

Erica said that they were planning to go to Kuai for two weeks. They planned to hike, whale watch, surf and just hang out.

Bram commented that he loved her choice and said he was sure that it would be a honeymoon to remember.

Erica smiled and agreed.

Bram then said that he was going home to spend a weekend relaxing.

Erica nodded and said that his relaxing always worried her because it seemed that was when he came up with the next leapfrog Fold idea.

Bram replied that he would try to keep it to a little jump.

Bram left work knowing that he was going to think through each scenario that would take place in the near future whether he wanted to or not.

Pat commented that everything was happening at one time and asked what she could do to help.

Bram thought for a moment and said that she should make sure they went on their normal walks, took time to go to the recreation center, relax by the pool and have great meals. He said that she was right that he was going to run through every scenario whether he wanted to or not.

He shared that he would be working with Marcus and Remi to set up remote labs to analyze samples of each of the water worlds. He wanted to keep the fact that they could get that kind of information about planets millions of light years distance, a secret. He would appreciate her keeping an ear out to make sure it was indeed being kept secret.

He went on to say that there was going to be a lot happening that he was not going to share with the Fold community because if the information became public, the safety of the site and the members of the community would be jeopardized.

Pat nodded in agreement and said that so much of the Fold technology had advanced that what was known a month ago was now ancient history.

Bram asked whether she felt that Daryl and Harold could be trusted to keep everything a secret.

Pat replied that they would be as tight lipped as she or anyone else of their closest team members.

Bram then asked Zoe to have all the bodyguards meet with him in the study after they had dinner. He wanted to make sure that they understood the magnitude and critical importance of keeping what they knew away from their bosses.

Zoe asked what the content of their reports should be.

Bram replied that the content would be the truth about the support they were providing but there would be no mention of anything about the technology.

Erica commented that was very much like the current reports they were sending in, but it would be good to set up a standard report and then vary it a little so that each report sent in would seem fresh.

Bram agreed that what he did not want was to have the FBI leadership curious about what was going on at the site.

Zoe suggested that Bram have a discussion with the General and with their Marine bodyguards about secrecy. She said that they didn't necessarily know the details of the technical progress and capability, but they got the sense that progress was being made at a rapid pace.

Bram said that he would follow her advice and set up a meeting with the General and together they could get Castor and Donna to understand the need for secrecy so they could ensure their partner Marines would be tight mouthed.

The weekend was as deep as he had thought it would be. Pat was his anchor to the world of reality and made it possible for him to come to the surface and take in two beautiful days.

What was clear in his mind was that the capability to go to another Earth like world would be a great way to ensure that he could protect the community from the turmoil that would come at them in the near future when the world learned about what the Fold technology meant to the status of the current economic environment.

The money and political communities would want to gain control.

The religious communities would most likely be vengeful. He felt this to be especially the case when they found out that the Aliens were in appearance similar to whales.

He felt justified in having asked Marcus and Remi setup the bubble labs to include both the water worlds and the Earth like ones.

The future as always would be whatever it was meant to be, but he was going to make sure that whatever happened he and his Fold community would have the means of self-defense and would have the means to get out of harm's way.

He knew that in the very near future his preparation would be tested. He had no idea what the test would be, but his team would persist.

<u>Chapter 26: Space Labs</u>

By the end of the following week Bram, Marcus, and Remi had the two space bubbles that held four labs each complete minus all the test equipment that Bram had asked Erica to procure.

They had decided on a distant solar system to park them. Only they had the coordinates.

Bram scheduled the first Fold to each of the six worlds. He purposely excluded a Fold to the Alien planet since he did not know whether they had the ability to detect objects in their solar system.

The water worlds all looked acceptable. They gathered all the data possible from their remote locations and then returned to the Fold compound and downloaded their data for analysis.

Once they had the water world data downloaded, they did a Fold to each of Earth like planets and gathered the same data.

In total they made eight Folds in two days.

Bram looked at Pat and Amy and commented that they were looking much younger and that the Fold process seemed to be turning back the clock for them.

Pat laughed and said that she did feel better than ever but doubted the younger look.

She then commented that she had scheduled Zuri during the upcoming Christmas break to send her out multiple times on one day then rest for a day and then go through another cycle of Folds.

The rest day included spending time with the site psychologist to talk through her feelings about the change that would be happening.

She had arranged for Elizabeth, Linda, and Orlando to go out on the first three cycles. If the Fold process was repairing her body and more cycles were needed they would repeat the sequence.

She said that Nuro and Jina had expressed their concern about the potential repair process. They had talked with Zuri, and she had insisted that she be allowed to try. They said that they would pray for a miracle.

Bram smiled and said that all he wanted for Christmas was to see Zuri walking.

Amy said that such an event would be a miracle, and she was hopeful that it would happen.

Bram suggested that Pat have a structural diagram of a healthy girl her age put into the bubble computer that it could use as reference. He was not sure how the Fold process accomplished what it did, but he figured he would put that information in the same location as the Fold control system equations were located.

Pat highlighted a problem that Elizabeth had surfaced. If the process worked Zuri could not return to the current University that she was attending. If she were recognized the power of the Fold process would be at risk of being discovered and then there would be a full attack on the program.

Bram suggested that if the miracle happened, they try to get Zuri into one of the Ivy League schools or into Oxford.

Pat said that she would get Elizabeth to see about Oxford it was her alma mater, and she would have good connections there.

Bram said that the analysis of the data gathered so far would take place in the Viewing Room where Lori had arranged for two teams of analysts to share what they had learned from their initial review.

Zoe commented that the circle of people that knew about the worlds that had been discovered was growing. She was having the backgrounds of all the analysts checked again. She commented that they were among the most trusted lab members who had been with the project from its beginning.

Bram thanked her for her proactive actions. He agreed but said that he needed to get the analysis going. The actual physical of the physical samples would be used to confirm what they learned in the next few days.

If they had a water world that met the specifications that had been defined to support life then he would send the reply to the Aliens.

And then they would Fold to each of the water worlds and send down sampling bubbles to gather physical samples.

Daryl and Harold once again celebrated the fact that the analysis of all three water worlds confirmed that they met the criteria that had been established.

Bram reinforced the fact that they were great hunters and shared they would make the next Fold visits to each of the planets.

He smiled as the two nodded and quietly thanked him for the opportunity.

Erica had come in toward the end of the meeting. She said that she had good news and bad news.

Bram smiled and said for her to start with the bad news.

Erica replied that the bad news was the cost for the instrumentation was ridiculously high.

Bram smiled and replied that if that was the bad news then the good news was going to be great news.

Erica smiled and said that the General had sent three helicopters to fly to Seattle to pick up all the instrumentation and it would arrive the following morning.

Remi was the one that reacted in the fashion of pumping his fist in the air as Daryl and Harold had now made popular. He said that his team would have the Lab bubbles ready to go by the end of the week.

Bram said that once the Labs were on location, the necessary coordinates would be available so that the sample bubbles could be Folded into their clean sterile environments.

Immediately after that the next sets of Folds to the water world would occur.

The work on the lab bubbles consumed Bram for the next two weeks. Then Pat remined him that Erica's fishing trip was coming up on the weekend.

Bram replied that he was ready for the Rushing River. He scheduled the placement of the two labs on the following Wednesday and the revisit of the water worlds for the next day.

Success seemed to be in the air. The week ended in a rush, and everyone turned their attention to the wedding.

Erica was on the first of the helicopter flights to the Rushing River. She and the General flew in together with the Admiral. They were all staying at the lodge. Folks were staying at two other lodges in the area and would be transported there to Mike and Mary's lodge by the Marines.

After his arrival and getting situated in his and Pats room, Bram took the opportunity to sit on the veranda and chat with the General and the Admiral. Mike joined in and it was clear to Bram that the three were of the same vintage and liked sharing their "war" stories. He tuned out and envisioned each of the upcoming scenarios that would occur after Erica and Gerry tied the knot.

The Admiral touched his arm, and he came back to the surface. The Admiral commented that his favorite Captain had given him his resignation and was planning to take a role with the Fold organization and work for Bram. He said that it had surprised him since he had figured the Captain would spend his career in the Navy. He was on the list to be promoted. The Admiral asked what role could possibly pull the Captain away from the ocean.

Bram thought for a moment, he smiled and then said that the role information was above the Admiral's pay grade, and he could not divulge it, but the Admiral could be assured that it involved the ocean.

The Admiral laughed and said that Bram would have made a great officer in the Navy.

Bram thanked him for the compliment and added that the General had already put in his bid to make him a Marine and he didn't want to offend either of them in any way.

The Message

Pat came out to the porch with Amy and Erica and joined the conversation. She commented that it was at this lodge that she had caught her big fish and that she was especially glad to see that Erica was making it a custom.

Amy added that she had learned that Lacy was planning to continue the custom.

Bram smiled and said that he was impressed with the actual fish Pat had caught and then later he had been confused by the fireworks and somehow ended up on her hook.

The General laughed and said that his two Marines, Orlando and Castor informed him that it was Bram that had been dishing out the fireworks.

Bram nodded and said that it was an accident and that he had his eyes closed the whole time.

Mike added that he had been there and couldn't get a shot in because Bram had rushed to point and wiped out all the attackers.

Castor had been standing on the porch with Donna as they stood guard. In a loud voice, he commented to her that Mike had correctly described the scene. He said that he and Orlando were too slow that day and Bram made them look like new recruits.

Bram looked over to Pat and asked if she wanted to take a walk up the river.

He watched as Castor and Donna took the lead, Bob, and Thomas took the rear.

He looked at the Admiral and commented that being alone meant alone with four other very close friends.

The General nodded and said he sympathized and added that there were as many Marines as wedding guests.

Erica thanked him for the precaution, but she doubted that it would be as exciting as what had just been described.

The following morning was the wedding breakfast that touted a breakfast special that Mike said was being called Pat's special. He added that there were also eggs to order and a variety of muffins and rolls.

The wedding was scheduled to begin at exactly noon and then an early reception meal at two.

Bram looked at Erica and knew that she had become the person she was meant to be. She was confident and she had become admired for her leadership style that focused on developing those working for her, she radiated happiness.

Erica looked over at him, smiled and gave him a thumbs up.

Later a few minutes before twelve, he called on everyone to go to and assemble in the field across the river. He waited until everyone was at their seats and walked up to the platform that would serve as the alter.

He was about to start the wedding when Lacy stood up and shouted in a loud urgent voice, that they should all get into the Rushing River.

He knew immediately something was very wrong. He pointed to the river and said follow me. He grabbed Pat by the hand and pulled her with him.

He stopped at the edge of the river and looked out to a far mountain where a bright glint caught his eye. He shouted at Lacy and pointed to the far mountain.

She gave him a thumbs up.

He then jumped into the river and made sure the wedding area was clear.

Lacy shouted for everyone to get down into the water as deep as possible.

Bram had just pulled Pat to him and then pulled her under the last thing he saw was two bubbles firing and then an overhead explosion and what seemed like a fire storm drove him under as well.

He immediately stood up and looked over to see Lacy talking on her phone.

He heard her say that they should capture their attackers, if possible, but any resistance should be met with elimination.

He then shouted that he would complete the ceremony right where they were.

He went straight to does anyone object to this union and then declare Erica and Gerald husband and wife.

He pointed to the lodge and shouted that the way out of the river led straight to a warm shower.

Then Gerry, in full dress uniform, picked Erica up and carried her out of the river and into the lodge. The Admiral and General followed and then the rest of the wedding party got out and headed toward their rooms.

Mike shouted that the wedding lunch was still on and would be on schedule.

One of the Marines spoke briefly to Mike, who then turned to Bram and said he was going to bill him for another door to the cave. He smiled and said the steel plates that he had added were bent but they had saved the cave.

Bram laughed and said that if all the attackers had accomplished was to destroy his door, he was going to give Lacy the largest raise that she had ever received.

At lunch, Lacy announced that the attack had come from the mountain on the other side of the valley. She had sent six armed bubbles to that location and had surprised three men who tried to shoot the bubbles out of the air. The return fire had kill all three of the attackers and the General had sent out a unit to that location to secure the site.

Bram thanked her for the update then he said that her quick action had saved the day. He then jokingly said that he would send her the bill for the damage that the second rocket had done to Mike's cave and would have her budget pay for it.

Lacy knew immediately that Bram was pulling her leg since she was on his budget and waved her hand through the air and replied that she had saved his hide only to have hers nailed to the wall so she was going to see if the General would give her a place in the Marine Corp.

Bram laughed and said that she might also want to ask the Admiral to be a rear Admiral and see if she could double dip.

Then Gerry stood up and said that there would never be another wedding like this one. He had found inspiration and found his soul mate on the banks of the Rushing River. He figured being married in its waters was the highlight of his life.

Erica stood up beside him and said that she agreed and said that she had caught the big fish she was after in that same river.

Bram raised his glass of wine and said that he had a toast to the bride and groom. He wished them a lifetime of happiness, of prosperity and of good health and that they would come back to work as quickly as possible.

Everyone cheered.

A helicopter was waiting to fly them back to the Fold compound and then they would be driven to the airport to fly out to their Honeymoon in Kauai.

Pat suggested to Bram that they stay an extra day at the lodge and decompress. She felt that the day's events was more than had been expected.

Bram agreed and let everyone know that if they wanted to they could remain for an extra day as well.

The General and Admiral both left as scheduled. But before leaving he instructed the Marines to remain vigilant and make sure Bram was kept safe.

Lacy let Bram know that she was going back to the Fold compound to open an investigation into the attackers. She wanted to know how they had been able to find out where Bram was going to be and how they were able to get the rockets that had been used.

Bram thanked them and then watched two helicopters leave.

Mike suggested they go take a look at the doors to the cave and that afterwards they sit on the veranda and relax for the remainder of the day.

He suggested doing real fishing the next day.

Bram said that he was interested in the door that he had paid for and then afterwards the porch seemed like the place to be.

Chapter 27: Transformation

Bram returned to the Fold compound and went full throttle in getting the Space Fold Labs functional and ready to put in place. It took longer than he anticipated but he rationalized that the Fold project was pole vaulting technological heights and exploration that would make them triple gold medalists champions in the Olympics.

He knew that every team was functioning at top capacity and capability.

Erica reminded him several times that he was moving all the efforts, each of which were major efforts, faster than any similar project had ever moved.

Pat told him to ease up a bit and let him know that as soon as Christmas break occurred, she had arranged for Zuri to return so that she could begin cycling through a series of Folds.

Bram said that he had never experienced an emotionally trying feeling like the one he had when he thought about the transformation that Zuri might experience.

He said that he thought it would be equally hard for Zuri and they should make sure she got the support that would help her during the transition of her body.

He asked about Zuri's admittance to Oxford.

Pat said that Elizabeth had received confirmation from her alma mater that Zuri was accepted into their program and that Orlando had also received confirmation that he could transfer in, but it was on a provisional basis that required him to keep above a three-point five grade point average. She said that Orlando had jumped up and down and then he had pushed Zuri around the campus shouting out.

Three-point five, Three point five
    Tra, la, la
Not so hard
For the bard
    Tra la le
Oh my, Oh my can this really be!
How can this be?
It's all downhill.
It's all downhill.
How can this be?
    Tra, la, la
    Tra la le
How can this be?

Bram laughed and said that he missed Orlando leading the way as they jogged in to work but he was pleased that he had been accepted to Oxford. He said that he agreed with Orlando that it was going to be a downhill run for him. He knew that Orlando was currently carrying a four-point average while still carrying out his responsibility to guard Zuri.

The Message

He asked Pat to schedule him on as many of the Fold cycles that he wanted to go on.

Pat said that she was sure that he would end up going on as many as Zuri. She said that she was not sure how he would take Zuri's physical transformation, but she was sure it would be positive and that he would help Zuri handle the transformation.

Bram agreed. He said that it would be good to have him at breakfast and describe the hoped-for transformation so that Orlando would have time to think about it and be prepared.

Pat said she would arrange for the breakfast.

Bram let her know that he was going to examine the space bubble that could hold an Alien. It was being built in the same hangar where Wheels one and two had been built. The bubbles were two hundred feet long and seventy-five feet wide. They were being equipped with water purifiers, aerators and chemical balancing units that would maintain the fluid at peak condition for the Aliens. He said that he was sure that it would hold two and maybe three.

He would have to make sure with the Aliens that such a bubble would be acceptable. In the long term he hoped to get the Aliens to make their own bubbles, but he was uncertain of their manufacturing capability.

The next day, Jose Estrada, the builder's project manager, met Bram at the airport. He greeted Zoe and Eric and then led the way to a waiting black van. On the way to the hanger, he thanked Bram for having asked for him to be the project manager of the giant bubble and asked about its design specifications.

Bram replied that currently he could not divulge that information but when he could, he would make sure to include Jose.

Jose said he would deliver the Bubble on time and at cost.

Bram thanked him and said that around Christmas, he planned to Fold the bubble to its destination and the hangar would be available for what he was thinking would be a second bubble order.

Jose said he looked forward to a second order.

There was a car entrance to the hangar that the van drove through. Bram got out and the size of the bubble towering over him and filling the hangar overwhelmed him. He had been expecting "Big" but what he now saw was "GIGANTIC."

He followed Jose as they walked outside of the bubble. The walk around it took about half an hour.

Jose stopped to show what at first appeared to be seamless joints but on a closer look you could see the intricated joint design that ensured the integrity of the joint.

Then they stepped into the bubble. What Jose called the tail end, was where all the equipment that would maintain the chemical and physical condition of the fluid that would be inside.

Jose pointed out tubes that ran the length of the bubble that had holes in them to ensure that the fluid condition was maintained throughout the bubble.

Several large viewing screens and computers were at the front of the bubble that Jose pointed out.

Bram asked how long the remainder of the commissioning of the bubble would take.

Jose commented that the deionized, distilled water would take almost a month to fill the vessel. Then the temperature and circulation control would be commissioned and finally the various chemical chamber functions would be tested. He said that in all it would take the remaining time before Christmas.

Bram said that the timing was perfect, and he appreciated the detailed testing that Jose had planned.

Bram looked at his phone and realized that it was near one in the afternoon. He then asked where they should go to have a late lunch.

Jose suggested his favorite Mexican restaurant. He said that the timing was perfect, and they would not have to wait to get a table.

After the lunch, Bram again thanked Jose and then went to the airport and caught the short flight back to Portland.

He was met by Castor and Donna who took point as they led the way to curbside. He noted that they had worn civilian cloths and their weapons were in holsters beneath their suit jackets.

The black van was at the curb parked in front of a similar black van and behind another black van.

Castor opened the sliding door and Zoe and Eric got in back as Castor walked around and got into the driver's seat and Donna closed the side door and got into the passenger's seat.

Bram heard Castor instruct the drivers in the other two vans and then the ride to Dallas got under way. Bram was glad that it had only been a day trip and that he, Zoe, and Eric had been the only ones on that leg.

The following week was Thanksgiving.

Bram, Marcus, and Remi made several bubble Folds to check out the coordinates for the Fold space labs. The location they finally agreed on was one that had a phenomenal view of a bright multicolored spiral galaxy.

Since this was to be a secret location that only they knew about and that nothing would be written down, they each selected their back up person who would be given the coordinates in the event one of them died.

Bram said that once the relationship with the Aliens and the existence of potential expansion worlds for Earth's population became common knowledge the location would be made part of the Fold record.

Finally, Zuri's Christmas break began, and she arrived home.

Bram had invited her and her family to Sunday breakfast. He had also invited Orlando and Mallica as well.

Pat let him know that she had invited Linda and Lacy.

The Message

After breakfast Bram asked Pat to describe the effect that the Fold process seemed to have on living things.

Pat described the various tests she had conducted with plants, fish, rabbits, goats, and pigs of various sizes and how she had made sure the Fold effect was always a positive one.

She looked at Zuri and said that she was hoping that it would have a positive effect on her, but she said she was not sure how that would actually occur and what the changes would be.

Elizabeth asked Zuri if she wanted to see if it would help her.

Zuri gave a laugh and said if pigs almost the size of Orlando got healed, she figured she should try to see what it did for her.

Bram said that she would always have someone making the Fold with her and asked who she would like to accompany her.

Zuri looked around the room and said that anyone in the room was welcome but that on the first couple of Folds she would prefer Orlando, Elizabeth, and Linda.

She looked at her parents and said that once things seemed to be going well, the two of them should go with her. If things did not go well then, they could all cry together.

She looked at Bram and said that he would be welcome on every Fold as well.

Bram thanked her for including him but said that if the Fold process worked the way he anticipated, he would be crying most of the time and figured that the macho Marine could handle the situation better than he.

Orlando laughed and said he would most likely be the one crying. He joked that his role of being her guard was at stake.

Pat speculated that they would all be crying. She then suggested that the Fold process begin at nine the next morning.

Orlando was at breakfast Monday morning. He said he had a ditty to sing on the way to the compound.

> *Zuri's on the way*
> *On the way*
> *What a bright,*
> *A bright wonderful day.*
> *Zuri's transformation day*
> *I say transformation,*
> *You say transformation.*
> *Zuri's transformation day*
> *On the way*
> *On the way*
> *What a day.*

Bram took his breakfast plate and rinsed it off at the sink and said it was time to get it on the way and led the way out the door.

They all repeatedly sang the ditty as they jogged to the compound. As always, the entire contingent of Marine guards joined in.

Bram accompanied Pat to the bubble that would be repeatedly used. He asked where she was Folding to.

Pat said that she had worked with Marcus to determine the Fold coordinates and then they had made sure that it was a clean space environment by repeatedly Folding scout bubbles to ensure a safe location. She said that the coordinate was behind Neptune where they figured their activities would not be discovered and would not require too much power.

Bram complemented Pat on making safety the top priority.

Zuri was pushed in by Orlando and he helped put Zuri into the seat designed to hold her.

He got into the bubble.

Linda entered the bubble and took the seat on the other side of Zuri.

He nodded when Linda commented that she had held Zuri's hand for several years when things were looking bad and that she wanted to be holding her hand when things began to improve.

Bram remembered well, the look on Linda's face when he realized Zuri was a genius and he asked her to be on his team. Later when he wanted to promote Lacy, she had recommended her sister who she said was a super organizer and would make a great support for him.

Linda was indeed super organized, but she was also very intuitive about what his next request for her help would be and often delivered it immediately.

He felt that it was appropriate for her to be on Zuri's first transformation flight.

After each cycle, Pat and the site physician would examine Zuri and the site phycologist would spend a few moments talking to her.

They both reported that some positive change was occurring, and that Zuri was handling it well.

Bram noted that the hands and feet were the first physical parts to show improvement. He saw immediately that Zuri's hands were no longer in a clutching position. Instead, she was wiggling her fingers and laughing.

Linda had a beaming smile and tears in her eyes.

Orlando was making a ditty about hands and feet.

Once Pat had listened to the two Doctors, she signaled for another Fold cycle.

Bram thought he had prepared himself, but he was amazed by the change that he was witnessing. By the sixth Fold cycle Zuri was able to stand on her own but she was unsteady, and it was clear that she would need to learn to walk. Her arms seemed to be fully functional and her neck and back seemed to be straightening.

He had tears in his eyes as the day ended and Zuri asked to keep going.

Pat said that she felt the same way, but she said that the Fold cycle would be on hold for a day and then they would continue with another round of Folds.

Pat said the following day would be spent at the pool where Zuri would get some water therapy exercises so that she could train her rejuvenating body how it should function. It would be a day for Zuri to learn to move her legs and begin the process of learning to walk.

She said that she had arranged the therapy so that Zuri's body could adjust and so the subsequent Folds would then be able to make additional improvements.

Zuri nodded and thanked her. She said that she also needed time to let her mind absorb what was happening. She said she was afraid that she was dreaming.

She looked at her parents and asked how they were doing. She asked if they would be in the pool with her and then in the bubble on the following day.

Jina came over and gave Zuri a hug as did Nuro. Neither of them could speak but kept giving her hugs. Finally, Jina said that they were overwhelmed with the miracle they were witnessing.

Zuri looked over at Orlando and said he was fired as a wheelchair pusher, but she was hiring him to teach her to walk, jog and run.

His beaming smile and the tears running down his cheek were contrasts of emotion and he gave a thumbs up but was not able to say a word.

Bram commented to Pat that he had never seen Orlando at a loss for words until now, but he identified with his emotions.

By the end of the week Zuri was a transformed person. Her facial features had changed, and she resembled a young Jina but as Pat commented to Bram she had a radiant look that made her beautiful. She was now taller than her mother by at least two inches even though she was only twelve.

She took to the water and learned how to swim and said that her legs, arms, and shoulders all ached from what she was doing.

Orlando suggested that they design an exercise program to get her new body into shape. He promised to make her as tough as a Marine.

Zuri laughed and said she wanted to look more like Zoe, Pat, and Amy.

He smiled and said they were as tough as any Marine.

Everyone agreed that the physical change was a miracle.

On Christmas morning at the planned breakfast Zuri arrived with Orlando in the lead. He made a formal announcement that Princes Zuri had arrived.

Zuri walked in with Linda holding her left hand, Jina holding her right hand and Nuro bringing up the rear.

Zuri stepped forward, did a slow turn, bowed, and then walked slowly to each person and gave them a hug.

She came to Bram last and whispered in his ear that she was forever grateful that he had pulled her in when everyone else was ready to give her up.

Bram whispered back that she was the miracle that he had always prayed to witness. He said that now he knew why he had been given the vision to create the Fold process.

Later Bram had let Mallica know that he planned to send their reply back to the Aliens on the day after Christmas.

The Message

In the morning he was surprised to see Mallica, Orlando and Zuri at breakfast. Zuri explained that she wanted to be part of delivering his second miracle to those distant beings.

Orlando said he was there to make sure they had a ditty to jog in with but that on this morning, the jog would be a slow walk so that Zuri could make it on her own.

He then shared the ditty.
> *Zuri's walking, give us room.*
> *Zuri's walking, sing this tune.*
> *Zuri, Zuri has come home,*
> *Wham Bam, it's no scam,*
> *Wham Bram is the man.*
> *Zuri's walking,*
> *Stop you gawking,*
> *She's just walking.*
> *To a Bram miracle tune.*

Bram led the way out and was surprised that every person that had a major role was standing and waiting to go in with him.

Pat said that she had invited them to go in and be part of the historic moment when the message went out.

Linda led them into the auditorium. She said that after the message was sent, Chef D'Carluca had his staff ready to serve breakfast in the auditorium and in the cafeteria.

She pointed to the camera crew at the back of the auditorium and said that everything would be taped.

Bram stood and looked out at the auditorium.

He thought for a moment and then asked Remi to join him. He asked if Remi remembered the preamble to the message that would be sent out.

Remi looked at Bram and then out at the audience. He said that the words he was about to say were from the lips of their very own Fold Peace Whisperer, Bram.

"Welcome we are friendly but fierce. We embrace intelligence, we embrace grace. We embrace every race. We help those in need. May we all live in peace."

Bram then asked Mallica to join them and share the message as it would sound to the Aliens.

She stepped forward and pointed over to Hoang who played the message slowly in Alien and she repeated it in English.

Bram then added that he was adding the fact that a water world had been located and that the initial exploratory vessel would be available to take their first alien explorers there.

He then looked over to Tran and gave the signal to send the message.

Bram was sure that there would be extreme surprise and wonderment on the Alien world.

He looked forward to their response.

The End

<u>**Preview of Fold Wormhole**</u>

Chapter 1 Return to the Desert

The Marine guards stationed at the desert compound had been notified to clear the helo pad and then standby for an early arrival of a group of people. The guards were on their desert rotation from the Fold compound located in Dallas, Oregon so they were familiar with the Fold technology, but they had never witnessed a Fold bubble departure or arrival. It was for them one of the more exciting mornings on guard duty.

Then the bubble appeared and hovered a few inches off the ground. They recognized two of their own, Castor and Donna as they got out of the bubble and took up the front position. Then a very beautiful young woman emerged who they had never seen before. She was followed by another of their own, Orlando.

Then they recognized the helo pilot that periodically flew one of their gunships back at the compound.

She was followed by the person they knew as the genius and his partner.

The last two that got out they knew as two of the FBI bodyguards assigned to protect the genius.

They watched as the group walked away in the dark of the morning and headed out into the desert.

The night was pitch black. Millions of stars twinkled overhead that seemed to be behind a thin white veil covering the face of heaven. Bram couldn't see his hands in front of him. He took the lead up the almost invisible path. His feet knew the way through their body memory.

The bright shimmering star light made the surrounding grasses and sage brush appear alive as the light morning breeze caused them to waver and the limited number of leaves to rustle.

He was followed by Pat, Zuri, Amy and then the rest of the protection detail.

Einstein was in his pocket.

He let everyone know that Pat, Zuri, and Amy were the only ones going to sit on the boulder that he had sat on during the development of the Fold equation. The four of them would watch the sunrise from the place where he had finally realized that he had made the breakthrough. A breakthrough that now he believed was guided by another hand.

He had thought of this outing as a way to bring Einstein for a visit to his home and to share with Zuri that instant of time that led to the miracle that she represented.

Somewhere, in one of the cracks in the boulder, was where Einstein had previously lived. Now at least five years old, Einstein would once again get to visit home.

Bram joked that Einstein had guided him in the quest to develop the Fold equation.

When they got to the boulder, Bram helped Pat, Zuri, and Amy up and then he sat down in his usual spot. He took Einstein from his pocket and placed him down beside him.

Einstein circled around once and then disappeared down the side of the rock.

Pat asked if he would come back.

Bram said that he thought so but only when the sun broke over the horizon and its rays hit the boulder.

Zuri smiled and commented that she was honored to visit the place where Bram had sat and thought through the maze of equations that had transformed her from a very disabled person to a one with a normal body. It was, she said, a body about which she was still learning. She said that it was like a stranger returning to her home after an extreme remodeling and not recognizing most of what she saw. In her case everything about herself felt different and unknown.

Bram replied that her transformation was for him the grand reward, for his efforts here in the desert. He added it was a reward that would carry him through the rest of his life.

Pat gave Zuri a hug and said that her physical transformation was a positive reward for everyone working on the Fold project. They all believed that they had witnessed a miracle.

Amy added that she had first learned of the Fold capability sitting on the boulder and thought at the time that she had witnessed something that could never be exceeded. Then she had witnessed Zuri's transformation and knew that she had witnessed the real miracle of the Fold.

A thin bright line cut across the dark night horizon as the sun light broke over the mountains to the east and the star light seemed to wane. The line travel across the desert as if seeking the boulder. It worked its way like a thief in the night sulked up toward an open window. Its first streaks of light hit the boulder and slowly worked its way and worked upward like the thief climbing in the window. It seemed to slow as if trying to find its way the way a mountain climber would look for hand holds as she made her way up the cliff.

A few moments later Einstein came out and surprisingly another mouse followed him.

Pat commented that it seemed that Einstein had found a mate.

Bram nodded and put out two crumbs and said that he had probably lost his Fold confidant to a love affair. He said that Einstein deserved to have such an affair.

Einstein got up on his two hind legs and Bram lowered his hand. Einstein got into his palm and then the second mouse did as well. Einstein circled and lay down and the new mouse did as well.

Zuri commented that she could not believe what she was seeing.

Bram lowered his hand and both mice got out. Einstein then led the way down to the crack from which he had come and disappeared.

The Message

Bram commented that he would return in a couple of months to see if Einstein would return to greet him.

Small bubbles, holding some tea, a sweet roll, and some cherries, appeared. There was one for every person in the group.

Bram said that they should enjoy the sunrise snack that Marcus had arranged and then take a walk in the desert.

Amy got up and as she went down the boulder said that she would be picking them up in a helicopter and bringing them back for a full lunch.

Bram left some crumbs on the rock and then led the way out to the desert.

He was heading out one degree from true north. That was one degree more than the last time he had made such a walk. He knew that Amy would know where to take her helo. He was silent as he thought about what seemed like only yesterday but then all of the achievements that had taken place since that time seemed to be flashing through his mind.

He felt lucky to have made the discoveries that had so far kept getting better and better and it had reached a point that he was not sure where it would take him next.

Pat quietly asked if he was OK.

Bram smiled and replied that Einstein had been a good partner in his many developmental surges. He gave Pat a hug and commented that giving Einstein a hug and getting a reply from him was always a short coming and that Pat would have to step up and take up the slack.

Zuri had been walking behind them and was thinking about the wonderful relationship the two had and her heart stopped when by chance she saw the rattlesnake. She stopped and quietly said that the two soapy people walking mindlessly ahead of her should pay attention and not tangle with the rattle snake they were about to walk into.

That caused everyone to stop. Both Bram and Pat looked to where Zuri pointed with her stick to where the snake was laying in the rays of the sun. It was still lethargic from the cold of the night.

Orlando said he would take care of the snake, but Bram stopped him and commented that the snake must just have moved into the sun's rays but had not yet been able to get warmed up. He said they were on its turf and should respect its territory.

He thanked Zuri for having been alert and then led the group around the snake.

He then related the story about having walked out from a center point and having recorded the terrain at one-degree increments until he had been able to match the topography he mapped in his mind and computer to a specific location in the United States.

He said that it had taken him a year and that today they were walking out along the three hundred and sixty first degree line.

Pat asked why the location had been so important to him.

He replied that it was a matter of principle. He was angry that sufficient security could be provided to so many important people, but he had to be treated like a criminal who was sent into isolated confinement. He was sure that it had to do with the fact that the folks had decided his ideas would be extremely powerful and they had wanted to ensure that the power it represented would not leak out of the country.

He pointed out that the leaks so far had come not from those associated most closely to the Fold project but from the very people worried about the leaks.

Zuri asked what he had done when he finally determined the location.

He replied that he had confronted Jeffrey and Erica and threatened to leak the desert location to the media. He made the point that the confrontation with the two was the beginning of the change that led to the social environment that they were now living in at the Fold compound.

He highlighted the fact that the confrontation had changed his relationship with Erica and subsequently changed her life.

Up until that time Erica wanted to be in control and thought that he wanted her role. She was upset because Jeffrey had given him the best apartment to live in. She believed that she was not being respected.

Pat commented that she had talked to Erica before coming back to the desert and had learned that for Erica the return to the desert would have been a return to a time that she now considered a dark time that she had successfully escaped and that she preferred leaving it in the desert.

Bram nodded and said that Erica was now living a different life with a new set of values and had found her soul mate and would most likely be happy for the rest of her life.

They had been walking for almost two hours when Zuri commented that she could not see the helicopter, but she heard it.

Bram pointed to a dark spot that seemed to be just above the ground that was fast approaching from the center point that was the compound buildings.

He commented that Amy had always flown her helicopter very close to the ground so she could pick him out as she passed over him.

He shared the fact that when he had some sort of place to hide he would do so on her first pass and then continue walking and wait until she realized that she had missed him and returned to pick him up.

It was a game of cat and mouse between the two of them the whole time they had been in the desert.

Pat shared that Amy had shared the fact that she knew that the two of them were always playing a cat and mouse game that she had learned to enjoy. It was, she said always the most fun part of her day.

The Message

Bram smiled and said that it was also a great way for him to start each day and that game had earned Amy the privilege of being the first person with whom he had shared the Fold breakthrough. He had taken her to the boulder and there he had introduced Einstein to her, and they had the same breakfast snack that they had just shared earlier.

Zuri commented that Bram had a desert experience that became the fabric that was still guiding the Fold program and one that she now personally embraced.

Bram smiled and commented that it was a very positive influence in his life and that the fabric of that life had been woven by his mother when as a young boy, she repeatedly told him that he had to treat others the way he wished to be treated. She had also said that if he embraced that one saying, his life would be rich whether he was a pauper, a wise man, or a genius.

He added that he tried to practice that philosophy even when he had the urge to kick some people in their derriere.

Pat laughed and said that most people would just say that they had the urge to kick some people in their butt.

Zuri asked what word she would when she attended Oxford University.

Pat said that she thought Bum or arse depending on the social situation.

Bram laughed and said that they should get into the hilo and enjoy the ride back to the compound.

Amy landed her Hilo in an open area and waved them onboard. She had Zuri sit in the front seat. Once everyone was in and had their safety harness on, she handed them each headsets.

They all got in and watched as Orlando led the rest of the group on foot back toward the compound. He had them singing some ditty and led off at a good jog.

Bram then told Zuri that she was about to experience a hair-raising flight that he had to endure every morning before working on the Fold equation and that she would learn why he finally had to make a breakthrough. He said that Amy had frightened him into being successful.

Amy laughed and then took off and flew out away from the desert compound. She flew just above the surface at a dizzying speed. She had arranged with Orlando to fly out long enough to let him get back to the compound.

Zuri shouted that she wanted to live to enjoy going to Oxford.

Bram laughed and said that Amy would make sure that Zuri was so afraid to fail that she would graduate at the top of her class.

Amy took a sharp bank and headed back to the compound. She did a little up bob and then set the helo down at the center of the landing pad.

She looked over at Zuri and asked if she had enjoyed the ride.

Zuri nodded and said it had been much, much more exciting than the Wheel One flight to the back of the moon.

The Message

Bram added that the flight in from the desert had always been exciting for him and that he had made sure that Amy went to astronaut training in an attempt to train her to be a normal pilot. He now realized that it had not worked.

Amy said that flying a helo had been and still was one of the most enjoyable things that she did. She said that she had convinced the Marines back at the compound to let her fly one of their gunships on a regular basis. It had allowed her to keep up her flying skill during her time back at the Fold compound.

Bram said he would now worry about who was flying the protection helo when he jogged into work in the mornings.

Pat said that she had just thought of a good ditty for their next jog in

> *Who's that flying in the sky.*
> *Who's that flying way down so low.*
> *Is that someone that we know.*
> *If its Amy then it's so.*
> *Who's that flying in the sky.*
> *Is that someone that we know.*
> *Yo, Ho, Yo, Ho*
> *Look how low, Look how low.*
> *Fly crazy, Ho, Ho, Ho.*

Bram pointed to Orlando, Castor and Donna who were standing with Zoe and Eric at the side of the helo landing area. He commented that they had made good time getting back and he was sure that they would all have a great lunch before heading back to the Dallas Fold compound.

The return to the Fold compound via bubble was scheduled after their lunch.

Chapter 2: Alien Engagement

Sunday morning Bram rode the two-person elevator to his basement office. He made himself a cup of pour through coffee and sat down at his computer. He worked his entire equation with negative time to see if it would give him an insight to what might happen. What he learned was that his equation using negative time seemed to go in a circle or at least it became nonlinear and perhaps be a spiral. It seemed to defy definition or relation to one particular shape.

Pat, Zoe, and Eric came in and said they had been worried about where he had gone and that he had broken the protection protocol.

He nodded and said that it had never registered when he got on the elevator to come down to his office. He suggested they put in a camera and alarm so that when he did it again they would immediately know.

Pat reminded him that they had agreed to go to the neighborhood recreation center for lunch where Melisa had gathered some of the younger children who they were going to play various games with.

Bram knew that his time thinking about negative space was over for the day.

He woke up on Monday ready to attack the day. On their five thirty in the morning jog into work, Castor took up the ditty that Pat had shared when they had gotten off the helo in the desert.

> *Who's that flying in the sky.*
> *Who's that flying way up high.*
> *Who's that flying way down low.*
> *Is that someone that we know.*
> *If its Amy then it's so.*
> *Who's that flying in the sky.*
> *Is that someone that we know.*
> *Yo, Ho, Yo, Ho*
> *Look how low, Look how low.*
> *We just wonder why it's so.*
> *Fly crazy, Ho, Ho, Ho.*

Both he and Donna pointed to the helo overhead and Bram watched as it came down low to one side and wiggled and then went back up. He had not been able to see the pilot but figured it was Amy.

At that moment he was thinking about the response he was waiting for from the Aliens. It had been sent to them the day after Christmas. He figured that it would take them a few days to react to the message. The few days had passed, and he hoped a reply had been returned.

He, Marcus and Mallica were scheduled to check the location where they had originally intercepted the Alien's first message to see if a reply had been sent back.

Linda welcomed him back and reminded him about his meeting and asked about the rest of his day and when he wanted to update his two-week calendar.

Bram suggested that updating the calendar should take place in the late afternoon. He asked that she set up a meeting with Remi and check with Jose to see when he could take possession of the first giant bubble.

He then asked to get a meeting set up with Erica to discuss the building of another bubble and to check on any other financial issues.

Linda gave a small laugh and asked if this was just today's items or was it the two-week items.

Bram said he would be in his office to start the day and then he would meet with Marcus and Mallica.

Bob and Thomas took their chairs as Bram pressed the heat lever on the water pot.

Bram sat down at his desk and put his hand at the center of the Milky Way Spiral picture that was under the glass on his desk. He was thinking about the Wormhole equation and the negative space aspect of the reversing process. He was anxious to investigate what going into negative space would mean.

He fired up his laptop and reviewed the equation yet again. He had it burned into his mind and really did not need to see it but doing so let him imagine what might happen. It was like having a book in his hand that allowed him to feel the weight of the story. He was trying to envision the resulting shape of his negative equation.

Linda's call that he had ten minutes before his scheduled meeting with Marcus and Mallica brought him out of his speculation about the negative part of space. He realized that he had spent almost an hour deep in thought and that he had not made the tea that he had intended to make.

He looked over at Bob and Thomas and realized that the two of them had used the hot water to make themselves tea and had made him a cup as well, but it was still sitting at the refreshment center.

Unlike Zoe that was willing to pull him up from the depth, these two were not willing to take that chance.

He smiled and thanked them for the tea and said that it was time for them to go with him to his next meeting.

Marcus and Mallica were waiting outside of his office and suggested they go to the lab where the bubble that had been sent out to see if the Aliens had responded, had just been returned to its holding area. They had arranged for Remi to retrieve the computer recording. He had volunteered to review it on his computer.

The Message

Bram thanked them for getting everything ready. He hoped that there would be a response.

Remi greeted them and said that there was something on the computer, but he had resisted getting into it until they all arrived. He pointed to a large screen and said he would now open the folder with the message.

When the message came on the screen, Bram had an immediate smile on his face. The first line was in English, "Greetings, we on Swoosh are elated that intelligent beings have received our message and were able to respond to us using our language. We are very impressed. To be offered aid dried our eyes and caused us to surface and breach."

Then the messaged changed to the alien language and provided more information about themselves, their population numbers, and the number of species in their world. There was an explanation that they did not have physical structures as had been described existing on Earth. They were amazed that the human species lived on land and breathed air directly.

They added that the energy required to send the reply had exhausted their energy resource and it would take at least another journey around their star to rejuvenate it.

They then gave some data about the condition of their star.

Mallica commented the lack of power and any significant structures had signaled her that rescuing the Aliens and transporting them to another water world had just gotten more complicated.

Marcus wondered how a species that could think deeply and develop a Fold message transmitter would not have developed the ability to build a large energy source.

On Earth, electricity, gas engines, and steam engines all existed in abundance. Often the power source had preceded the use it was eventually used for. He said it was hard for him to understand how the technology to send out the Fold message had been developed.

Bram agreed that it seemed inconceivable, but reality said that it had been done. He speculated about the whales and the dolphins and wondered if they had superior thoughts but were not able to develop the technology to communicate with humans.

Mallica then brought them back and asked about the response and pointed out that Earth would have to supply the short term capability for the Aliens on Swoosh to begin to make the move to another water world.

Bram agreed. He pointed out that the first transport that would hold two maybe three of the Swooshians was ready for delivery. The three of them had to agree on the delivery coordinates and then make the Fold from the hangar in Seattle to the coordinate.

Marcus suggested a coordinate near the Alien water world that they had previously used since it would save time since he would not need to verify the spot did not have a field of debris.

The Message

Bram agreed and let Marcus know that the Fold would happen that afternoon. He had a meeting with Erica with the objective of her ordering a second bubble. He asked Marcus to call Jose at the building site to verify the coordinate of the bubbles center.

Then they would meet at three and Fold the bubble out to the coordinate near Swoosh.

Mallica asked whether they would respond to the reply from Swoosh.

Bram suggested that she get a message ready that asked the Aliens for the current chemistry on Swoosh and how soon the Swooshians would be ready to check out the new water worlds that met the parameters that were agreed on.

Mallica suggested they also ask how quickly the Swooshians were planning to make the transition to a new world.

Bram agreed and added that with the current Fold capacity it would take more than their lifetime to get just a small percentage of Swooshians to a new planet. He said they would need to figure out a way to setup a transport system that had higher capacity and one that did not rely on the Earth for the materials or the manufacturing of the bubbles.

He asked if she and Marcus might take that on as a project. They could recruit other folks, like Remi or anyone else that could add the knowledge they needed to set up a remote bubble production system.

Mallica said that a project like that would be exciting for her. She said that she was up for it and would get a group together to flesh out who needed to be on the team.

Bram thanked her and said that Marcus already had his hands full with determining where bubbles should Fold and making sure the Fold location was clear of debris. He expected that Marcus would be extremely critical in determining the coordinates for a bubble factory.

Marcus agreed and said he was excited about suggesting locations within the Swooshian solar system that might position the production facility near the materials needed to make the giant bubbles.

He then added that perhaps some even better locations would be in some other solar system near a planet that had the materials critical in making the bubbles.

He said that once he was given the ingredients from which the bubbles were made, the files with the data from the previously discovered planets could be examined and an optimum location could be selected. Perhaps the facility could be on the surface of such a planet but at a minimum it could be nearby, and materials mined and sent out to the production facility.

Bram said he had heard enough, and he was going back to his office and begin to work on his next project.

The Message

He was walking back to his office thinking about the negative realm of his equation when Erica intercepted him near the cafeteria.

She asked if Bram knew that it was lunch time.

He shook his head and said that it seemed that the time was flying.

Erica suggested that he follow her, and they would meet up with Pat for lunch.

Bram followed her into the cafeteria and waved at Pat who was sitting by herself at their usual table.

Erica had selected an Italian salad and was almost immediately on the way to the table.

Bram was not sure what he wanted. He looked over the offering and went for a slice of beef, some asparagus, and a small, baked potato. He carried his tray out to the table and then decided that he wanted a lemonade to go with what he had selected.

Pat asked how his day was progressing.

Bram commented that he seemed to be constantly behind in what he had been planning to get accomplished.

Erica waited until Bram had finished and was sipping his lemonade and then asked him what their meeting was about and could they have it now.

Bram smiled and said that it was a very short topic. He was having the current bubble moved out of the hangar in the afternoon and he was interested in getting another one on order.

Erica nodded, made a note on her phone, and then said it was done. She then said the order would be in by the end of day.

Bram thanked her and said that her meeting was one that had happened quickly and ahead of time. He said that when he got back into the office, he would be able to focus on his next project.

He was leaving the cafeteria when he decided that where he needed to go was to the Lab and see if a bubble was available that he could use. His turn toward the Lab caught Castor and Donna by surprise and they hustled to get back in the lead and then asked where he was going.

Bram apologized and said that he had decided to see if a bubble that he could use was available.

Remi had left the cafeteria on Bram's heal and overheard the exchange. He said that he had several bubbles ready, but they would need the Fold coordinate programed in.

Bram replied that he was going to use the Neptune coordinates and that once they were programed in he was going out to try an experiment.

Remi asked about the experiment.

Bram shared that he was going to nibble at the impact that negative time had on the Fold reverse equation.

Remi asked why he did not send out the bubble on its own.

Bram said that he had done that previously and that there was nothing recorded on the visual or the coordinate calculator.

Remi shook his head and asked if there was a way to hook up a second bubble that could pull him back.

Bram said that he did not know how to program such a bubble and said that he felt that once he had a personal experience he would be able to figure out how to navigate the negative space region.

Remi then suggested waiting until morning so that Bram would have an entire day.

Bram thought about it and said that the suggestion made sense and they should plan to use the next day to do the initial exploration of the negative Fold space.

He spent the rest of the afternoon deciding what he wanted to learn in the negative Fold space.

That afternoon as they were riding back to the house, when Pat asked what he was planning for the next day, Bram shared that he was planning to venture into the negative Fold space.

He was surprised by the silence that followed.

He asked why there was no reaction.

Pat replied that she was thinking through what was bothering her and she would share her thoughts after dinner.

Bram found it hard to wait. Finally, after dinner he led the way down into his office and sat down on the two-person recliner. He was pleased that Pat sat down next to him and said that she was ready to share her concern and to ask him to do several things when he ventured into the negative Fold area.

She said that she was afraid that the scientific laws that were more or less absolute in their current reality would not hold in the negative Fold reality. She then asked how he thought time and space would function in the negative reality.

Bram admitted that he was not sure about anything in the negative Fold reality.

Pat asked whether he would consider waiting before Folding into the Negative.

Bram replied that he had considered that but there were no additional actions or developments that he could envision so he was planning to make the negative Fold to see if he could personally learn what was going on.

Pat then said that she wanted him to take enough food and water for a week with him.

She asked if he could use his body to gauge time. Or was there a way for him to separately keep track of time other than his computer.

She had no idea how he would be able to gauge distance and asked if he had an idea.

Bram thanked her for the food and time ideas and admitted that he was relatively clueless about everything that he might encounter.

He mentioned that her questions had triggered several ideas that he would act on in the morning.

<u>About the Author</u>

Ronald E. Mueller
remwriter95@gmail.com

Ron grew up in what is now Flint River State Park in Southeast Iowa. The 170-year-old house Ron lived in is built into a hillside. It faces a 125-foot-high cliff towering over the little Flint River. The house and the land talked to him about; the passing of time, the struggle to conquer the land, the struggles people faced and the wonder of nature.

He climbed the cliffs, crawled into the caves, dove from the swimming rock, collected clams from the bottom of the pond, gigged and skinned frogs for their legs. He trapped muskrats for fur, hunted raccoon in the dead of night, and with only a stick hunted rabbits in the dead of winter.

His young life was outdoors, and nature tested him.

He walked to a one room stone schoolhouse uphill both ways. A stern but warm-hearted teacher, Mrs. Henry was instrumental in shaping his character as she shepherded him from the fourth to the eighth grade. A Montessori before its time. It was a great way to grow up.

His experiences inter-twined with snippets of fantasy lend themselves to the adventures he leads the reader through.

Ron Mueller

<u>Listing of Message Characters</u>

Amy	Wellington	NASA astronaut
Bob		FBI bodyguard
Bram	Nielson	Protagonist
Castor	Suarez	Marine guard
Cedric	Stetson	Fishing boat
Daryl	Nazda	Backup Pilot Bubble 1 Pat Pilot
Donna		New Marine guard
Edward	Sharp	Site Marine Commander
Elizabeth	Miller	humanist philosopher, .
Eric		FBI bodyguard
Erica	Wilson	Initial archrival
Ester	Mannerly	Nasa quality inspector for the two wheels.
Gerald	Gerry	Sooner Captain Erica's husband
Harold	Redat	Backup Pilot Bubble 2 Amy Pilot
Jeffrey	Mikelson	Boss that is patient,
Jina	Juma	Mom
John	Morgan	NASA director Jefferies Boss
Jose	Estrada	project manager wheel one and two
Lacy	Stetson	first office support. Ted's daughter
Lester	Tilson	Marine Major General Fold security
Linda	Stetson	Ted's oldest becomes Bram's support.
Lori	Middleton	Lab, workshop supervisor
Luke	Stetson	Fishing boat Ted's son
Mallica	Evenston	World class mathematician
Marcus	Smith	World class astrophysicist
Marial	Stetson	Brought Picnic lunch -- Cedric's wife

Mary		Rushing River Inn Owner
Melisa	Etrius	Organizer of the Fold neighborhood activities
Mike		Rushing River Inn Owner
Myla	Smith	
Nuro	Juma	Dad
Orlando	Gutieres	Marine guard
Patricia	Fleming	NASA astronaut Bram's mate
Raymond	Daedlus	Husband to be of Lacy
Remi	Hardwood	Direct bubble assembly Lab technical
Rita	Stetson	Brought Picnic lunch - Ted's wife
Samuel	Natorly	US President
Serena	Windal	Fold phycologist -Marine Therapist
Ted	Stetson	Fishing boat
Thomas		FBI bodyguard

The Message

Published by: Around the World Publishing LLC.

www.ingramcontent.com/pod-product-compliance
Lightning Source LLC
Chambersburg PA
CBHW060316100726
47907CB00002B/429